CAUGHT UP!

A **Winston Chapman** Novel

Copyright © Winston Chapman

BLACK PEARL BOOKS

CAUGHT UP!

A Winston Chapman Novel
Is Published By:

BLACK PEARL BOOKS

P.O. Box 361985 · Decatur, Georgia 30036-1985

Copyright © Winston Chapman

All Black Pearl Books titles, imprints and distributed lines are available at special quantity discounts for bulk purchases for sales promotion, premiums, fund raising, educational or institutional use.

Special book excerpts or customized printings can also be created to fit specific needs. For details, write to Black Pearl Books: Attention Senior Publisher, P.O. Box 361985, Decatur, Georgia 30036-1985 or visit website: www.BlackPearlBooks.com

BOOKSTORE DISTRIBUTION

Contact: **Black Pearl Books, Inc.**
              P.O. Box 361985
              Decatur, Georgia 30036-1985

Discount Book-Club Orders via website:

www.BlackPearlBooks.com

ISBN: 0-9728005-0-6

Publication Date: July 2003

Cover Credits

Design: MARION DESIGNS
Photography: OHM/MARION DESIGNS
Model: CRISTAL
Additional Assistance: JESSICA HOYTE & LUV LOVE

PRINTED IN THE UNITED STATES OF AMERICA

Acknowledgements

First and foremost, to my lovely wife who's inspired, cheered and pushed me to the finish line. It's embarrassing for an author to not be able to put feelings into words. But that's how much you affect me. I'm blown away by your beauty every single day. Your have an incredible mind and a genuine soul! And of course – I think you're sexy as H-E-double hockey sticks. Thank you for giving me a beautiful daughter. I'm lucky and I know it! We gotta be the definition of love, 'cause I even love the way we argue. XOXO!

My Publisher, **Black Pearl Books**, you've been a pivotal part of my success. My editor, **Zion Banks**, thanks for your candor – next time, it ain't necessary to curse so much at me.☺ My Publicist, **Felicia Hurst** thanks for tireless promotion.

Thanks to **Cristal**, the *Caught Up!* cover-model that leaps-off the cover and has made this novel the most-touched book in bookstores. To the Award-Winning Photographer, **Ohm** -- I still can't believe you were willing to shoot for me. But, I'm glad you did! Also, Special Thanks to Jessica Hoyte & Luv Love.

To all my book-industry supporters, **Best Black Fiction Dotcom**, thank you for ranking *Caught Up!* - **#1** !!! To the numerous **early book reviewers** from around the country – through rewrites and title changes, there's always remained a special place in my heart for you.

To the **Black Bookclubs** – Much love goes out to you. It is the enduring spirit that you possess for literature that's making big changes in this business. Special shout-outs to: **Busaro Nayo Book Club** (Philadelphia), **Sexy Ebony Book Club** (Brooklyn, NYC), **Sister To Sister Book Club** (Sicily, Italy).

To all the **Black Bookstores** across the country that have loyally supported black authors, long before others found that it was a viable market – I thank you! **Special Thanks To:** Mutota, Fanta & Nsenga at African Spectrum & Oasis Bookstores in Atlanta – The 1st stores to launch *Caught Up!*. I couldn't have done it without your help!

To various **Media**: Radio, Newspapers, Magazines and Newsletters – Thank you for your reviews, interviews and promotion.

To the **Black Colleges**, thanks for the love, but don't forget to pick-up the text books, too!☺

Acknowledgements-Continued

To My Author Friends, Carla J. Curtis & Valerie Rose - Thanks for your insights! **Special Shouts To:** Charles & Suzette Brown! **And To My Boyz**: Gary Beasley & B-Wood (Brandon Woodard).

To My Brothas In Writing: Michael Baisden, Eric Jerome Dickey, E. Lynn Harris, Nelson George, Donald Goines, Timmothy McCann, Walter Mosley, Omar Tyree, Carl Weber, Franklin White & many others – Thank you for clearing the path and making it okay for a brotha to write!

To The Readers: I pride myself on being very accessible, evidenced by my 41-City Tour. Drop me an e-mail about anything. Leave a phone number, as often as I can, I do actually call some readers back. - *Winston@WinstonChapmanBooks.Com*

To My Family: **Dad** – Thanks for instilling courage, the entrepreneurial spirit and the desire to take risks, in me. And, for the knowledge of understanding how to determine a calculated risk! **Mom** – Thanks for the creativity and pushing me & Gary into public speaking. There's so much more I could thank both of you for, but it would exceed the length of this book. **My brother, Gary** – I don't know what to thank you for? Just kidding! It's good to know that I have a brother who'll tell me when something stinks or not! **My Sister-In-Law, Karen** – Thank you for your kind-spirit and for being crazy enough to marry Gary! I'm sure nobody else would've! **My Mother-In-Law, Father-In-Law & Brother-In-Law (Terrence Hurst)** – Thanks for the warm welcome into your family. **My Under-18 Nieces & Nephew (Randal, Asha & Dameon)** – Y'all know y'all ain't got no business reading this, but somehow I'll bet y'all are reading this right now – Ohhh, I'ma tell y'alls mamas!

If I've forgotten someone, I'm very sorry! Make sure to bring it to my attention, so that I may give you proper recognition in my next novel. I definitely realize that no man is an island. And, no one becomes successful – alone. So, if I've overlooked you, I'd like to offer my sincere apology using the words of Rev. Jesse Jackson, *"Charge it to my head and not my heart!"*

Last but definitely not least – my entire family & friends! Thanks for being honest & supportive!

Winston - Winston@WinstonChapmanBooks.Com

CAUGHT UP!

The Life CHAPTER ONE

I couldn't believe I had gotten myself into this situation. Was old enough to know better. My mom always said, *the choices you make, will determine the quality of your life.* I was looking straight in the face, at the possibility of losing mine. Or at best, the loss of any life that would even remotely be described as quality.

It's the middle of the night, here I am scantily clad, sitting on a street curb, wrapped in a borrowed jacket with the letters APD stenciled on the back, answering a detectives questions, while trying to shield the blinding glare of the squad car's flashing lights.

◆◆

This dreadful nightmare all began just two years ago. I'd stormed out of my mama's house in Des Moines, Iowa -- vowing I'd never come back. Took with me the $746.29 I'd earned over the past summer working at the same diner that my mom had *schlepped* greasy food for the past 19 years. Determined I'd not be sentenced to that same life, I headed straight to the Greyhound bus station and bought a one-way ticket to Atlanta.

Made my choice of city *on-the-fly*, looking at a US Map, while standing in line at the ticket counter. Chose Atlanta because it was one of the places I was sure I'd connect with my roots. People who look like me. Understand me. Relate to me.

Thought about Chicago -- too dirty. Thought about New York -- too big. Washington D.C. was too hard to figure out, where it actually was on the map. Besides, Atlanta was a warm-weather city. And, it didn't hurt that it was so close to Florida.

As a black girl growing up in Des Moines, I never felt I belonged. Felt like a permanent guest everywhere I'd go. Being adopted didn't help. And being adopted by a white woman helped even less. Not to mention, I was obviously a product of an interracial relationship.

Though, everyone in town seemed to try to help me belong. It was just that, their need to make me feel at home, made me feel that much more like an outsider -- *the Special Negro*.

My soul and spirit, not to mention my smile had grown weary of pretending that I didn't feel different from everyone else. So, that was it. I decided I had to get out of there.

After graduation, I worked all summer at the diner. Listened to my customers, my neighbors tell crude racial jokes over the *cup-of-joe* I'd just served them. If ever I happened to wander by or be wiping off a nearby table just as they reached the racial-joke punch line, they'd simply turn to me and say, *"Oh, no offense, Raven?!"*

Like that made it alright? Like it was okay to insult my heritage, as long as you didn't mean it towards me?

There were only two other black girls at my high school. Shamika and Mercedes. Yet, they didn't nearly receive the *Special Negro* treatment that the white folks in town gave to me. Best I could figure was three reasons.

First, Shamika and Mercedes had not grown up here. They'd moved here, when their parents decided to escape the mean streets of Chicago, to pursue a more tranquil life in a smaller town. That, to the rednecks 'round here, nearly makes them foreigners.

Secondly, they were not light-skinned like me. Actually, I'm not that light. It's not like you can see my veins or anything. And, I don't turn red when I blush. But, compared to the other two black girls, you'd think I was Halle Berry because they were dark-skinned. A very pretty, smooth dark color, almost like coal.

Thirdly, their parents were black. Never understood how I somehow gained points in the eyes of the community by having a white mother. Somehow, I must be tamer. Less threatening. My light complexion and my so-called "frizzy" black hair made me almost an "honorary white girl". That is, just as long as I didn't rock-the-boat.

It's so funny how the folks in my town conveniently make use of their blinders. I felt I looked more like the black girls than any white girl. I had a big butt like theirs. My hair is nappy, not frizzy, like theirs. My skin got ashy like theirs did. And, I felt alone, like they did.

But, if you ask anybody in our town if there's stereotyping in our town? -- They'll tell you, *"Hell no! We all get along 'round here!"*.

Even the white boys I briefly dated were more interested in the *taboo* of the black side of me. I saw how they peered at my round, high-riding backside. Yet, at the same time, they hid behind the safety of the fact that I had a white side, too. With me, they could have their cake and eat it too. Lust after black beauty without it being evident.

Most guys decided to pursue me because they viewed me as some hidden Amazonian treasure. Every single guy I dated attempted to sleep with me on our first date. Absent was the romance I'd over-hear my white-girl classmates speak of.

No matter how honorable I thought the boy was at the beginning of the date, they all ended the same way. Grabby hands trying to expose my breasts to eager eyes.

It wasn't so much the grabby hands that I minded, as it was the *reason* for the grabby hands. It was never even an innocent true physical attraction. The kind where you actually like the person, but the extreme physical attraction makes you try to speed things up.

No, it was never anything close to that. Which would have been okay, I guess. These guys' assertions and advances had nothing to do with me, Raven, the person. Had more to do with the black-girl-Raven.

Quite easily, I could read the curiosity written in the pupils of their eyes, as they'd attempted to raise my shirt or sweater: *I wonder what this black girl's titties look like? Are the nipples different?*

Some even skipped the first step of trying to cop-a-feel on my tits, before viewing them. It was like they didn't care to feel them as much as they were curious to see them.

I believed that they figured my natural *jungle sexual instincts* would somehow be revealed in privacy. They were very wrong. And usually ended up going home with a sore pair of *balls*.

◆ ◆

I have to admit, sitting in the plastic-molded seat of the Greyhound bus station, I was a bit nervous about leaving the only place I'd known. Began wondering if I was making a mistake? At the same time, I knew if I didn't go now, I'd end up like everyone else in Des Moines. Satisfied with only talking about the big plans they had when they were young. And annually modifying their excuses for never actually doing it.

Working in a diner, you hear these excuses and stories just as many times a day as you refill coffee.

The faces are different, but the excuses are the same. *'I was going to become an airline pilot, but my girlfriend got pregnant and I had to support the family'* or *'I was going to go-to/finish college, but I had to pay the mortgage'*.

Then this type of comment is usually followed up with some type of half-hearted commitment to *one-day* complete the dream. *'Yeah, after the kids graduate, I'm gonna ....'* - you fill in the blank. Actually, neither the speaker nor the listener really believes a word. Yet, both shy away from disputing the validity. Instead, it just becomes a good game of reciprocating coffee conversation -- *you listen to my lie & I'll listen to yours.* Just one of the ways people in Des Moines make it through another unfulfilling day.

Though I was excited about getting out of Des Moines, I was not looking forward to the 48-hour bus ride to Atlanta. It seemed as though my bus made stops in every small town. Sometimes going west rather than east. But what could I expect for only $39?

As the bus pulled into Kansas City, Missouri for an hour-long layover, I began recognizing just how sheltered I'd been. Didn't even know there were two different Kansas City's. One in Missouri and the other in Kansas.

Got the feeling I was getting closer to my goal of being around more black people. The K.C. bus station was almost entirely filled with black folks. More than I'd ever seen at one time.

After a brief freshening in the just-barely sanitary bathroom, I found the Door #4, where my new bus would be boarding. I sat down next to a very pretty black girl, who looked a little older than me, about 21 or 22.

"Are you going to Atlanta too?", I said attempting to strike up a conversation.

Her nose was nestled in a romance novel. After a slight delay, apparently so that she could finish the sentence she was reading, she responded.

"Oh, um, yeah. But, I'm not taking the bus. A friend of mine is just meeting me here. We're gonna drive down.".

She was the color of burnt caramel with very striking features that perfectly matched her concise manner. Long, expertly flat-ironed hair that fanned out easily whenever she looked a different direction. Had a slender build, except she had logic-defying curves for someone of her size. The very tight, sleeveless, designer T-shirt she wore followed the contour of her torso like it had a road map, stopping just above her naval. The words on the front of her shirt stretched across her chest like a billboard. Though the words actually said *Tommy Girl*, when I first saw them, to me they read, "Look Here!". She had an almost elegant, hip-hop-Jennifer Lopez style.

"Watcha going to Atlanta for?", I bluntly asked.

"I'm a model, actress *and* a singer, on my way to be in a music video.", proudly she responded, though she attempted to be *ho-hum* about it.

Craftily, she did not mention whose video, so that I'd be enticed to ask more about her.

"Really! Who's video?", I took the bait.

"M.C. Krush.", she said. Again, matter-of-factly.

"COOL! Cool, cool, that's cool." , repeatedly I chanted with declining exuberance while nodding my head. Was beginning to recognize that I was sounding like someone who ain't-never-been-nowhere.

It was too late to un-do it, but I'd try anyway.

Sensing my interest had plateau-ed, she kept the subject going.

"Yeah, it's cool sometimes. But, we work long hours, too...... I'm sorry, I never introduced myself. I'm Nia Moore.", she said, resting the book in her lap while extending her newly manicured hand to me, in just the manner a star would while connecting with one of their fans.

"Nice to meet you, I'm Raven. Raven Klein.", I said, without paying too much attention to the painted designs on her fingertips.

"Are you in the entertainment industry?", Nia asked.

I blushingly laughed. "Who me? No!", I said, shaking my head.

"Why do you say it like that?"

"I don't know? I just don't think anyone would mistake me for someone on their way to becoming famous."

"That's not true. I thought maybe you were a singer or a model."

Okay, now Nia was just being polite. I never thought of myself as bad-looking, but a model? *Come on now*. It's not like, I *wasn't* in good shape. I had a slim waist, perky breast and a shapely bottom.

But Nia, *oh my goodness*, I was nothing like her. Her arms were toned, definition in the shoulders, forearms and biceps areas. Plus, she had that thin-shapely look going for her, like Tyra Banks. Just enough meat in all the right places. No excess anywhere.

I've noticed models, at least black models, seemed to have contradictory physical features. You know, narrow hips, yet a protruding curvy backside that stops where the thigh begins. No *Bu-thigh* issues, where the butt is not distinct from the thighs. And they all have flat stomachs, narrow lower torsos leading up to a ballooning bust, accented by strong-looking but not over-bearing arms.

"So what you going to Atlanta for?", Nia questioned.

"Just a change of scenery.", I said vaguely, uncomfortable *with the shoe on the other foot* and me being the subject.

In Iowa, people read signals. Not true for city girls, I was finding out firsthand.

"Change of scenery?", Nia said, dramatically leaning backward, simultaneously contorting her face like she either resented my vagueness or didn't understand or both.

"Change of scenery? Whatzz that mean? Are you visiting, moving or what?", boldly she continued.

Feeling intimidated and not wanting to be on her bad side, even for the short time I had left to wait for my bus departure, I decided to come clean.

"Yeah, I'm moving there. Just didn't wanna live in Iowa, anymore."

With a huge grin, clapping her hands together and alternating stomping her feet, she said, "IOWA!! Girl, I didn't know any black people lived in Iowa!"

Passively and semi-humorously, I tried to make light of the moment, "Yeah. Well, there aren't anymore black people in Iowa. I was the last one."

I didn't like my town either. Obviously, that's why I was moving. Yet and still, I felt like a stranger shouldn't be allowed to make fun of Des Moines.

When her laughter had subsided, I could see that Nia really meant no harm. She wasn't cold-hearted. And could tell, she could read my face.

"Girl, I'm just fuckin' with you!", she said, while giving me a side-to-side rocking, sisterly hug with one arm. "So, where in Atlanta are you going to be living?", seamlessly she transitioned the awkward moment away.

"Actually, I don't know yet?"

That hug, made me feel more comfortable sharing information.

"YOU don't know yet?", she said, tempering her tone down by the end of her sentence. Didn't want me to close up, I guess.

"No."

"Well, Raven, do you have family living there?"

"No."

"Do you already have a job in Atlanta?"

"Um, no."

The concern on her face made me even more nervous. Nia paused her questioning for a moment. Then she took a deep breath, chewed on her upper-lip while her eyes rose inside her eyelids in thought, like she was trying to figure out a geometrical problem. Her eyes quickly scanned me over then rose inside her eyelids again, like she was double-checking the answer. Then she resumed speaking in a very calm, *please-believe-me* voice.

"Okay, listen....", she whispered, placing her hand on my knee, "..... my agent, the guy who's picking me up, keeps a two-bedroom apartment rented for me in Atlanta. You seem like a nice girl. I probably should not be doing this, but, I think you're gonna get eaten-up if I don't. What I'm trying to say is that you can stay with me until you get on your feet."

Surprised by the offer, tempted to take her up on it, I decided to decline.

"Thank you so much Nia, for your offer. But, I think I'm gonna be okay. I've got my own money.", confidently I spoke.

Biting her lip again, Nia glanced at the very expensive watch on her wrist. It seemed as though she was starting to lose patience.

"Raven. The A-T-L is a big city that you know nothing about. How much money do you think it's gonna cost to get an apartment?"

"I dunno, maybe, four or five hundred?"

Nia just lowered her head and shook it side to side.

"Try more like $800 a month. Plus, $800 security deposit. Plus, money to turn on the electric and gas. Plus, groceries for you to eat. Not to mention, dishes & pans to cook with. And, we ain't even talked about no furniture, so you can have a place to sit or sleep. That's over 2-G's right there! OH! And how you gonna find an apartment with no car! OH! Better yet, how you gonna qualify for an apartment with no job or local references........".

Now, I was really worried. Most of the things Nia had mentioned, I'd never even thought about.

Noticing that her volume had increased during the explanation of how serious my situation was, Nia motioned for me to follow her outside.

From her purse, she pulled out a gold cigarette case filled with Newport cigs. Nia offered me one, but I didn't smoke. She turned away, cupping one hand around the lighter to shield the wind, as she lit up. Immediately, she began pulling hard on the cig, like she was stressed-out.

After a few drags, she began speaking to me as she exhaled the smoke away from me.

"Raven, I don't know what you're running from in Iowa, but I can tell you're not a bad person. You just have to understand, you're gonna see alot of things you never dreamed-of in Atlanta.", she said, contagiously nodding at me.

"I know.", I said, nodding back to her, now more worried than ever. Especially after hearing her long list of expenses that I failed to consider.

"All I'm saying is, I can help you. Everybody needs some help. You're a pretty girl. I'm sure my agent could even find you some work in the meantime. So, you might want to think about my offer before my agent gets here, okay? That's all I'm saying, okay?"

"Okay. Thank you.", I said, having already made up my mind that I must take her offer. But, I wanted to kill a little time, so that Nia would think that I had given it some serious thought.

Just then, a shiny black Cadillac Escalade pulled into the Greyhound parking lot and honked the horn.

Nia stomped out her cigarette, waved to the tinted window, sprayed a burst of breath-freshener in her mouth and surveyed the ground around her to make sure she had both of her bags.

"Well, Raven, that's my agent. Whatzit gonna be?", she questioned, tilting her head to the side while holding her muscular arms out to the side.

"If you don't mind, I would like to take you up on your offer. I promise I'll stay out of your way and pay my own way ....",
I unnecessarily rambled.

Nia interrupted my unnecessary rambling with a hug and smile. This time, giving me a two-arm embrace.

The car horn sounded again as we made our way over to the mammoth vessel.

As we approached, the trunk popped open shortly before the *Herculean* man exited out of the driver's side door.

Nia led the way. I followed far enough behind to allow her to have whatever conversation was needed to explain my presence.

The 6'4" - 250 lb. man wrapped his massive arms around her waist, planted a quaint peck on Nia's lips before bear-hugging her feet completely off the ground. Gingerly, he placed Nia back on the ground, while looking at me.

His embrace was ended with a playful pat on Nia's backside. To which, Nia responded with a hard punch to his arm that had no effect, as he tapped her bottom once more.

"Rico, this is my friend Raven. Raven, this is Rico.", Nia introduced us.

"Nice to meet ya Raven.", Rico said.

"Nice to meet you Rico.", I nervously responded, while shaking his hand.

Although he appeared to be of a gentle nature, while my hand was easily being swallowed by his, I couldn't help but think how easy it would be for his hand to crush mine, even by mistake.

"Raven's moving to the A-T-L. I told her she could stay with me.", Nia informed him.

"Cool! Let's roll!", Rico said, holding both of Nia's bags and gesturing for me to give mine to him as well.

While Nia was explaining the situation to him, I'd wondered if Rico would veto our deal? Thankfully, he didn't.

Rico loaded the bags in the back and it wasn't long before we were heading south on I-70, on our way to Atlanta.

Rico's Escalade was fully loaded. Chromed wheels, sunroof, gray leather seats and a pop-out television screen with a DVD player.

On the road to St. Louis, which would be our first stop on this 15-hour journey, I learned that Rico was a former NFL linebacker. Played his college ball at Georgia Tech. Even before he explained the knee injury that had ended his career, I'd already assumed something like that, as he looked far too young to be retired.

After his third season in the NFL, at age 25, Rico got injured playing in the Pro-Bowl game in Hawaii. Fortunately, he had just signed a guaranteed contract. The deal was for 6 years, the first two years were guaranteed. The total contract would have paid him $9-million. Plus, a signing-bonus of $4-million. Because he got injured before the season, he was entitled to payment for the first two-years ($1.5 million each year) and he got to keep the signing bonus. Rico was sitting pretty with $7 million.

I'd wondered earlier when I saw Rico hug and kiss Nia what the attraction was, but now I knew. Rico's not ugly or anything. Actually, he's very handsome. Thick eyebrows, long eyelashes and a perfect smile.

It was just a size thing, I guess. Nia, though tall at 5'9, most likely did not weigh even half as much as Rico. Even wondered how such a small girl could handle such a big man, if you know what I mean.

Rico owned two nightclubs in Atlanta, hence his involvement in promoting Nia's career. With his contacts from his NFL days still being fresh, he could open doors Nia knew she'd never make it through.

Didn't know if Nia was playing him or not? Or, if it was the other way around? They might be madly in love. I didn't know.

I'd never known anyone with a million dollars before. I guess, you just get suspicious when you're around some Donald Trump-type environment.

Wondered why they'd meet at a bus station in K.C. versus somewhere else? And, why they weren't flying instead of driving?

Turns out, Nia had been in K.C. for a modeling shoot. She'd be the *Beauty of The Week* in the next issue of *Jet* Magazine. Rico was in St. Louis, attending a former teammate's week-long bachelor party and wedding. They decided to meet at the Greyhound station, because Rico had already driven four-and-half hours coming up to K.C. to pick-up Nia and the Greyhound station was close to I-70, therefore he wouldn't have to navigate his way through downtown K.C. to get to her hotel. Besides, Nia had already checked out of her room.

It was around 7:30 PM when we pulled into St. Louis.

"Raven, are you in a hurry to get to Atlanta?", Rico asked.

"No. Not really?"

"I think we gonna stop at a hotel in St. Louis, if that's alright with you?"

Like I was gonna say no. They were my ride. Not to mention, Nia represented my living quarters in Atlanta.

"Fine with me.", I said, smiling back to him in the rear view mirror.

Rico put on his wireless phone earpiece. Apparently called a hotel, making a reservation of two rooms. Not rooms, *suites* is the word I heard him use.

We pulled into the Grand Marquis hotel. A very classy hotel. The staff clearly knew who Rico was. They treated us royally. A valet took the car. Not one, but two bellhops placed our bags on the gold luggage racks and led us through the marble-floored lobby, past the check-in counter directly to a private elevator.

As I watched one of the bellhops pressing the 25th floor button, the top floor in the hotel, I couldn't help but think about how drastic a change I was experiencing.

Less than six hours ago, I was riding on a nasty bus. Now, I'm about to enter a suite in a very classy hotel.

Exiting the elevator, I now understood the purpose of the two bellhops. One was for me! Seeing as our rooms were in opposite directions.

Before we parted, Rico slapped a fifty-dollar bill in my bellhop's hand and began to clarify things for me.

"Hey, Raven, everything's on me. If you need something, just call downstairs and they'll take care of you. Anything at all, order a movie, use the phone long-distance, order room service, need a ride somewhere in the hotel limo. Anything at all! I mean it!", he said authoritatively. Attempting to make sure, I'd not be shy about anything.

Nia, standing next to him, just smiled proudly before speaking.

"Why don't we go downstairs and get something to eat? Raven, I know you've gotta be hungry?"

I was. Not to mention tired from the twelve hours I'd spent on the bus prior to meeting Nia.

"That's cool. Thanks you guys!", I said, as genuinely as I could.

Thanks, didn't nearly seem quite enough.

"Alright, let's meet downstairs at 8:30?", Rico added.

Nia and I agreed.

In the restaurant, Rico repeated his, *its-on-me* comments.

I wanted to order something not that expensive, but it was virtually impossible. There was nothing on the menu that cost less than $22. So, I ordered the twenty-two dollar French Dip sandwich.

Midway through the meal, both Rico and Nia broke out their cell phones. Rico making plans to head out with some of his buddies still in-town from the wedding. Nia, no doubt, calling some girls she knew in St. Louis.

As we were leaving the restaurant, on our way to the private elevator, Rico was stopped by a well-dressed, well-built, handsome friend of his. They exchanged *man-hugs* that seemed like it hurt. Hard pounding on each other's back.

It was clear that this guy also knew Nia. 'Cause he smiled at her and turned the *switch* on his *hug-dial* from tough to gentle.

Then his eyes made their way towards me.

"Damn. Now who is this?", he commented, while extending his hand.

Nia rolled her eyes like she knew this *slickster* all too well.

"This is Raven.", Nia said, deliberately separating our hands.

"Well, it is certainly nice to meet you Raven. I'm Brian, friends call me BJ........."

"That ain't all they call you.", I heard Nia, silently echo in the background.

"............. Anyway, what y'all getting into? Y'all don't mind, if *I* tag along?", BJ invited himself.

"Man, we ain't gettin' into nothin'. I was getting ready to go hang out with Ty and K.C. -- you know Todd just got married this weekend."

"Bullshit!", BJ seemed surprised.

"Naw, I'm for real. If you wanna roll, we can roll?"

"That's straight!", BJ said, turning his attention to me. Reaching for my hand, he kissed the back of it and said, "I'll see you later, Raven."

"Yeah, whatever!", Nia barked back at BJ.

Rico was tickled by BJ's corny antics. He simply put his big *paw* on the back of BJ's neck and guided him away from me, towards the front door before shouting back to Nia that they may be out kinda late.

"Who is that?", I asked Nia.

"Gurrrll, nobody you wanna know. Trust me!", she said.

It wasn't like I couldn't see through BJ's phony facade. I was just curious as to who he was. And about the relationship between him and Rico.

For that matter, I was curious about *her* relationship with Rico. She kept referring to him as her agent. Yet, there was clear evidence that they had much more than just a business partnership. The kiss they shared. To say nothing about the room they were sharing.

I was definitely in uncharted waters. Nia was in, as she called it, *'The Entertainment Industry'*. Maybe this is the way everyone behaves in showbiz.

"So, Raven whatchew *fenna* do? Me and my girls about to head to Pleasers Club. Did you wanna come?"

"No, I'm real tired. I think I'm gonna go to sleep. What time are we leaving tomorrow?"

"Gurrll, I don't even know. But with Rico, you can believe it won't be before noon! Don't worry about it, we'll call you early enough!"

"I just didn't wanna be holding nobody up.", I clarified.

"You sure you don't wanna go to Pleasers? You don't know what you're missing?"

"Why? What is Pleasers?"

"Psst. It's just a club."

"What kinda club?"

"A strip club. Men dancers on one side, women dancers on the other side. That's probably where Rico an'em are going anyway."

I was tempted as hell to go. Had never been to a place like that. However, my body felt like it needed to sleep for a month.

"Naw, I don't think so ......"

"We ain't leaving the hotel 'til around midnight. You could go to sleep now, and I could come wake you up around 11:15."

The private elevator doors opened to our floor as we continued our conversation.

"Nia, I don't know?"

"Aw-right. But, you're gonna miss King Kong?", Nia toyed with me, as she slowly turned towards her room.

"Okay, I'll ask. What or who's a King Kong?"

"Can't explain, you'll just have to see it for yourself."

"No promises, but call me at 11:00.", I finally conceded.

The Night CHAPTER TWO

That night at Pleasers, the parking lot was filled with nothing but expensive cars. Mercedes, Lexus', Jaguars, Porches, BMW's, Audi's, and all the oversized expensive SUV's. Even saw a Ferrari.

Nia's friend was expectedly cute and sexy-dressed.

Tyanna had a look like Beyonce' from Destiny's Child. About 5'8, maybe 135 pounds, hair in micro-braids and dyed brown-blonde, a *meat-n-potatoes* backside and a bright-dimple smile across her bronze colored face.

She was the only girl, other than me, that looked like they'd eaten a decent meal in the last six months, or that weighed over 115 pounds.

I was kinda diggin' her style, too. And not just because her shape, closest resembled mine. Her approach was definitely eye-catching. She was wearing a camouflage-print spandex top with only one shoulder strap and four narrow horizontal splits, revealing a peak at her cleavage. Low-cut jeans with a chain belt. The jeans were cut so low, her tattoo was peeking out the back. Another tattoo was making its debut, on her chest. Tyanna even had a flashing-light naval button.

If I was a guy, I'da been confused as to where to look on her. She had a plethora of *look-here* items.

Nia's *look-here* area was easy to figure out. The same as at the bus station. Her titties. She loved tight shirts with writing on them. Her busty-ness always stretched the letters horizontally. And, her itty-bitty lower torso just magnified her bosom.

Nia and I probably wore the same cup size. But, because of her smaller frame, her endowment looked more dramatic. Not to mention, they were shaped perfectly round, like a firmly packed ball of clay.

Tonight I could tell she didn't have a bra on. Which made me wonder, *Was her perkiness a result of some augmentation?* Maybe, I was just jealous.

As we walked from the parking lot, I noticed the line to get into the club was extremely long. But that didn't impact us as we were heading toward a side-door VIP entrance.

I was loving this type of life. Never waiting for anything. I didn't even get *'carded'* at the door. I was with Nia, and I guess that was good enough for the bouncer.

Inside the club, the hip-hop music was loud. Not to mention the combination of the screaming men and women.

The stage was in the middle. There was a wall that divided the stage in half. One side was filled with men watching women dance. You couldn't see the dancers on the other side of the wall. However, from around the side of the stage, I could see the excited men waving dollar bills.

We sat in a private booth that had better furniture in it than my mom had in her house. Black leather sofas, expensive-looking coffee and end tables, entirely enclosed by tinted glass. This was cool because it helped reduce some of the blaring noise from the speakers.

Shortly after sitting down, our shirtless, g-string male waiter came to take our order. Nia ordered a sex-on-the-beach. Tyanna, a blue-mother-fucker. When he turned to me to take my order, the giggles came out. The waiter's dick, hanging *very nicely* in his g-string, was directly in front of my face.

Nia stepped in, "Umm...she'll have a sex-on-the-beach, as well."

"All on your tab, Nia?", he clarified.

"Yeah."

Nia turned to me somewhat surprised by my reaction.

"Girl, how old are you?"

"19. Why?"

"Ooooo. I don't know if this girl can hang with us, Nee.", Tyanna jumped in.

"Why? How old are you guys?", I quickly responded.

"21", said Nia. "22", responded Tyanna.

"Oooo, Nee. We gotta get her a private dance with King Kong.", Tyanna proposed, very giddy.

Nia covering a smile with her hand, nodded *yes* back to Tyanna.

As the waiter returned with our drinks, I folded my lips in, to keep from giggling again.

Nia reached over to me with a twenty-dollar bill, "Here Raven, give this to him."

I attempted to hand it to him, but he moved his hands above his head, gyrated his lower body before pushing his groin closer to the bill in my hand.

"Put it in his g-string.", Tyanna leaned over and whispered to me.

As I did, looking up I caught him glaring at me with *very* sexy, serious eyes.

"Thank you.", he said, kissing the back of my hand.

"Alright, here we go.....", Tyanna said, raising her glass, waiting for us to do the same.

"Get ready to take it to the head!"

The way they were preparing themselves, I figured out, Tyanna meant we're supposed to drink it, all at once. Both Nia and Tyanna made it. I wasn't a liquor drinker, so it took me about three times to get my drink all the way down.

In Iowa, we drank mostly beer at parties.

As we downed drink after drink, the liquor started getting me bold.

"So Nia, what's the deal between you and Rico?", I slurred out.

"Ohhhpp. Nee, I think your girl's drunk.", instigated Tyanna.

"I am not. So whatzup? Is he your man or what?"

"Look at Miss Iowa, all up in my biz-ness.", Nia said with a smile.

"Naw, Rico ain't my man. He's just my agent."

"She thinks Rico's your man?", Tyanna giggled toward Nia. "I know what she needs. Raven needs some business of her own, instead of being all up in yours. I'll be right back!", Tyanna continued with a mischievous grin and a wink.

Tyanna returned with a cute-as-hell, brown-skinned male dancer. A 6-foot-two, mouth-watering piece of chocolate.

"Wooooo-oo!", Nia screamed, as they came through our door.

Tyanna quickly put her bottom back in the leather seat, so not to delay the show.

Costumed in a loin cloth, gold fig leaves looped around each bicep and a string of fig leaves around his forehead. He had a god-like chest that he could make bounce by flexing, a stomach that rippled like a *Ruffles* potato chip and arms like damn!

"Did you guys want the regular VIP dance or the Private VIP?", asked the dancer.

Tyanna and Nia looked at each other, turned in unison to harmoniously scream, "The PRIVATE!"

The man then went to our door and turned the lock. He started dancing over by Nia first. Then made his way around the room. Letting each of us spank his butt.

Next, he centered himself in the middle of the room. Paused for dramatic purposes. Then ripped off his loin cloth.

"Ohhhh my goodness!", screamed Nia, clapping her hands together.

"Damn, King Kong!", yelled Tyanna, even more excited.

I was just in shock. So, this was King Kong? Aptly named. I'm not lying, his dick had to be 14 inches long. Non-erect! And, it had girth too. It didn't seem real. Hell, the damn thing hung mid-way down his thigh.

This time, when Kong made his way around the room, it was much more sensual. Placed his dick in Nia's hands. Took two hands to hold it! Did the same with Tyanna and me.

I was hot as hell inside just holding that dick. Could see it in Nia and Tyanna too.

These were some wild girls! I was definitely intoxicated. By the liquor and by Kong.

His third trip around the room, he incorporated *our bodies* into the show. Caressing and sucking on Nia's titties through her shirt, until her eyes closed in shear enjoyment and her nipples were popping through.

Then he stood Tyanna up, facing her towards the sofa. Bent her over. Put her hands on the back of the sofa and began mocking *'doggie style'* with her. Keeping her in that bent-over position, he stood off to the side of her, reached over her backside between her legs and began stroking. Slowly across her jeans. Up and down. Then side to side.

It marked the first time anyone had been able to shut her up all night.

That is, until she moaned, "Uhhh-uhh".

After Tyanna made that passionate noise, Kong really went to work on her. Increasing his pace. Stroking the hell out of her, until Tyanna's body shivered, forcing her to grab his hand as she tried to straighten up.

By her lip-folded, eye-dazed expression on her face, *I knew* Tyanna had just cum. Hell, I was damn close myself just witnessing the action.

Nia giggled in the aftermath of watching him with Tyanna and in the anticipation of me being next.

"Hold out your hands.", Kong instructed me, as he poured some warm oil into my hands.

Placing his *thang* in my hands, his eyes signaled for me to begin stroking him. I did.

"Yeah girl! Work it girl!", shouted the renewed Tyanna.

"No, you work *her!*", choreographed Nia.

Kong obeyed. He began giving me the same treatment as Nia, manly caressing and nipple pinching through my shirt. Then he nibbled my neck, while his hand, now between my legs, rubbed me into ecstasy. Tightly held onto his neck as I couldn't help but to cum in my pants.

"Look at her face!", Nia enjoyed laughing to Tyanna.

Nia's comment made Kong cut my time short, as he returned to her.

Lifting up Nia's shirt, revealing her perfect *Playboy-magazine* breasts, he began sucking hard until her face squinted. Unbuttoned her pants, slid his hand way down deep. Deep enough to reach *pay-dirt*.

Just before Nia's body began convulsing, I noticed that Kong was only *semi*-hard. This guy was incredible!

Then I noticed Tyanna, shamelessly getting out of her clothes.

And so did he. He started to abandon Nia to go towards Tyanna, until Tyanna demanded, "Uhn-uhn. You're not done with her yet!".

With Nia lying on her back, he slid her narrow hips completely out of her pants and nestled his head between her legs.

From my viewpoint, all I could see was the back of Kong's head moving side-to-side, like he was saying *'no'*. And Nia's legs shaking and her body continuously jerking up and down. Her facial expression had no remnants of the sophistication I'd seen earlier in the bus station.

"Ahhh, shit. I'M CUMMING! I'm cummin, cummin', ummin'", Nia feverishly exhaled with glazed, wandering eyes. Her hands, desperately trying to push his head out of *that* area.

Tyanna was busy playing with herself as Kong, now fully erect, stood up to see who was next. There were no volunteers, so Kong decided it must be my turn. I guess, because I had the most clothes on.

Shortly after Kong had lifted my shirt, re-nibbled my already sore nipples and stroked me to a sequel orgasm, Tyanna made a comment.

"Okay now, somebody's gotta get fucked!"

There was a pause.

Tyanna continued, "I'm sayin', we bought the Private VIP, whozit gonna be?"

Silence. Nobody dared volunteer.

I thought, *Why don't she do it? She brought Kong back here? It was her idea?*

There was no way in hell, I was gonna attempt to handle Kong *inside me*! *I knew* he had too much for me. This man had just given three girls orgasms, at least once each, some of us twice, without being as so much as fully erect. Oh, hell no! I don't think I could ever be that drunk.

"Y'all scared!", declared Tyanna.

"Yeah we scared. Why don't you do it!", battled Nia.

"I ain't scared!"

"Then do it!", Nia, again challenged.

There was a brief pause before Tyanna said to Kong, *"Come on"*, as she positioned her body back against the leather sofa.

Judging by Tyanna's face, I think she *needed* Nia to challenge her into doing it with Kong.

As Kong unwrapped a condom, that when rolled-up on his massive dick looked like a thimble, Tyanna appeared to be having second-thoughts. But, I'd learn, she was not the kind who'd *punk-out*, even when she should.

Her normal *in-your-face* demeanor had humbled a bit. Softened, somewhat. And, her eyes never left his dick. Wanting to know its location at all times. Apparently, didn't want any surprise penetration. No more I guess, than a kid would want a surprise shot from a doctor.

Nia and I intensely watched. Unabated curiosity. Wondered what the outcome would be. Though, we were pretty certain of it. But, like a Mike Tyson fight we were still drawn.

As Kong positioned himself on his knees in front of Tyanna, spread her legs apart in a 'V', took himself in his right hand preparing to penetrate, Tyanna decided to forego ego and make a plea.

"Wait, wait, wait. Go SLOW! OKAY?! Very slow! And, not deep!", Tyanna said, staring directly into his eyes and nodding.

Kong just smiled at her nervousness. Reassuringly, he nodded back. He must've heard that type of apprehension, all of his life. Every girl he'd ever been with must've had the same reaction.

"I-yigh-yigh-yigh, ooo-ooo-ooo", Tyanna groaned, as he entered.

This match-up was already a no-contest. Not more than four to five, slow 4-inch-deep strokes into it, Tyanna was begging.

"Ooooo-ooo, Slower, slower, oh my gaa... oh my gaa... oh my gaa..... oh my shit...I...I'm....Cu...um...MING!..I'm...cum...mm...ming!"

Tyanna's thick legs were shaking. Her face, dually-pained with embarrassment of her duration and by the residual ecstasy, not yet fully released.

Still connected, Kong leaned back to give us a better view. And, out of pure desire to prove clear supremacy, decided to showboat for Nia and me. Pinched Tyanna's reddened nipples, to a now, full half-inch. Gave her, about an inch more of himself. Seductively moistened his thumb with his tongue, then placed it directly on her clit.

No need for a referee to declare a winner in this contest. A picture's worth a thousand words. He wasn't moving at all. No pumping. No humping. Nothing. Meanwhile, Tyanna was going crazy.

"Oh my gaa...oh my gaa...oh my gaa-aah.....OOHH, OH-Shit, Oh my gaa...Ohh-SHIT", Tyanna shrieked, as she tried to make eye contact with him between her jerking.

I have to give the girl credit. Tyanna's will, was very strong. Though, she *wasn't* fooling anybody. She was definitely Kong's puppet. He was no more than five, out of a possible fourteen inches deep and she'd already cum three or four times, in about a 90-second span. Yet, she hung in, as best as she could. I'll give her that!

Realizing that Tyanna's common-sense was definitely exceeded by her ego. An ego that *would not* allow her to concede on her own. Kong decided to do it for her. Slowly backing out his now creamy condom, signaling it was the end with a kiss to Tyanna's exhausted and flushed face.

Though, the whole thing lasted less than 10 minutes, judging by Tyanna's face, you'd've sworn it'd been two hours.

"Thanks baby! You were great!", he said so genuinely, I'd've believed him, had I not just seen it.

Then Kong turned to me and Nia.

"Anybody else want some?", Kong encouraged, holding up fresh condom packets.

Me and Nia, unplanned, had the same exact reaction. Moving away from him, shaking our heads, *'Hell No!'*.

"Thanks ladies!", Kong said, handing each of us his card. "Call me anytime you wanna have some more fun! I'm gonna have the waiter bring you guys some more drinks."

Looking over to Tyanna, he publicly announced, "Don't worry about it babe, I do this for a living! I'm an adult film performer. Listen, you're not bad, for not being a professional!"

Then Kong continued out a back door to our booth that I hadn't even known existed.

Shocked looks were on all three of our faces, after his revelation. It certainly explained why the three of us couldn't handle him. And, I guess his comment was of some consolation to Tyanna.

We took turns cleaning up in the private bathroom that was located in our booth before resuming our drinking. We were attempting to regain the high we'd all lost, due *solely* to Kong's visit.

Tonight, was very exciting. It was the kind of night where you wanted a souvenir. Although I was certain, my memory of this night would never fade.

I've always considered myself as a little on the wild side. But, I'd never had an opportunity in Iowa, like I did tonight.

This wild escapade was bonding us together. Guess it makes sense. When you orgasm in front of someone, it's only natural that you feel a connection. Like our own little secret, that only the three of us shared.

Later, we even felt comfortable teasing and mocking each other about our moments.

Nia teased Tyanna, "Girl, Kong had yo' thighs shaking like a 6.0 earthquake!"

Nia cracked up laughing. So did Tyanna. I just smiled, not sure of how far to take it.

"Aw, fuck you girl!", Tyanna said with a smile. "What about you, Nee. When that boy was lickin' yo' pussy, I thought you were having a seizure!", Tyanna continued by shaking her body and rolling her eyes to the top of her head, mocking Nia.

They both, giggled again.

"Oh, and don't think we forgot about you, Iowa.", Tyanna included me. "Iowa-girl trying to have an orgasm on the sly. I saw your lips quivering, while you were trying to suck in air. Sounded like a damn tuba player with asthma!"

We all fell out laughing and raised a toast to King Kong. Then headed back to the hotel.

Schooled CHAPTER THREE

The next day, I woke up at the crack of noon. Eyes badly in need of some *Visine*. I had cotton-mouth. My head was spinning from the *Sex-on-the-Beach*. Nipples *still* erect from last night's sex-on-the-sofa.

Had all the symptoms of a wild night out. The only thing I didn't have was any regrets. I'd had the time of my life. Felt free.

As I turned to grab the phone to order some food, I just about screamed when I saw someone sleeping in the other bed. I'd forgotten that Tyanna came back to the hotel with us last night. And, that she'd stayed in my room.

I ordered two servings of pasta before taking a long hot shower. By the time I came out of the bathroom, Tyanna was awake and the food was sitting on the table.

"Whazzup girl?", Tyanna greeted me.

"Nothing. I ordered you some pasta, if you're hungry?", I said, sitting on the bed, *lotioning* my legs.

"Thanks Iowa!", Tyanna responded. Then she seemed to notice the size of my legs as I was putting on my underwear. "Girl, I didn't know you were that thick. Girl, you gotta nice body!"

"Thanks. So do you!"

"So whatchya think Iowa?"

"'Bout what?"

"About last night?!"

"Oh, that was cool! I had a good time."

"I *know* you did!", Tyanna smiled.

"No, I *know* YOU DID! I don't know how you did it with King Kong?"

"I dunno either! Especially seeing as I don't get too much dick."

My eyebrows furrowed in confusion. She was a very pretty girl. I couldn't imagine *her* having a tough time finding men to screw.

"Well you could've fooled me. Even King Kong said you were good!"

"Psst. Please. That shit don't count. He was just being nice. He knew he wore me-the-fuck-out!", Tyanna contagiously giggled at the end of her sentence. Apparently, she'd just done a *visual-rewind* of last night.

"Yeah, he was good. But, damn. He is a porn star, after all. I'll bet he gets paid big dollars!"

"No. I mean, he probably makes decent money. But, not nearly as much as the women he's fucking in the movie! Did you know that some women in adult films make up to $5,000 per film?"

"Damn! That much! How do you know that?"

"Yeah, I looked into it once. But I don't think I could stand running into big-dick niggas like Kong."

"Yeah, I hear you!", I agreed.

"I mean, they ain't all big like that. I've been to a couple tapings."

"You have!"

"Yeah, it's no big deal. I've even been offered $4,000 by a producer to be in his film. Not like I was shame or anything. It's just, that they expect the girls to do alota shit. You know, anal stuff."

"Oh, hell no!"

"I'm saying, it ain't *that* bad. I've done it before. Privately. Actually, the best orgasms I've ever had were from anal sex."

"Don't that shit hurt?"

"Naw, not really. Well, no more than sex did, the first time I had it. You just start slow and use lots of lubrication. Start with fingers, first."

Okay, now she was giving me too much information.

"It still sounds like it hurts."

"I can't explain it right. You'll just have to try it for yourself someday."

"Yeah, I don't think so!"

"Whatever. Anyway, I turned down that producer's offer. He wanted me to sign to a four movie deal *and* start right off in the *'big leagues'*, with guys like King Kong. Not to mention, anal stuff. I'da done it, if he'd've started me off slowly. Start me on an amateur scene first. Maybe, some masturbation scenes, playing with toys or just messing around with other girls. Or at least, some smaller-dick guys, something slow like that.", Tyanna spoke as though she'd done her research.

I was speechless. Well, my mouth was. My mind was very noisy. *"So, that's why she said she 'doesn't get too much dick'. She must be bisexual?!"*, I thought. Also, my mind was hurriedly doing arithmetic. Four movie deal times four-grand was $16,000 she turned down. Damn!

Tyanna interrupted my silent calculations, "So, I hear you're staying with Nia in Atlanta. Are you modeling, singing or what?"

"Why does everyone keep asking me that? Do I look like a model?"

"Yeah!"

"No I don't. Models are super-skinny.........."

"I can tell *you* from Iowa. That's white models. Black models got some meat on their bones. Tyra Banks *gotta* booty, now don't she? Besides, you could be one of the background dancers in videos for all I know?

And you know, they gotta have something to shake to be in those videos."

"Well, thanks for the compliment. But, I'm not a model. And, you don't ever wanna hear me sing!"

"Well then, whatzup? Rico gonna give you a job at the club?"

"No. I dunno. I just met Rico. I was a waitress in Iowa, I thought I might ...."

"Girl, you better ask Rico for a job. You can get pee-aid! That's where I work."

Damn, I might wanna to talk Rico?, I thought. I wouldn't mind making enough money where I could easily turn down a 16-grand offer like Tyanna.

"What do you do?"

"Dance at Rico's club."

Uh-oh?, I thought. Assumed it was a strip-club. Didn't really want a career as a nude dancer. Though, I was already becoming hooked on Nia and Tyanna's lifestyle.

"Is it a strip club?"

"Of course. Why? Don't tell me you're shame of your body?"

"No, that's not it. It's just...... Is that where Nia works too?"

"Heee-ell NO! Nia, ain't hardly that wild!"

What was she saying about me? That I was?, I thought.

"Yeah, I don't know. I don't think I have the right type of body for nude dancing."

"There goes that Iowa-thinking again. You're going to Atlanta. Home of the big bootys. You definitely have the right type of body. I'm not gonna convince you. I'll call you at Nia's when I get back there. Take you to the club. You check it out. The easiest money you'll ever make!"

"Really?"

"Fo' real! Make a $1000 a week! Sometimes, five-hunnid a night! Nuttin but big ballers come up in Rico's clubs. Athletes, movie stars, singers. Ain't no sex goin'-on. Most of 'em are married and just wanna see some different pussy. That's it!"

Tyanna definitely had me interested.

While she was in the shower, I chewed on my cold pasta and thought about it. Still kinda wanted to see what type of job I could get without becoming a stripper. Though, I did realize I had no real qualifications.

Did alotta thinking.

It could be a good last resort! Wouldn't hurt to check it out! I'd be able to get a car and my own apartment fast!, I pondered.

Though, to be honest, I didn't consider myself of the stripper-mentality. Nor was I confident in my body or my ability to dance sexy. Wondered, would I be able to make that kinda money? And still, I had reservations on how *any* girl could make that much money *without* sex being involved?

After Tyanna's shower, wrapped in a towel, she continued her presentation on the stripping business.

"Okay, Raven listen. To be a good dancer, you really only need to know four basic dance moves. *The Booty-Jiggle. The Booty-Rub. The Tittie-Pinch* and *The Clit Peek-A-Boo.*", Tyanna said, unwrapping herself to began a demonstration.

"They ain't hard. *The Booty-Jiggle* is the hardest, but you can get it. Any woman can make her butt shake. But, guys wanna see the booty jiggle.", she said, turning her backside to me.

She stood tall, looking at me over her shoulder as she made her booty jiggle like *Jell-O*, continuously. Incredibly, she achieved this *without* great movement from her hips. Her legs were the source of the jiggle, but she'd use them sparingly, just to keep the jiggling going.

Curious as to how she was doing it, I tried it. Not as much success.

"Don't worry, you'll get it. It's almost like learning how to *hula-hoop*. More effort in movement, doesn't mean the *hula-hoop* will stay around your waist. Same with *The Booty-Jiggle*. But, you'll get it. Practice in the mirror at home."

Like Tyanna said, the rest of the moves *were* much easier.

The Tittie Pinch was simply, starting at your waist with your hands, in a swirling motion, work your hands up to your titties. Tightly gripping them both at the same time, you slide your hands to the peaks. Ending with a nipple-hardening, two-fingered pinch. Sometimes, tug the nipples until they snap back like a rubber-band.

The Booty Rub is where a guy is seated in a chair with his legs open. Standing inside his legs with your back to him, hands on his knees, you place the top of you butt in his groin. Keeping pressure on his privates, slowly you rub his stuff with your butt. According to Tyanna, the goal is to try to get him hard with this technique. She also called it the *'They fall in love with you'* move.

Finally, *The Clit Peek-A-Boo* was just that. Standing, facing the guy, you lean back slightly, stretch the skin above your pussy upward and force your clit to peek out. All of these moves are to be done with seductive, almost *'fuck me'* faces.

Intensely studying Tyanna's moves like a pre-med major at Harvard, I was startled by the knock at the door. Turned out to be Nia.

Seeing Tyanna re-wrapping herself in the towel, Nia, with raised eyebrows, squinted her nose and began speaking.

"Damn. Eww. Whatch'all doing?"

"Nothing.", both Tyanna and I said, the way guilty kids would respond.

"Anyway. Rico said he's gonna hang here in St. Louis for a couple more days. He offered his car, so that we could drive back. I told him, *Hell naw!* So, he booked us some airlines tickets. Our flight leaves tonight.", Nia said with a proud smirk.

"I'm flying back tonight. What time d'yalls flight leave, Nee?", Tyanna asked Nia.

"7:15"

"So does mine. What airline?"

"Delta."

"Damn! We *gotta* be on the same flight!"

"Cool girl! We can hang out tonight. Maybe even take Raven to *The Underground* or something?"

"Girl, I can't. I'm s'pose to work tonight. But, y'all should come by the club. I was telling Raven about it."

"Ohhh. Really?", turning to me, Nia said with a surprised glance. Turning back to Tyanna, she shrugged and offered, "I dunno? *Maybe*, we'll swing by for a *quick* minute?"

We never did. It wasn't Nia's scene. Now I could tell what Tyanna meant when she said that *Nia wasn't that wild*.

The wild night in St. Louis was an alcohol-induced aberration for her. Just as it had been for me.

The only one I was certain was a *freak* was Tyanna. And she wasn't the bad kind of *freak*. I guess, *freaky* would be the better way to describe Tyanna.

Arriving at Hartsfield Airport in Atlanta, I unknowingly redundantly kept thanking Nia for allowing me to stay with her. I thanked her on the shuttle train to baggage claim and in the cab on the way to her *2-bedroom apartment*, as she called it.

Turned out to be a 2-bedroom, 2.5 bath loft! On Peachtree Street! In the heart of downtown Atlanta!

Her unit had 14-foot ceilings, hardwood floors, floor-to-ceiling windows, an office (that could act as a 3rd bedroom), and a kitchen complete with stainless steel appliances and a *six-eye* industrial stove. It even had two levels. The bedrooms were located on the upper level, at opposite ends divided by a bathroom.

The next morning I was awakened by M.C. Krush's music blaring on Nia's high-tech sound system. Sleepy-eyed, I made my way downstairs and witnessed Nia dressed in spandex, going over, what I assumed to be her dance routine for the video.

I stood at the bottom of the stairs for the moment, not wanting to interrupt her, admiring her talent. She was quite a talented dancer. More talented than the booty-shaking she no doubt was most-likely hired to do in this video.

When the song ended, Nia, still breathing heavily was semi-startled by my presence.

"Oh! Hey, what's up girl! I'm sorry, I hope I didn't wake you?", she said.

"No. I was already up.", I lied. "You know, you're really good!"

Out of breath, Nia labored, "Thanks. I'm just trying to work out some rust. It's been a while since I've done a dance video. I just gotta get my body adjusted."

"Well, it looks good to me!"

"No it doesn't. But thanks anyway. I'ma 'bout to take a break and make some breakfast. Did you want some?"

"Yeah, sure. I gotta get dressed, so I can find a newspaper."

"There's a newspaper over there.", Nia said, pointing to the seat of her Soloflex exercise machine.

"Oh, thanks."

"What'ya need a paper for?", Nia questioned

"To look for a job."

"Ohhh?", Nia said confused. "From what Tyanna was talkin' 'bout, I thought you were gonna work at the club?"

Wasn't sure where I should go with this. Tyanna was her friend. Certainly, I didn't wanna offend her.

"I dunno. I appreciate it and all. But I just thought I might see what I could find, first."

"I hear you. I don't know how she goes to that club to take her clothes off for men. I mean, Tyanna's my girl and all that, but I don't call that work."

"Yeah. I guess the money's very good?"

"Still! Howzit feel knowing thousands of men have seen you butt-naked? You know, I've been with her at Kroger's when she's been recognized by some of her club-customers."

"Kroger's?"

"Oh, it's a grocery store here. I forgot that you're from Iowa. Anyway, these customers think they're being discreet, leaning over trying to whisper at her. But as loud as they whisper, they might as well've gotten on the store microphone. It was embarrassing! People in line in front of us, turning all around. Mamas, 13-year old boys and the cashier all looking her over. Even looking me over. Assuming I must be a dancer too 'cause I'm with her. That's the part where I don't think the money's good enough."

"Yeah.", numbly I responded, just thinking about it.

"Oh. Girl, I hope you don't *think* I'm trying to tell *you* what to do? I was just saying that it's not for me that's all. I know plenty of girls who love dancing! Hell, Tyanna's one. I mean, you do what you want. Try it and see if you like it.", Nia rambled.

"Uhm, maybe? I dunno what I'm gonna do?"

"My bad. I didn't mean to sound all negative. When I first moved to the A-T-L, I danced at both of Rico's clubs, *Slick-N-Thick* and *The Carmel Club*."

"You were a stripper?!"

"Exotic dancer! Yes, I danced for about seven days. That's how I met Rico. He auditioned me."

"You gotta audition?"

"Yeah! What'dya think? They can't have just any-old-nasty-looking-fat girls dancing up-in Rico's club! Some of the smaller clubs don't care -- they're just happy to get *any girls* who wanna dance. Not Rico's. His clubs are the best in town. Most expensive. Most celebrities. And, the most money for the dancers.", Nia marketed Rico's club to me.

Then she looked me over, up and down, around my sides and said, "Gurrll, witchyo butt, you don't *EVEN* have to worry! You'd make it. NO PROBLEM! Trust me, I know what Rico likes!"

You do, huh?, I wondered.

Nia didn't have a big butt. A shapely small-to-medium sized one, *So, why was Rico still kickin' it with her, if he only liked meaty bootys?*

After Nia had changed her tune about dancing, I decided I'd give it a shot. Knew there was nothing in the Atlanta Journal Constitution newspaper that'd pay me more. Plus, I was in a hurry to get my own place, my own transportation, my own space. I didn't foresee Nia and I having any problems. And was very grateful for what she was doing for me. Just wanted to rely on nobody but myself.

Over the next couple of days, I rehearsed the moves I'd been taught by Tyanna. Learned a couple more from Nia, who surprisingly wasn't philosophically against teaching to me what she *said* she'd never do again.

Think Nia enjoyed *playing* choreographer. Made her feel special, like in the bus station. And it gave her a brief taste of her dream. Even if it was only fantasy.

When Friday finally came, both Nia and I were prepared. Nia, for her MC Krush video shoot. And me, for my audition with Rico.

Nia let me borrow her new Ford Mustang convertible to go to my audition. At 7a.m., I dropped her off at the video shoot site. It was in an upscale area of Atlanta called *Buckhead*.

Though the videos are only 3 to 4-minutes in length, Nia knew they sometimes take several long-hour days to shoot. Therefore, I'd certainly be done with my audition, which was at noon, before she'd be finished with her video shoot.

When I arrived at *Slick-N-Thick*, I was extremely nervous. Though, less nervous than I'd've been if I hadn't already known Rico. Yet, I was still nervous.

Rico was very charismatic. Gave me a *by-the-hand* guided tour of the club. As we walked through the enormous luxurious building filled with people preparing for another day of business, bartender's stocking the bar and cleaning crew vacuuming, Rico explained some of the rules.

Then he introduced me to Bernice, the *House Mom*. She's the woman who looks-out for the girls. Not physically. That's the bouncer's job. But anything else the girls needed, from costumes to personal issues between dancers. She's also the person that makes out the work-shift schedule and collects the fees the dancers must pay to the club.

Oh yes. Even though the dancers are the reason the club attracts so many customers, dancers are technically *Independent Contractors* and must pay a fee for the *privilege* of shopping their goodies to the clubs' customers. Almost like leasing space.

The industry term for this fee is *'Tip-Outs'*. And, it isn't cheap!

Every night a dancer works, they pay the club $20. House Mom gets $10 more. The music DJ gets a minimum of $20 or 10%. If you have a good night, you're s'pose to give him more. Supposedly, the DJ gets no salary other than tips from the dancers. I didn't like the fact that on some nights, when over 100 girls were in the club, the DJ could make more money than any dancer, without having to take his clothes off! That's why most girls never give him anymore than the mandatory twenty. Bouncer's get a minimum of $10 which I didn't mind at all. I could see the value in tipping the bouncers. They protect you - walk you to and from your car. But the rest of these people, I didn't think it made any kinda sense.

Just to go to work, it cost a minimum of $60. That meant, the first six dances you do are free!

When we finally reached Rico's gorgeous office, located in the very back of the club, we sat down and talked for a bit until he was ready for me to audition.

He sent me to Bernice to get a costume and to change into it.

Upon my scantily-dressed return, Rico was seated in his leather chair, behind his desk that had a computer on it and a series of video monitors that covered *every inch* of the club.

"Did you bring your own music?", he asked.

"Umm, no. I didn't know ....."

"It's alright. I've got it covered.", he said, pushing the power button on his 100-CD office stereo system.

I stood-up in preparation to begin my audition when a voice came over his personal intercom system.

"Excuse me, Rico. I have a call for you on Line-1.", said the mysterious young-sounding voice. Apparently, his secretary.

"Chante', I thought I told you to hold my calls. I'm conducting an audition.", Rico barked like it wasn't the first time.

"I know. But it's Clive Sparks. He says it's very important!"

"Okay Chante', I'll take it.", Rico reluctantly replied. Turning to me, he apologized, "I'm sorry.... um...um....Raven...", he said, struggling to remember my name. "......You can have a seat, I'll only be a minute."

It was colder in his office than it'd been earlier. But then again, I guess, I had more clothes on then.

I sat in a leather chair in front of his desk, looking at his football-days pictures and trophies that were the only office decoration. And pretended not to be listening to his conversation with Clive.

I could only hear one side of the conversation anyway.

"What's up, Clive...............What?!.........No, Nia's trippin'...........Don't worry about it. I'll handle it. I promise ....No........I said I'll handle it................So, I'll handle it .... Alright, bye.", Rico finished his brief, to-the-point conversation, by forcefully hanging up the phone.

"Sorry, about that. Whew. Okay, I'm ready.", he exhaled tension.

Again, I stood up and prepared to dance. While the coolness in his office exaggerated my peaks, which I assumed to be a plus, it also exaggerated my shivering nervousness.

"Raven, you seem nervous?"

"A little.", I confided.

"Well, don't be. You got a great body. Turn around.", he said, motioning with his finger.

"Damn! Baby definitely got back! And the titties to match!"

I smiled, still somewhat uneasy. And, not knowing what to say back.

"Okay Raven, here's the deal. First of all, you have to come around the desk to audition. Just like you'd be doing in the club."

"I'm sorry, I didn't know where you wanted me to stand?", I said, feeling the *jitters* resuming.

"It's alright. You didn't know. Just relax!"

"Okay."

"Now, the way my auditions work, is simple. If you can make me *hard*, you've got the job. If you can't, then how you gonna excite my customers? Huh?".

I just shrugged my shoulders.

His comments served to place *even more* pressure on me.

"Don't worry. I already think you're sexy. So, it shouldn't be that difficult for you.", Rico attempted to ease my tension.

After he pressed the play button, I began moving as sensually as I could at this early hour. I slowly slid my arms out of the straps on my top. Could see Rico, unknowingly lick his lips in anticipation. Just the confidence-booster that I needed. Leaned on him. Brushed my not-yet-revealed cleavage up his chest until his head was between them. With my back to him, I took off my top. Spun around with my hands covering up my breasts. Just teasing him some more. Then, I went into my *Tyanna-taught* routine. The *Tittie-Pinch*. Removed my bottoms, then did the *Booty-Jiggle*. Segued into the *Clit Peek-A-Boo*.

By the time I got around to doing the *Booty-Rub*, Rico didn't have to say a word. I could *feel* I'd just gotten the job!

As I started to get up from my seated position in his crotch, Rico reached out around my waist to pull me backward on to him again. Guess, he wanted me to continue my grinding. So, I did.

Turned out to be sensual for me too. Feeling the power I had. Or, the power he had. And not just the power in his pants.

We grinded for a few more minutes. Even after the song had ended. I closed my eyes. Continued rubbing my booty against his manliness. In my mind, pretended I was getting some of it. Made it easier to be sexy.

Meanwhile, Rico was busy *palming* both my titties upward to the sky. Pinching and twisting me to extreme perkiness. To say nothing of my now moistened state.

His huge hands made my 36-C's feel tiny. Rico slid his left hand, between my legs to check my *status*, I guess. Stroked just enough, to get the *beginning shivers* out of me and then abruptly ended it.

"Well, you got the job!", Rico said, surprisingly in a professional tone of voice, as he guided my body off of him.

Didn't know what had just gone on, so I just said the obvious.

"Thanks."

"You can start tonight. I'm giving you a $200 costume allowance. You can see Bernice.", he said rather coldly I thought for just having *felt me up*.

I was feeling abandoned a bit. Eventhough, I had no real reason to feel that way.

With my costume in my hand, arms folded across my body and apparently nothing else to say, I turned to exit his office, very confused. Before leaving, I hurriedly started putting on my clothes.

"Hey, Raven. Come here.", Rico said, motioning with his head.

I walked over. He stood up, planted a kiss on my lips. Hugging me, he whispered, "You were very good! I'ma take care of you here.", he assured me with his firm embrace.

Felt a little better. Before those words and that affection, I'd felt like I was on one of my *typical* dates back in Iowa.

Before I left the club, Rico gave me his private cellular phone number. Told me to stay in touch with him. Spoken in a manner of expectation. Talked about a possible dinner sometime.

Felt really guilty opening Nia's car door. Though Nia *denied* any personal involvement with Rico and I wasn't sure what Rico and I were doing -- it still didn't feel right.

Flip The Script CHAPTER FOUR

In November, it had been three months since my audition with Rico. I was making decent money working at the clubs. Not the type that Tyanna had sworn I'd make, but good enough for me to afford the latest styles and sample the expensive life.

I was still living with Nia, who'd *somewhat* fallin-out-of-favor with Rico since the day of the audition. She didn't talk about it much though. But, I knew the deal.

At the MC Krush video shoot, she'd gotten the star role. Thanks solely to her connection with Rico, and Rico's connection with the Grammy Award-winning video producer, Clive Sparks.

Rico had done the *I'll-owe-you-one* with Clive to get Nia the treasured, feature role. It'd mean lotsa screen time in the video. This is what she'd always dreamed of. National exposure that just might catapult her own career. Reminiscent of former Laker-girl, Paula Abdul and *In Living Color-Flyy Girl*, Jennifer Lopez. Both had *blown-up* after becoming background dancers in Janet Jackson videos.

MC Krush, though not as big of a name as Janet Jackson, was definitely the star of the moment. His hard-hitting latest CD, *Don't Touch My Sh***, had gone double-platinum.

The video being shot was for his hot new single, *Bitches and Switches*. A song that was low on any meaningful substance. But a hit in the hood, with its hard beat and sampled lyrics from the nostalgic R& B song, *Jamaican Funk*.

I never knew more than the song's catchy hook lines. *"My bitches bring me riches and do my dishes. The snitches, end up with stitches, while I hit my switches.*

Best I could figure, the song was a superficial *ballers* claim, that he only cares about the girls that make him money (the bitches), and his hydraulic-designed car (the switches).

The video called for the star-hoochie (Nia), to take off her shirt in the video.

The set was designed exactly like *Arnold's* on the old TV show, *Happy Days*. MC Krush, dressed in a leather jacket and white T-shirt, portraying the role of a black Fonzie, was to snap his fingers. Simply by MC Krush's snap, Nia was to take off her shirt.

Obviously, they weren't going to actually show Nia's titties on TV. They'd planned to use some blurring just enough to distort the picture into legal content. Yet, it'd still be clear that the girl was naked as she'd continue bouncing around as though she'd been hypnotized by MC Krush.

Nia refused to do the scene.

They'd already spent alot of money and time shooting most of the other scenes, of which Nia was also the star-hoochie. So, starting over was not an option. Plus, in typical star baby-ism, MC Krush was whining about completing the video. Threatening to walk-off, if they didn't finish soon.

Nia had caused a great deal of problems in just about everyone's eyes. But, she held firm and didn't do the topless scene.

The producer had no problem replacing her with one of the hundreds of beautiful back-up dancers that eagerly volunteered for this chance.

An appalled Nia said they'd lined the girls side-by-side. Had them all get topless as Clive and MC Krush shuffled their way down the line, looking for just the right *fullness* for the scene. Even had some of 'em doing bouncing dance moves to check-out their firmness and how they'd look on camera.

I don't know if Nia was right or wrong? Maybe a little of both.

Though, I did *feel* her on the topless *thang*. Who knows, where the video footage might end-up someday?

At the same time, I could feel Clive and Rico. Nia should've checked out the deal, so not to waste Rico's favor and Clive's time and money.

When the video was edited and first appeared on MTV, Nia was still in much of it. Apparently, Clive could not convince MC Krush to re-do the other scenes.

In the video, Nia hadn't been totally cut-out. However, Rico was a different story.

The night of the video shoot, Rico had come by our loft pissed off! I mean, really pissed off at Nia. Could hear the half-hour screaming session very-well from my room upstairs.

Was frightened for Nia. Knew I'd never want a 250-pound man that mad at me. Even kept my finger in a *ready-to-dial-911* position. Though, it never was necessary.

When Nia finally was verbally broken down to tears, Rico left. But not before telling her he'd *never* help her again with her career *and* threatening to kick her out of the loft that *he* was paying for. Even took the car keys to the Mustang.

I guess he was trying to prove a point. To add further injury, he'd given the car to me. Just, so that Nia could see it.

I didn't feel right being used as a weapon, but what could I do? Say no? Then Rico would surely kick both of us out. And what would that prove?

Plus, I knew part of the reason he'd given me the car was, he knew I'd take Nia where-ever she needed to go.

He just told me that she could not drive it. Which was a non-issue, as Nia seemed to have lost her desire to be a star.

Over the past two-months, Rico's distancing from Nia, *was* taking its toll on her.

Without Rico's support, she'd lost her luster. Her previously well-groomed hair, frequently fell short of its model-silkiness. Her clothes, never neatly pressed from the cleaners. She'd even picked up a few pounds. I thought she looked good with the extra weight, but I knew it wasn't good for her business, which didn't seem to matter anyway. Nia had not been to a single audition since the break-up. I guess, you could call it a break-up?

Delicately, I tried to offer her help as she'd done for me.

Not viewing herself as a needy, charity case, Nia stubbornly refused, sometimes. Other times, I'd just do it anyway without asking. Just take her clothes to the cleaners and return them to her closet. Leave a newspaper with red-circled audition dates on her bed.

Didn't work. Nia never tried. Satisfied to sit around in sweatpants and a sweatshirt watching *Divorce Court*.

I think Nia thought Rico was going to be the one to come back to apologize and not her.

Rico was a mild-mannered giant of a man, but definitely not a weak man. No push-over. Maybe, that's where Nia was underestimating him.

I don't know what they ever had going on? But, Rico was definitely not the type to be *pussy-whipped*!

Couldn't believe how long it was taking her to figure this out. Maybe she had? Ironically, maybe *her* ego wouldn't allow her to believe that she *didn't* possess the magical, finger-snapping control over Rico that was trying to be displayed in the MC Krush Video, she'd shunned. Or, maybe she was hoping that I'd smooth things over?

Through this difficult fall time of year, Nia never harbored a grudge towards me. At least, not one that I could detect.

She seemed to be crystal-clear that *her* problem didn't include me. It was between her and Rico. And, she didn't even care that I was driving, what had previously been *her* car. Or that Rico and I were still cool.

In fact, we were very cool. Just a week ago, I'd come back from a vacation in Miami with Rico. First-class everything. Sun, sand and the nightlife.

After our trip together, I'm sure Nia knew Rico and I were *hittin' it*.

Actually, Miami *was* the first time Rico and I had sex.

Though, I never confirmed it to her. Remembering how she'd describe him to me as her *agent* when we first met.

Besides, she'd *never dare* ask. Probably didn't wanna know. And because *now,* the script had been flipped. It was as though, *she* was living in *my* place. Not hers.

Still I could tell, after our Miami trip, Nia figured she'd let her *golden-goose* slip away to me.

Tyanna and I had fallen to a *no-more-than-hello* speaking terms, whenever she'd visit after the incident between Nia and Rico. She thought that I'd somehow betrayed Nia by accepting the car.

Tyanna was no longer dancing at the club. Having, in a fit of disgust, gone into Rico's office to tell him that he'd *dogged* Nia.

Rico never fired her. She'd left on her own, in a failed attempt to force a reconciliation between him and Nia.

Like I say, I think people mistakenly thought that Rico was weak.

From Precious, another dancer at *The Carmel Club*, I'd heard that Tyanna was now doing internet-modeling. Basically, nude still-pictures. Not porn. But I *know* the money was vastly less than she'd've been making if she were still dancing at Rico's clubs.

According to Precious, Tyanna had sold her *Jaguar*, moved out of her condo and was now living at one of the weekly-rent motels on Memorial Drive in Stone Mountain.

It was so ironic how all our fortunes had changed in just a few of months.

Had no desire to be in competition with Nia or Tyanna. At the same time, I *wasn't* gonna give up *my* good fortune for an argument that *didn't* even involve me.

◆◆◆◆◆◆◆◆◆◆◆◆◆◆◆◆◆◆◆◆◆◆◆◆◆◆◆◆◆◆◆◆◆◆◆

It wasn't long before I'd surpassed even Nia's achieved status with Rico. It had been several weeks since I danced for money. Rico had *unofficially* promoted me to a manager position.

Now I was *'privy'* to the most intimate dealings of the club. Counting money and sitting-in on private meetings.

Everyone knew that I was Rico's right-hand. DJ's, bartenders, bouncers and the house-moms. Whatever I said was gold.

Could tell the dancers resented me. However, they respected me. Or maybe, feared me enough not to dare cross me.

I describe my new position as *unofficial* because I didn't have a name pin or anything. Had no specific salary. No specific duties. And, I *was* paid in cash among other ways.

All my needs were taken care of. Sometimes, Rico would give me a lump of cash totaling $2,000. Other times, he'd surprise me with glittering diamond jewelry.

Most recently, he brought home to me a shiny-new, blue convertible BMW. Leather seats, CD and the whole-nine.

To Nia, this latest gesture represented the permanent closing of the door between her and Rico.

The next morning, I came downstairs to an already awaken Nia. She'd not gotten up *this early* in months. Noticed several bags parked at the door and two others she was almost done packing.

"Nia! What's up, girl?"

"I think I'ma move out.", she said with watery eyes.

"Why?! What's goin' on? Wait. Put that stuff down. Talk to me, Nia!"

When she looked up, one tear had made it to her cheek that she quickly wiped away with her palm.

"I'on know. I think I'm in your way, here. I mean, you got your thing going and I ....", Nia tried to finish, but an avalanche of tears kept both palms busy.

Rapidly blinking my eyes, trying to keep from crying as well, I walked over and gave her a firm hug.

"Nia, you ain't in my way. Remember, you're the one that helped me at the bus station in Kansas City. Listen. I'ma help you, but you gotta let me! Okay?", I said motherly, leaning back to look her square in the eyes.

"Okay.", Nia softly sniffled.

"Girl, this is about Rico. Ain't it?", I said, no longer beatin'-around-the-bush.

"I'on know?", she said, shrugging her shoulders and shaking her head.

"Yeah it is. Girl, Rico don't hate you. He asks me about you all the time", I lied.

"Yeah?", Nia responded, looking a little better.

"Yeah! Y'all just had a misunderstanding that just lasted *far* too long. That's all. And you know how men are. You hurt his pride, you know. Kinda made him look bad. Hmm? And to a man, that's worse than shooting him. You know what I'm saying?"

Nia, head hanging, nodded to let me know that she was still listening.

"I'm sure we can work this whole thing out. Let me talk to Rico. Let me see what I can do, okay?"

Again she meekly muttered, "Okay."

"Okay, I'ma talk to him. But, you gotta promise me *you* gonna be cool about it. You know he goin' wanna act like he won. Talk to you like you're five -- you know how he does. And, it ain't even 'bout that. But, just let him say his thing, so that we can get this situation straightened out. Alright?"

"Okay."

"In the meantime, don't ever leave again. Talk to me, okay?"

"Thanks Raven!", she said, offering a warm hug back to me.

"No problem. You my girl!", I squeezed her back. "Listen, why don't you take this money. Go get your hair, nails and toes done. Want you to look good tonight, when Rico comes by. Dress sexy, too."
It had been a conversation that we'd avoided for months. Felt like, the least I owed Nia, was to make an attempt for her.

Wasn't worried about Rico getting back with her. He was long past that. But, he might still help her career-wise because I *know* he did like her.

Later that day, I met Rico at The Shark Bar on Peachtree for lunch.

"What-up Rave!", he said, leaning over the table to kiss me on the cheek.

Loved how he never seemed to lose excitement in seeing me.

"Nuttin'?", cutely I returned.

"Lookin' good as usual, boo!"

"Thanks. Hey listen, I wanna talk to you about, Nia?"

Rico's face, immediately changed from excitement to disgust.

"What now? Whatta 'bout Nia?"

"Oh, it ain't nuttin' bad. She's just feelin' real low..........."

"Good! She should! That bitch made me look bad! I can't have that shit, you know?"

"I know. And, she's knows that now! And, she's sorry. She didn't mean to make you look bad. That wasn't *it*, at all."

"Yeah, well, whatever. Don't matter now, anyway.", Rico calmly said, waving a waitress over.

I could tell I was getting to him. He wasn't nearly as passionate. Thought it was my style, but it could've been the fact that nearly four months had passed.

"I know. That was a long time ago. But, she's still very hurt by the way the whole thing went down. I'm saying, Nia was still crying this morning."

Rico's attention was peaked by that revelation. Could almost see, Rico was both pleased and impressed that he affected Nia that much, after all this time.

"Can you do a favor for me?", I said, feeling I'd sufficiently softened him up. "Can you talk to her? She wants to talk to you. She would've

asked herself, but she thought you'd turn her away. Can you do it for me, baby?", I finished with a tilt of my head and begging eyes.

Rico, in contradictory form, was shaking his head *'no'*, as he respond, "Okay. Tell her to come by the club ...."

"What I meant to say was, will you come by the house to talk to her?", I tried to amend the deal.

"What?! Naw. She wanna speak to me, she can come by the club, tomorrow. That's it. And, if she don't come tomorrow, you tell her never to come. That's it, baby. That's the best I can do."

Knowing that he meant it, I didn't press further and agreed on Nia's behalf.

◆ ◆

The next day, I helped Nia get ready for her meeting with Rico. Worked on her hair. Vetoed outfits she picked out to wear.

Nia was self-conscious about the weight she'd gained. Therefore, she felt the sexy outfits that were her staple, no longer looked good on her. It wasn't true. Not at all.

I coaxed her into snug jeans that accented her newly-gained, thicker derriere. Added a lightweight, long-sleeve top that tapered to the waist and was cut-low enough in front to see some of her cleavage.

I thought, *In order for this to have the best chance to work, Nia had to be sexy. Intriguing. But, not overtly. Just enough, to soften his edge.*

Nia appeared more nervous than she did for the video shoot. Clearly, this meant alot to her.

When we walked into Rico's office, he leaned back in his leather chair, legs crossed, tapping his pen on the side of his shoe.

"What's up, Rico!", I said, energetically. Trying to get this thing off to a good start.

"How you doin' babe?", he said to me. Then one-word addressed Nia, "Nia?"

"Hey, Rico.", Nia said, sounding very nervous.

"Why don't we all sit down.", I suggested, seeing that Rico hadn't intended on offering.

"Rico, Nia's here to ...."

Holding his hand up to pause me, he interrupted, "I see her, Rave. She grown. She can speak for herself."

I went over to close his door and sat in a nearby chair. Close enough to intervene should the situation turn ugly. Yet, far enough so they could do their thing.

Taking the cue, Nia began to speak, "Rico, I am......."

Again, he interrupted. "First of all, let me say, I'm glad you came to see me today. And, you look good, Nee! Very good!", Rico said with a sly grin, then he motioned for her to get up and take a spin, so that he could get a better look.

Nia sincerely said, "Thanks, Rico.", before obliging his spin request.

As she was spinning, our eyes had a quick conversation. Mine told hers, *Everything was gonna be alright.* Hers, responded back, *I hope so.*

I thought it was gonna be a long conversation, judging by Rico's *Godfather* approach. Sitting behind the desk. Cross-legged and acting all cold.

Surprisingly, he abandoned that approach for his more characteristic jovial style.

"I see, you done gotta a little butt, now.", Rico engaged with a smile.

"Umm-hmm."

"It looks good on you!"

"Thanks. Listen Rico, I am *so-oh* sorry about disrespecting you. I didn't mean to. I just didn't wanna do......well...... ......I'ain't know, it was goin' make *you* look bad. Otherwise, I'd've just gone-'head and done it. I never meant to *dis* you. You mean too much to me. You always have. I'm just tryin' to say, that I wanna be cool with you, again. I hope you can forgive me, 'cause I really do mean it. I'm sorry.", Nia rambled, like she'd been saving it for four months.

"I'm glad to hear you say it. You know Nee, had you just been straight with me about it, I'm sure we could've worked it out. But, it's all gravy, baby! I just need to know that whoever I'm *lookin'-out* for, is also *lookin'-out* for me. Ain't that right Rave?"

Rico surprised me, by addressing me at the end. Didn't care for him using me to compare against Nia.

"Oh yeah, babe.", I echoed.

"Well, I just want you to know, that I *do* have your back. I just made a stupid mistake, that'll *never* happen again! Anything you need, just call me.", Nia continued her pleading.

"I believe you. I believe you.", Rico said, elbows on the desk, rubbing his chin with one hand.

"Thank you."

"You really mean what you said?", Rico baited her.

"I do, I do!"

Turning to me, Rico surprised me with his question.

"Rave, don't we still have a dancer position open, from that girl we just fired?"

"Yeah?", I said, in a confused tone.

Rico turned back to Nia.

"Well, I'm short a dancer?", he said as a vague invitation to test her just-promised loyalty.

"Ohh-kay.", she said, nodding her head.

Nia was obviously, a little disappointed. And so was I. Hadn't expected that! Rico knew, she didn't wanna dance. It was just his way of making her earn her way back into his good graces. He wanted it not to be easy. But this was a little *below-the-belt* for me.

"Cool. Rave, in a minute you can get Nee all set-up to start tonight. But first, can you give us a minute alone?", Rico asked.

"Oh, sure."

When I opened the door, I'd purposely let the knob leave my hand. That way, it'd stay open as I waited outside.
Moments later, Nia came over to close the door. Apparently, instructed by Rico to do so.

Though they'd been in there about nine or ten minutes, I didn't *really* think anything was going-on in there. Wasn't worried about it. Just wondered, *why I couldn't be in there?* After all, I was the one who set this whole thing up.

Like I said, I wasn't *too* worried about it. Though, when the door re-opened and Nia came out, I gotta admit, my eyes scanned her tight shirt to see if her nipples were erect. Evidence of some funny business. They were not.

"Wazzup, girl?", I questioned as we walked.

"Nuttin'. We're cool now.", Nia said in a daze. Still thinking about the job she'd been volunteered to.

"Nee, don't worry 'bout it. Nee. Nee. Psst. You know Rico just fuckin' with you a bit, right?"

"Yeah. Maybe?"

"Nee? C'mon? You know Rico ain't goin' having you dancing long. He just testin' you girl! Hell, he might just wanna see if you'll come back tonight ready to work, then tell you that you don't have to?"

"I'on know. I mean. I'll handle it, it's cool."

Nia hoped I was right. But, I wasn't. Nia was back to square-one. Doing what she'd said she'd never do again. Making the situation even more uncomfortable was the fact that I was now *her* boss.

Nia'd replaced one of the best money-makers at the club, Passion. A 5'6, 125-pound, Halle Berry look-a-like girl, who just *knew* she had it all.

Hate to admit it, but she kinda did. Best body symmetry in the club, for sure. Perfect breasts, without augmentation. A Georgia-peach round butt. Neither too big, nor too small. Hour-glass waist. And, blemish-free skin.

She was the girl that *everyone* wished they could borrow *at least one* specific body part from. Hair, thighs, butt, breasts, eyes, smile, calves, nipples, lips, skin-texture, nose, toes, ears, feet -- you name it, she had the best of it.

The problem was, she *acted* like she knew it. The good side was, the customers knew it. They knew they'd have a hard time finding a better-looking creature anywhere. Therefore, she had a large group of regulars who'd come to the club *just* to see her.

For that purpose alone, she *was* valuable to the club. Her customers paid a cover-charge, bought drinks and ate. All of which was money that went to the club.

She definitely had it all. A Mercedes in the parking lot. A home in Marrieta, GA. That is, until Passion made the critical mistake of fuckin' with me.

I'd selected her, along with several other dancers to be in the annual club calendar, we'd be giving away to customers in about a month or so, on New Years night.

Passion had been in the calendar the past three years. On the cover, the last two.

This year, things were different. I was in charge of the calendar shoot.

I'd even updated the calendar idea to include a computer disk. We'd have 40 different thumbnail images of different dancers that could be used as a screen-saver for a computer. Made plans to sell these CD's all-year-long for $10 each.

It was a way for the guy to take our girls home, in more than just his memory!, was how I had pitched my idea to Rico.

Rico, absolutely loved the idea!

On the day of the shoot, that bitch told me that, *she's s'pose to be on the cover, like she's always been.*

I told Passion, I hadn't made a final decision. But, I'd let her know when I did.

Then, she snapped. In front of all the other girls, just got ghetto on me!

"*You'll* let me know, my ass! Bitch! I'on *even* know *why* you be tryin' to act like *you* runnin' shit? This is *Rico's* pull-lace, bitch! Ree-Cose! Not yours! Four months ago, you were just a dancer, *just* like all of us. And, not even a good one! The only difference is, I guess, you suck a good dick! Bet you can suck a big fat one, too. What'cha do back in Iowa, practice dick-sucking on corn-on-the-cob? Is that how you got good at suckin' big dicks, HO! Ev'rybody here know, that's the *only* reason Rico got you *playin'* boss lady, bitch!"

Passion was probably speaking the sentiments of the group. But, no one else, outwardly showed support. Nor did anyone attempt to halt her tirade.

Because Passion was such a money-maker, she felt immune to any potential reprimand. In her mind, there'd be little in the form of punishment. Maybe a fine. Maybe.

Surely, Rico would side with her, she thought. After all, she'd been here three years. Me, just four months.

To tell the truth, I wasn't sure as to what Rico's reaction would be. But this incident *had* to be handled. If it'd been anybody else, I'da fired them right on the spot.

From *jump*, Passion had always tested my authority. I never made too big of a deal about it, because I figured she was *too* important to the club. And, I didn't want Rico *thinkin'* I'm being stupid, by startin' a beef with the club's #1 girl. Like it was some, jealous girl-shit.

When we got to Rico's office, he'd already heard about it. It was in the next few minutes, I found out *just* where I stood with Rico.

Passion, with tons of hand-waving, eye-rolling, neck-twisting attitude, attempted to *bogard* her way into telling her side first.

"Rico, this girl's been trippin'! All the girls been saying it. She acting like a queen, all up in everyone's face and shit! Excuse me, for cursing. All I'm sayin' is, I've been here three years and I'ain't never ...."

In a very deep voice, Rico told Passion to *Shut up!*. Intimidated Passion to silence with a serious glare, the way I imagined him doing to an NFL football quarterback.

"I just need to know one thing, *HAS* Passion been following your rules?"

I hesitated to answer honestly. Could feel Passion looking over at me.

"Yes or No, Rave?"

"Well, Rico, most of the time she does........."

"That's a NO.", Rico said without hesitating. "Passion you're fired! Get your shit and go! And, if you *even* think about *doing* some damage to this place, *I'ma be* the one you goin' deal with! You hurrd me?", Rico warned, without bias to gender.

Passion, thoroughly shocked, did as she was told. No doubt, she planned to appeal later, after things cooled down. Figuring, she'd apologize her way back into the club.

Passion was lucky that she had options. With her looks, she definitely could find work at another club. Hell, she was the star at the best club in Atlanta. No doubt, Passion'd be able to make real decent money, even at the smaller B-level clubs.

However, as Passion was packing-up her things, clearly written on her face was uncertainty. At that moment, she knew, she'd never be rolling in dough, unless she somehow got back-in at Rico's clubs. And that path led right through me.

I never understood why dancers would treat the club so nonchalantly. They had to have known that the lifestyles they led were due to their youthful *body-n-appearance* that wasn't goin' last. And, that they were fortunate to be working at a *good-money* club.

So, why would anyone mess that up? Especially, if you've bought a house, a car or have kids to feed.

Actually, some girls did *'get it'*. I'd say, 'bout 15% of 'em. Most of them, were medical students or law-school students, who needed to make fast money for school. They had a purpose for dancing. A bigger goal.

Most dancers' goals, never exceeded anything more than a car. Even that, you'd be surprised how many dancers don't even have that. They spend up to $40 on a taxi, each way. Or, rent a car for a week, from a rent-a-car place that don't require a credit card. They'd pay much higher rates than they'd get on Priceline.com. Plus, they always *ended-up* going over the mileage allowance and wind-up paying $350-$400 a week renting a car. Hell, they could buy a used car from an auction for five or six hundred! Some of these girls are not the *sharpest tool in the shed*!

Playing The Game CHAPTER FIVE

It was the beginning of December. Nia was still relegated to a dancer's role at the club. And, wasn't making much money either.

Though Nia had all the physical gifts to make good money, she lacked the demeanor of a dancer. A certain sex-appeal that expanded beyond the realm of the body.

The *fellas* wanted a girl that was, first of all, fine.

Secondly, they wanted girls to make them feel special, like *they* were *'Big Willie'*.

And lastly, they wanted the fantasy that they could possibly *hook-up* with you outside the club.

The big money-makers mastered all three elements. Good money makers had two of the three. Nia, really had only the first element, her appearance. Though she *was* trying. But the guys could sense she was faking it.

And then there were the other girls that actually used the club to market their own *Private Enterprise*. They'd make their *real* money after they left the club, if you know what I'm saying?

I'd also started my own, *Private Enterprise*, unknown to Rico. I'd been setting up bachelor parties. Not dancing myself. Instead finding the girls.

My contact was Sergio, a male barber in East Point. I'd met him at *Slick-N-Thick* back when I was dancing. He'd pay me $500 to provide three girls, which was easy money. Never had any problem finding girls despite it being a bachelor party.

Most girls *don't* wanna do bachelor parties for two reasons.

First, the expectation is much different than a club. You *will* be handled. Might even have to do some shows with sex toys. You know, dildos and stuff.

The second reason, the money. The crowd is always smaller than a club. Normally, 15-20 guys. If they ain't ballers, then you could end up wasting your time.

The good side to bachelor parties is that you work less hours and have no club fees to pay. And for the dancers with a *freak-streak*, it's private and you might be able to '*get-on*' with someone, for money or for fun.

Fortunately for me, I had a good set-up with Sergio. He knew if he ever booked a party with me where my girls didn't make money, I'd never do it again for him. Especially seeing as the girls worked for tips only. The $500 went to me alone.

It worked out good for Sergio too. He knew he'd never be able to access the beautiful girls that I could. Or convince 'em, to do a party for tips only. Let alone be able to set it up on a moments notice.

◆◆◆◆◆◆◆◆◆◆◆◆◆◆◆◆◆◆◆◆◆◆◆◆◆◆◆◆◆◆◆◆◆◆◆

Three weeks had passed since the firing of Passion.

She'd just called my cell phone that morning, apologizing and pleading for me to let her come back to work. Giving me the anticipated *sob-story* about her $1800 mortgage payment and her $600 car note.

Eventhough I didn't really like her, I'd become an astute business-woman hangin' around Rico. She was good for business! *And, customers had been asking about her!*, I had to admit to myself.

Told her I'd think about it and call her back sometime today.

Thought about pullin' a *Rico*. Maybe I'd make her dance for me *on-the-side* for a while, before letting her return. Make her work her way back into *my* good graces.

I wanted to break her down a bit. Knew she'd turned her nose up at bachelor parties 'cause she felt that she was *too good* for that sorta stuff.

Back when she was still working at the club, she'd even made some customers that *wanted* to buy a dance from her, wait. Arrogantly, she'd go to the bar, drinking water until *she* decided that they could have a dance.

Passion was a masterful game-player whom had never been on the wrong side of the fence, as she was now.

Maybe I should teach her a lesson?, I pondered.

Besides, it didn't hurt that I knew I'd get more money from Sergio for her to perform.

Around 10am, I walked into *The Carmel Club* to pick up the money I normally deposited at the bank.

Inside Rico's office, a man was seated in front of his desk.

Knocking on the door frame and leaning in, I said, "Excuse me Rico. Is the deposit ready to go?"

"Almost. It'll be just a minute. C'mon in.", Rico invited. "I want you to meet somebody."

The well-built white man in his mid-30's stood up and turned around.

Immediately, my eyes were drawn to his belt line and the badge that was clipped on it.

"Raven, this is Sergeant Fillmore.", Rico introduced.

"Stanley. You can call me Stan!", the man altered Rico's introduction.

"Nice to meet you.", I said.

As we shook hands, peering over Stan's shoulder, I could see Rico making eye-conversation with me. But, I couldn't make out what he was trying to say.

"Nice to meet you Raven.", Stan said with a smile and a purposely-luring caress of my hand. "Rico's told me alot about you!"

Now, I was concerned. I'd never heard Rico mention *his* name.

And, what had Rico told him 'bout me?, I wondered, attempting to not allow it to show on my face.

"Well Rico, I'm not gonna take up any more of your time. I see you got things to do. But let me know about what we talked about soon, okay?", Stan spoke in code to Rico.

"Yeah. Just call that number I gave you around 2:00.", Rico responded.

"Will do. Take care. Nice to have met you Raven. I'll talk to you guys later.", Stan said, with one arm raised as he exited Rico's office.

"What's going on? Who was that? Whatzzee want?", nervously I questioned.

"Gurrll, relax. Close the door and sit down for a minute. I need to holla at you."

"What's up?"

"You know how they've been tryin' to close the strip-clubs in the A-T-L, right?"

"Yeah, I heard about it. I know. They've been cracking down on the clubs that are doing prostitution."

"Well, that's part of it. You know *the law* says a dancer can't get any closer than 2-feet to the customer. Which is bullshit! They know *ain't nobody* goin' come into *no* club, buy dances and not get some kinda physical contact. They gotta get somethin'! They just put that rule in, so that they can enforce it on the clubs they want to. Every club does the *booty rub*!"

"Umm-hmm?"

"Stan is the man that's goin' keep us from ever having that problem. You know what I'm saying?"

I did. But then again, I didn't.

"We gotta take care of him, and he'll take care of us. Know what I mean?", Rico added with raised eyebrows.

I just nodded. Though, I really had no clue. Thought it'd be revealed during our conversation.

"So, I need you to do me a big favor, Rave?"

"What?"

"Don't worry about the deposits today. I'll take care of all of that.", Rico said, reaching into the top drawer of his desk.

Pulling out a stuffed-full envelope, he handed it to me and continued.

"I gave Stan, your cell phone number. I need you to meet him, where-ever, and give him that envelope. Can you do that?"

Looking at the envelope, attempting to use x-ray vision to see its content, I responded, "Yeah, I can do it. I guess?"

"No, don't guess. Can you do it or do I need to get Nia?", Rico, not-so-subtly threatened.

"No, I'll do it!"

"Good! That's my gurrll! You know all this stuff stays between us, right?"

"Yeah?"

"The other thing is, we wanna keep Stan on our side. Keep him looking out for us. So, I want you to *take care of him*. You know what I'm saying!", Rico said, with another eyebrow raising expression followed by a wink.

I *thought* I knew what he was saying. But, I'd hoped I was wrong.

"Shit, you a big girl. This shit's important! You know what I'm saying. If you don't, then I've got the wrong girl working for me!", again he dropped yet another threat.

Putting the envelope in my bag. I left his office. Sat in my car for a moment. Hands to my forehead, in thought.

Rico's asking me to bribe and sleep with a cop!, I couldn't get it out of my head.

I'd thought he and I had become too close for this kinda shit. I mean, I could understand the money. But, why did it have to be me to sleep with the cop? Then again, maybe Rico knew it *had* to be me, because he could trust me.

My vacillating was interrupted by my cell phone.

"Hello?"

"Raven? It's Passion. I'm not tryin' to bother you! I was just calling you back to see if you'd made a decision yet?"

"Oh, no. I'ma have to call you back..........", I said.

"Okay. No problem! Take your time, I'm home all day. I'll just wait for you to call me. Okay, bye Raven."

"Hey, Passion! Wait, don't hang up!"

"I'm still here."

"How long would it take you to get from Marietta to Downtown?"

"Right now?"

"Yes, now!"

"In traffic, about an hour."

"Okay. Need-ya to meet me at the Westin Hotel at 1:00. If you help me, I'll get you back in at the club soon.", I promised vaguely.

"Help you with what?"

"Listen, I ain't got time to explain. Do you want to be back at the club or not?"

"Yeah, but....."

"Then meet me in the lobby at the Westin at 1:00 sharp. Bring your dance outfits. If you ain't there, you can forget about *ever* dancing at the club. Understood?!"

"Okay. I'll be there!"

"You'd better be!"

Felt a bit of *De Ja Vu* after hanging up the phone. Wondered if I was making the same mistake as Nia. Rico told *me* to handle it.

Got back to my loft around noon. Nia was in the shower. Thought about asking her to help me out. Knew I could trust her, much more than Passion. And she did owe me one. But this type of thing was way out of Nia's range. She didn't even feel good dancing. Now how she gonna be able to pull this thing off?

Who I really needed was Tyanna. But, we hadn't talked in months. And even after I reconciled Nia and Rico, she still was harboring a grudge against me. That girl was very strong-willed. But she would've been perfect for this assignment. She thrived on excitement and danger.

I forced any thought of Tyanna out of my mind, 'cause it just wasn't gonna happen. Especially not at the last minute.

The way I saw it, I had three options.

First, Passion, whom I wasn't sure if she'd go through with it or not. Or, how well could I trust her. Thought about my mom's fool-proof recipe to keeping a secret: *Don't tell anyone!* But on the other hand, the girl was hungry. And, people *will* do most anything when they're in need.

Next option was Nia. My friend. She was in turmoil enough just being naked at the club. *How am I gonna ask her to be* a prostitute for one *night?* Oh, and a free prostitute! Though, she might do it? Especially, if I told her Rico was involved. But I wasn't feeling good about doing that. Plus, Tyanna and I would never get back together if she heard I'd done something like that!

Of course, the only other option, was me.

Decided, I'd play it by ear. Meet Passion at the Westin Hotel, as planned. If I use her, good. If not, then no big deal.

◆ ◆

When Passion arrived in the lobby, right on time, I'd already gotten room keys to two adjoining rooms. Paid the $169 per room cost out of my own money.

I might've been making too big a deal out of this whole thing. I mean, Stan wasn't going to turn us in, 'cause he'd also be going to jail.

But, just in case, I'd rigged the video camera Rico had given me, in one of the rooms. Rested it on the window ledge. Faced it towards the bed. Covered the rest of it with a towel.

I felt better knowing, I too, would have a card in this poker game.

"Hey what's going on Raven?", Passion questioned, as we walked to the elevator.

Wondered how much I should share with her?

"Oh, I just got a private dance party for a *very important customer* of the club."

"Okay. Just dancing, Raven?", she said, trying to clarify.

Not wanting to tell her out-right in the elevator and having no way to be vague or stall until we were in one of the rooms, I just lied.

"Yeah. Just dancing."

When we got to my two rooms, 2304 and 2306, I opened the door to 2304. It was the room with the camera in it.

My cell phone rang. I told Passion to get dressed in her outfit, before answering the phone.

"Hello?"

"Hi, Raven?"

"Yes."

"It's Stan."

"Oh, hey Stan!"

"Did Rico talk to you?"

"Yeah. Everything's cool. I'm at the Westin. Room 2306, if you can meet me here?"

"Yeah, sure. Give me twenty minutes."

"Okay, I'll see ya soon!"

I was surprised how open we were speaking on the cell phone. With him being a cop, I'd thought we'd be using code names and shit. Maybe I'd seen too many episodes of *Columbo*.

Passion came out of the bathroom, prepared.

"Who we dancing for?"

"You mean, who you dancin' for?", I corrected her. "It's not important. All you need to know is he needs to be *satisfied*! *Very SATISFIED!*"

"Just dancing, right?", she muttered.

I started stealing Rico's lines.

"Look Passion. You a big girl. Satisfied means, satisfied! Whatever he wants. He's too important and he'll be here in a few minutes. I'm going next door. I gotta talk to him first, before I bring him over here. Just relax. We'll be over here in about 30 minutes."

Passion said nothing. Looked scared.

"Don't screw me Passion!", I warned.

"I won't.", finally she spoke.

I exited through the door that joined our rooms together.

When Stan came into 2306, he suspiciously began looking around, before we did any talking.

"Did you have something for me?", he asked.

I gave him the envelope. He immediately put it in the inside pocket of the blazer he was wearing.

Reality was in the air. Could almost smell it. And, definitely saw it. When Stan opened his coat, I saw the black gun holstered at his side.

This was definitely not Iowa. Much bigger than lewd country-bumpkin jokes at the corner diner. This was for real.

Stan made himself comfortable in a chair.

"Raven, come here.", he motioned me over to him. Opening his legs to allow me to stand right between them, whispering, he questioned, "I think you got something else for me?", as he gripped my butt.

Placing my hands on his chest, I played along, knowing that I was gonna pass him off to Passion in a minute. And knew he wouldn't mind the switch. Passion was a white man's dream.

Stan placed his gun on the table, turned me around, to have me sit in his crotch. It'd been a while since I'd done the *Booty Rub*. But, it's just like riding a bike. Stan was hard in record time.

I guided Stan over to the adjoining door. Opened it to reveal a lingerie-garbed Passion, lying on the bed.

Stan was very pleased. In a hurry to transcend rooms, he nearly forgot his gun was on the table.

Next, I sat Stan on the edge of the bed and namelessly introduced him, "This is Passion."

I sat in a nearby chair after giving Passion the eye. Thought whether or not to leave. Decided I better make sure, by staying.

Passion started him off, with the *Booty-Rub*. Her eyes bulged. I assumed, she didn't know he was already *hard*, as she sat on him.

Stan rubbed his hands up and down her, like he was searching her for clues. Covering every inch of her body.

Peeled down her bra, man-handle her a bit. Pinched her erect before sliding his left hand into her panties.

Wasn't looking before, but Stan had on a wedding ring. He must be married.

I could see that Passion was uncomfortable with me being in the room.

Too bad!, I thought. I couldn't afford a possible *mess up*. And, she had a high potential for that. It was the reason she was here in the first place -- she'd *messed up* with me.

Stan pushed Passion upward to standing. Pulled down his pants to reveal that *only* the arm-of-the-law was long! His little pinkish-tan dick was only about four or five inches *max*, in length.

He leaned back on his elbows as he waited for Passion, who looked over to me in hesitation. I just turned away.

Passion did what she knew Stan was expecting. Knelt between his legs and began sucking his little dick.

It wasn't long before she had him groaning and ready to explode.

"Wait! Wait!", he said, grabbing her hands, not wanting to waste himself yet.

Passion attempted to sneak in a few additional strokes. Figuring, this might be her way to avoid intercourse, if she could make him explode now.

Somehow, Stan managed to contain himself. He spun Passion's back to the bed and danced his tongue all over her. Licked her like he was in love. Slow and careful. Even Passion, seemed at times, to lose track that *this* was an *assignment*.

What Stan's *gun* lacked, his tongue more than made up for.

Passion was attesting to that right now, with her squeaky moans and body-jitters. He'd licked *my* presence into an insignificant state. Passion could only concentrate on handling the next wave of ecstasy. Her trembling hands, undecided whether to push his head away or see just how much more she could take.

Finally, he slid her to the edge of the bed. Raised her legs and entered. Clearly, his depth was anti-climatic. In Passion's face, I could tell it wasn't *doin' it* for her. He was just too small.

Stan tried her on top *and* doggie-style. Not much improvement. I wanted to tell her to fake it, but I hadn't thought that far ahead.

Didn't matter anyway. Like a good cop that *always* has a back-up plan, Stan did. A different position. One I had never tried.

Stan turned Passion on her side and raised her top leg resting it on his shoulder. Straddled the bottom leg that was hanging off the bed at a downward angle. It was like, he had Passion doing a vertical split. This made it easier for him to get all the way in.

Small dicks, girls with nice butts and doggie-style, *never* go together. The booty gets in the way.

Passion didn't need to fake *anything*, anymore. He was *puttin'* it to her.

Moving much better than I'd expected for a white boy. Spanking her backside with one hand, while softly *thumb-brushing* her clit with the other.

They exchanged heated moans for another five minutes before they almost simultaneously declared their climaxing.

"I'm cum-ming.", Passion admittedly groaned, with new found respect for Stan's ability.

"Oh, me too! Uhhgg- Sheee-it.", Stan returned. His flushed red face was all contorted. As his body seemingly appeared to be going through electric shock treatment.

I was experiencing a mental orgasm. Having accomplished my goal by *sub-contracting* the worst part to Passion, who'd done her job *very* well.

Plus, I had my protection in the form of a video tape. Not to mention, a bonus. I'd never thought about how the same tape, could also be held over Passion's head.

Before Sgt. Fillmore had left the hotel room, he'd given me his card. Told me if there's *anything* I needed, to just give him a call.

Jealous of this witnessed offer, Passion tried to slide her way in.

"Don't I get a card too?", she asked.

I shook my head *'no'* to Sgt. Fillmore and sternly stared at Passion.

Couldn't really blame her for trying. I mean, she *had* done the dirty work. And if anyone deserved a *hook-up*, it was her. But she had *no* idea of the deal that was *actually* going down. So I made sure it stayed that way by sending Stan out the door without anymore contact with Passion.

"Okay, Raven, tonight stays between us, right?", Passion said, with surprising concern.

"What?", I toyed with her.

"You ain't gonna tell nobody 'bout what I did this afternoon, right?", she continued, feeling the need to explain more clearly.

"Girl, it ain't no thang! Nobody cares!", I uttered, still fuckin' with her.

"Aw, C'mon, Rave. Please, don't tell anyone! C'mon, I helped *you* out!"

"Awright, awright, awright. Girl, I was just fuckin' with you! I ain't goin' say nothing!"

I enjoyed watching Passion, squirm a bit. Made her seem less perfect.

Actually, I'd gained a degree of admiration towards her. It was true. She *had* helped me out. But I wasn't going to let her know how much!

"Okay, Rave. Can I come to work tonight?", eagerly she asked.

I decided to *renege* on our deal. At least, partially.

"I'll tell you what I'ma do. I *need* you to work a bachelor party for me tomorrow. After that, then I'll start you back at the club three nights a week."

"Aw, Rave. *You* said, if I did *this* for you, that you'd get me back in. You *promised* me!", Passion begged.

"I *am* getting you back in! It's just goin' take a little time to get you all the way back. I've already hired someone that took your place. But, I *need* you at the bachelor party tomorrow. Do well for me there and I'll get you in, three nights a week. At least *one* of the three days will be a Friday or Saturday night!", I said holding my arms out like it was a *take it-or-leave it* offer.

"Hmmph. Al-right.", Passion said, as though she was disappointed. But, realized she really had no choice but to accept my offer.

At that time, I really had no *master-plan*. I could've brought Passion back fulltime with no problem. Rico wouldn't have minded. I just wanted to make sure Passion was clear that *I* was in control.

Plus, I was beginning to see the value in keeping her hungry. As much as she hated tonight, she knew tomorrow would be worse.

Tonight was with *one* guy in an elegant hotel room. And, a *white* guy, at that.

Tomorrow, it'd be with more guys. Black guys, who might recognize her later at the nightclubs or the grocery store. Certainly, they'd be talking about it. Though she *knew*, she'd not have to fuck anyone, unless she wanted to. Still, it was almost a certainty she'd have to do some other *wild* shit. Masturbation. Letting guys nibble and squeeze her. Maybe even some *dildo-involved lesbo-shit* with other dancers, if the guys requested it.

Normally, I never went to the parties that I set up. Just got the money and that was it. But I couldn't resist going to see Miss Perfect dealing with her situation.

She handled it quite well. Did what she *had* to. Even the things, she didn't wanna do. I was impressed. Hated that I'd gone. Was almost beginning to actually like her!

The next night, Saturday, was Passion's first night back at the club.

I walked her back into the dressing room personally. Wanted the other girls to know, it was *me* who allowed *her* to come back.

Didn't wanna hear no rumors that I wasn't in control. Or leaving a door open for Passion to make another mistake, by trying to *act* as though *she'd* won our battle. Even though, after what she'd been through, I don't think she'd've been that stupid again!

"Listen up! I've decided to bring back Passion. She'll be here three nights a week right now.", I declared to the room-full of half-naked girls. "Welcome back Passion.", I said, giving her a hug.

Some of the girls were excited to see her. Others were not, remembering the arrogance of the *old* Passion. Or maybe, thinking about how their money might change, now that Miss Perfect Body was back. Which ever was the case, I didn't care either way. As long as they knew Passion was back under my terms!

Amidst the excited screams of those welcoming Passion's return, Nia pulled me aside, having just gotten off of her cell phone.

"Raven! Raven!", she said tugging at my arm.

"What's up Nee?"

"Tyanna's in jail!"

"Whaatt?! For what?"

Looking around, Nia said, "I'on't wanna talk here".

We went into the office and shut the door. The loud music was still seeping in, but I could hear her much better.

"What happened Nee!"

"I guess. Well, you know, Tyanna's been doing that Internet-Modeling, right?"

"Yeah?"

"Well, I guess, she tried to turn it into an Escort-Service."

"Whaaat?"

"I'on know all the details. She just called me from jail. Wants me to bail her out, but I ain't got $600?"

"Don't worry 'bout it. I'll go get her!"

"Thanks, Rave!", Nia said with relief.

I left the club immediately. Went home to get Sgt. Fillmore's number. While I was there, I popped in the tape of him and Passion. Hadn't had a chance to even make sure that I had something visible on the tape.

Then, I called Sgt. Fillmore, told him I had a good friend that'd been arrested. He researched it and called me back. Told me he knew the arresting officer very well. And, he'd be able to have the charges dropped in a day or two.

I knew I'd owe him another night's *good-time*. Didn't wanna use Passion again. And it *sure-in-hell* wasn't goin' be me! I was over-looking the obvious. Tyanna'd have to pay him back herself.

I still had to pay bail until the charges were actually dropped. After which, I'd be able to get my money back.

Tyanna looked surprised to see that it was me who'd bailed her out.

"How you doing Tyanna?"

"Fine."

"You alright?", tentatively I probed.

"I'm fine.", she said. Pausing before saying, "I guess I .... Well ..... Thanks for bailing me out Raven."

"Hey, don't worry about that. I'm just glad you awright!"

"Where's Nee?"

"At the club. Hey, listen. I know we all kinda *fell-out* for a while. But, everything's cool now! I mean, you ain't gotta do that shit. You *know*, you can come back to the club, anytime!"

"I don't know 'bout that ....."

"Even if you don't wanna come back to the club, I got some bachelor party shit going on-the-side. Good money! You ain't gotta be doing that shit, you know what I'm saying?"

"Yeah. I know."

"Oh, I almost forgot to tell you. I got them to drop the charges against you!"

"Whaaat?! How'd you do that?"

"I gotta friend in the APD."

"Cool! Cool, cool!", Tyanna breathed genuine relief.

"You ain't gotta do nothin'. It'll be done in a couple days."

"Cool. Thanks Rave.", she said. This time, with even more sincerity.

"Well. I guess, I shouldn't have said, *you* ain't gotta do *nothing*. I mean, you might have to give him *'some'*. But he'sa white boy though!"

"Sheee-itt! No problem! I don't care if he's King Kong!", Tyanna giggled.

She'd gotten to me with that one. Belly-laughed for several minutes. Hadn't thought about that wild night, in a long time.

Not wanting to leave business dangling, I set up the *payback* night the next day at a different hotel. I was present again.

Though Tyanna and I had just reconciled, I wanted to make sure there was just *payback* going on. Didn't want Tyanna offering any info about me.

Tyanna just did her *thang*. *'Broke him off something proper like'*.

This time, she was on the winning-end of a *No-contest* battle. I'm talkin', wore him out! Simply had *too* much for Stan. Too much: ass, style, and stamina. Not to mention, the *desire* to *put-it* on him, that Passion had lacked.

◆ ◆

Monday morning, I'd dragged myself downstairs to an already awakened Nia watching the video tape, I'd forgotten to take out of the VCR.

"Rave, what's the deal?"

I rushed to the VCR and ejected the tape. Like she hadn't already seen it?

"What's up Rave? That was Passion, I recognized her. Whatchew got a porno thang going?"

Still reluctant to give more info than was absolutely necessary, I dodged it.

"No, it ain't like that!"

"Then what's *it* like?"

"I wish I could tell you, Nee. But ......"

"But what? .... You don't trust me?!"

"Naw, it ain't that....It's just.... Okay, listen. If I tell you, you gotta promise not to tell anyone! I mean, no one! Not even Tyanna!"

"Okay!"

"You know, the police officer who's getting the charges dropped against Tyanna. That's him on the tape with Passion."

"Whatchew doing black-mailing him?"

"Naw, nothing like that. We gotta deal worked out at the club that keeps us from dealing with all those fines they've been giving out at other clubs."

"Damn?!", Nia excitedly screamed. Seemingly impressed and surprised that I could be that savvy. "Wait a minute. How come Passion's on there if he's dropping the charges against Tyanna? And, how'd you get the tape?"

"Passion was before Tyanna went to jail. I hid a camera in the room. I just got the tape for my own protection. Passion don't even know 'bout the tape. Neither does Tyanna.", I let slip out.

"You gotta tape of Tyanna?"

Too late to lie, now.

"Yeah. That's how she paid him back for dropping the charges. See, that's why you can't tell her."

"Damn, Rave. I'idn't know, you were *smooth* like that! Got *Poe-lease* on *your* payroll and shit! Check *you* out!"

Hadn't expected her reaction. But, she was getting a little too impressed for my liking. Made me wondered, if she'd actually be able to keep this to herself?

"No bullshit Nee. This ain't no game! Keep that shit to yourself!", I warned her.

"I will. I will. I promise. Dammmmn. Well, shit! Now, that you done told me everything. You don't mind if I finish watching the tape, do you? Wanna see if Passion's *any* damn good, like she acts?"

"She ain't all that! But, here.", I said, tossing the tape to her. "This'll be the only time you'll see it! Now if you *wanna see* a white cop begging, just watch the tape of your girl Tyanna *wearing his ass out*! It's in the blue case, right next to the VCR."

I'd failed to heed my mom's advice about keeping secrets. But I trusted Nia. Could tell her loyalty was with me. Even more so than with Rico.

I'd proven myself to her. Helping her to *get in* again with Rico. Though he still wasn't helping her with her career. But, I'd made the effort and that's what counted. Proven it with Tyanna too. Most people who Tyanna had *dissed* would never have bailed her out. Let alone, get the charges dropped for her.

And now that Nia was viewing Tyanna's tape, her hands were no longer clean either. How's she gonna tell when Tyanna'd be mad at her too?

I was safe!, I thought.

My Turn, My Time CHAPTER SIX

It was June of the next year, the start of my first, full-summer in the A-T-L.

I'd been working for Rico for about 10 months. Made his clubs more of a success than they'd *ever* been.

I'd just finished a record-revenue generating promotion. An amateur stripping contest I called *The Shake It Fast* contest. Named it after the song by rapper Mystikal.

Successfully, I'd attracted 73 amateur women dancers to partake in the contest. All of them vying for the $1000 grand prize.

The club had receipts of over $22,000 for that night alone.

Despite all that I'd done for Rico, I was realizing I *really* had nothing to show for my efforts.

True, I had nice clothes and jewelry. A gorgeous loft and car. But, everything really belonged to Rico. And he could take it all back, anytime he got ready.

The only cash money I had was $7,000 in a shoe box in my closet. Most of it from my coordination of bachelor parties.

I was looking for more security. Maybe a piece of the club. I thought I deserved it.

Hell, I couldn't even *qualify* to buy a house if I wanted to. Any money that'd been paid to me was in cash. Had no W-2's.

I thought, after the most successful day in *Slick-N-Thick's* history, it might be a good time to talk with Rico about me further. Knew he'd certainly be in a good mood.

Nia was still working at the club. Holding out for the promise that Rico might once again help with her career. But he really had no intention on doing so.

Back in May, I *hooked-up* Nia with a record producer that'd ventured in the club. Set him up in a complimentary private booth. Went back in the dressing room to get Nia and to tell her who was in the booth. Suggested, that she try to make her own *'break'*. *Dance for free in exchange for an audition*, I advised her.

Apparently, she'd done *something* right. Must've conquered her normally-tame dancing-style.

I don't know what went on in the booth. But Nia's set to record a demo-CD at the end of the month.

Now I was looking to make my own *'break'* with Rico.

◆◆◆◆◆◆◆◆◆◆◆◆◆◆◆◆◆◆◆◆◆◆◆◆◆◆◆◆◆◆◆◆

The morning after the *Shake It Fast* contest, I went into Rico's office.

"Hey Rico."

"Rave! There's my girl!! Whatzzup baby!", Rico excitedly greeted me with a bear hug and a butt-feel. "Girl, you got that magic touch. First, the Calendar's on CD's, now the *Shake It Fast* contest! I'ma have to take you somewhere special! Whatta 'bout Jamaica? Huh?"

I didn't want anymore bonuses. I wanted a job. A check. Moolah. Like Puff Daddy says, some *Benjamins*.

"Jamaica's cool. But, I wanna talk to you.", I said, attempting to pry my behind from his grip.

"Yeah. yeah. I wanna talk to you to!", he said, walking over to close the door to his office.

When he returned, he wrapped me up again and began kissing me. He'd not made a *pass* at me in over 2 months. We weren't mad at each other or anything. He just hadn't *done it*. I guess the outstanding money from last night was the aphrodisiac that had him horny today.

His current passion for me made me defer my comments. Choosing instead to take full-advantage of the attention I was getting. And truth be known, my body sorely wanted and needed *it*.

After a spontaneous *romp* on the desk in his office. Naked and wrapped in a cuddle with Rico on the office sofa, I forged ahead with the original reason for my visit.

"Hey, babe?"

"Hmmm."

"I've been thinking about things."

"Umm-hmm"

"Do you like the way I've been running the club?", I asked.

"Yeah! You know I do. You've been doing great!"

"I was just thinkin'. I mean, it ain't no thing. But, I wondered if I could be paid on the books. You know, like a salary."

"Huh?"

"Well, it's just that I can't get a credit card. Get a bank account. Rent a car. Order stuff on-line, like airline tickets or nothing. If I was paid a specific salary, then I'd be able to do these things and not have to ask you for money."

"If I paid you on the books, then you'd have to pay taxes on the money!"

"I know. I don't care!"

"Well, and so would I. Because any money that's paid through the books is reported to the IRS. Right now with the loft, the car and everything else, I figure I'm paying you the equivalent of about 70-grand. So, I don't know. Let me think about it, okay?"

His key word was, *equivalent*. Though, it *was* true. $30,000 a year for the loft, but I shared it with Nia. $7,500 a year for the car. $5,000 a year in groceries and *eating-out* money. Trips we'd taken, about $10,000. And, I'd say another $13,000 between clothing, jewelry, hair & nails and visits to the spa. So, he was pretty close. It was just, I couldn't access any of the actual money.

Satisfied that he'd consider it, I hummed sweetly, "Okay.", and nestled back into his arms.

If he'd ask me to marry him, I'd not worry about it at all. But, I'd become a realist. Rico was the consummate bachelor. And I didn't think I loved him as much as I loved how well we worked together. Although, I did care about him, alot!

Though prior to that impromptu romp, I'd not had any *dick* over the past two months. I'd have to be *crazy* to think Rico'd not had some *pussy* in that same time.

He'd always respected me. Didn't bring any *hoochies* around me. Nor, did I suspect he was *fucking* anyone in either of the clubs. I just knew he wasn't going *too* long without some sex. Seeing as I hadn't given it to him, I assumed he had another source somewhere.

◆◆◆◆◆◆◆◆◆◆◆◆◆◆◆◆◆◆◆◆◆◆◆◆◆◆◆◆◆◆◆◆◆◆

Tyanna and Passion were dancing for me regularly at the bachelor parties that I was still booking. The combination of Passion's unbelievable body and beauty along with Tyanna's *freakiness* was certainly good for attracting repeat business.

Passion was doing it, plain and simple, for the money. Still only working the three nights at the club. She was desperately trying to hang-on to her lifestyle.

Tyanna was, well, Tyanna was just *freaky*. She enjoyed the excitement and the attention.

Over the past couple of months, Passion had become the *unofficial* fourth *musketeer* in our group.

Me, Nia, Tyanna and Passion, had even taken a four-day-trip, down to

New Orleans during *Mardi Gras*. This trip put the night in St. Louis to shame.

For a few days, all we did was drink and party. All day and all night. On Bourbon Street.

Prior to New Orleans, I wasn't a *weed* smoker. Neither was Nia. But, we all indulged.

During the last night, Tyanna came back to our room with what I believed was *crack*.

What'd I know. I'm from Iowa. The only drugs I knew about were *marijuana* and *crack*. Mostly from TV.

Anyway, I knew I *wasn't* going to try no shit like that. I'd seen, too many *Behind-The-Music* features on VH-1.

Turned out to be a drug called *X*. Short for Xtasy. Was s'pose to heighten sexuality. *The best high ever!*, claimed Tyanna.

Tyanna's sales-pitch didn't convince me. However, I was surprised when Passion agreed to sample some. Followed by the reliably-hesitant Nia.

After a few minutes, I could see the effects in all three of their glazed eyes and smirky-smiling faces.

Under the influence, Tyanna revealed that she *was* bi-sexual. I'd kinda suspected it. And, it wasn't uncommon for strippers to be *'bi'* or gay.

"Sometimes I wanna be dicked. Sometimes I wanna be licked.", she released, to a giggling room. "What, don't tell me y'all ain't never thought about it!", Tyanna defended her bisexuality.

There was uneasy silence. No one wanting to admit that they'd *even* thought about it. I knew I had.

"Okay, y'all know y'all lying!", Tyanna said glancing around our hotel room.

Though I was very drunk myself, what happened next was unbelievably sobering.

"Alright, we'll see who' lying?!", Tyanna said, taking out a note pad, from the desk and writing something on it. "Pick a number, 1 thru 3.", she continued.

"Two.", Nia answered first.

"One.", I answered, unsure of what we were doing.

"Three.", Passion delivered, having no choice.

Tyanna turned the piece of paper around, showing that she'd written on it, the number three.

"Okay, so what's that mean?", Passion questioned, sitting on the edge of the bed.

"You've never been even a little attracted to another woman?"

"What?! Psst.", Passion said, not *clearly* denying it.

"We'll see in just a moment!", Tyanna declared.

Tyanna had Passion move to an upright position, at the edge of the bed. Then, she began doing a *strip-tease* dance for her. But not touching Passion.

After a few short moments, we could see how tough it was for Passion to try to *ignore* Tyanna's sex-appeal. Serious-faced, Tyanna kept moving dangerously close to her. Never making actual contact.

Then Tyanna, like a *mime*, still not touching, circled her hands around Passion's chests. Moving two of her fingers together in a pinching motion.

It wasn't long before Nia and I giggled at the sight of Passion's nipples piercing through her halter.

Tyanna had proven her point.

Passion couldn't claim that the arousal had been *touch-induced*. She *had* to be thinking *something* sexual about Tyanna.

Tyanna repeated her *magical levitation* experiment on both, me and Nia. With the same perky results as Passion.

Then invited Passion and Nia to perform the *magic*, on her. Except when *hers* did levitate, she placed their hands directly on her peaks. They obliged. Caressing. Squeezing. Pinching.

Passion became the first to abandon caution and started nibbling. Nia, feeling the *taboo* had been lifted, also joined in.

All three of them went at it like crazy! Taking turns on each other. Kissing. Titties in mouths. Hands between legs. Fingers, pinching. Butt-squeezing. Crotch-rubbing. Finger-probing. Tongue-tickling. Booty-spanking. Passionate-moaning. Begging-groans. Climax-claiming.

Continuously, they'd encouraged me to come over. I wasn't real interested in that. Wasn't *feeling it* like them. Yet, I must admit, I was feeling sensations watching it. Throbbing in my peaks, among other places.

It must've been the *X* that buried *their* inhibitions. Well, at least Nia's and Passion's inhibitions.

After about 25-minutes, when they'd *finally* satisfied the last one, the three of them rested on the bed, unembarrassed and giggling.

It was the type of laughter, you could only *appreciate*, if you'd been drinking the same drink. In this case, if you'd also taken *X*.

Like I say, I'd always kinda figured Tyanna liked women. Ever since her comment about my big legs back in St. Louis. But, I'd never expected to see Nia with another woman. For that matter, a prissy Passion!

Just went to show me that anything is possible under the right circumstances.

◆◆◆◆◆◆◆◆◆◆◆◆◆◆◆◆◆◆◆◆◆◆◆◆◆◆◆◆◆◆◆◆◆◆◆

Being paid on the books wasn't possible. According to Rico.

It's a control issue, I thought. Knew it soon as he said it.

Could see it, in his eyes. Rico's a guy who always looked you square in the eye. Especially, during disputes.

But with me, he never did. Instead, he fumbled around with papers as he gave me the news. He fumbled excuses just as badly. Talked about it being his accountant's advice.

Since when do accountants advise their clients to break the law by paying employees with un-reported money?

I knew Rico had consciously made a decision that he wanted to *make sure* that I remained with him. And continue to make him rich with my great ideas.

I was pissed. But I didn't show it completely.

Was hurt because I thought Rico trusted me. Loved me. At least cared a *hell-of-alot*. I felt used. Unappreciated. Trapped.

Decided I needed to start controlling my own destiny.

I'd been *asked-out* many times by guys in the club. Which happens, often. Some guys figure, they'll never get one of the dancers to go out with them, because they get offers all the time. So they try with any other woman who works at the club. Waitresses, bartenders, door-girl and me. Guess they figured we must all be *freaks* 'cause we work at a strip-club.

I never accepted any of these invitations out of loyalty to Rico.

But when Darren Sharper, a handsome #3-ranked heavyweight boxer asked me to go with him to a Destiny's Child concert, I thought, it must be fate. Seeing as I'd already adopted two of *Destiny's Child* songs *Independent Woman* and *Survivor*, as my own personal anthems.

Though Darren was from Atlanta, I'd never seen him in either club before. But I knew who he was. Had seen him fight on HBO at Rico's house. It was just a matter of time, before he became the champ.

On the night he asked me out, I noticed his entourage was having more fun than him. Turned out, he was training for a fight against the #1 ranked challenger. They'd come out to release some steam that had built-up, during his training camp.

While he spent plenty of time with autograph-seekers impressed by his 26-0 record, with 24 knockouts, I was more impressed by this 24-year old fighter's restraint. Despite his buddies' urging, and the fact that they were *making-the-day* for several dancers, Darren didn't purchase or accept a single table or lap dance.

And, it wasn't a money issue. As a recent Olympic champion, having been featured in fast-food commercials and having made $6-million from his last fight, I knew he could afford as many dances as his libido could handle.

At one point, Darren left his table that'd been swarmed by dancers, hoping to *get in* on the money that was flying from his table.

He came over to the bar and leaned against it, right next to me.

"How are you doing tonight?", he surprised me, by speaking.

"Fine. How are you?"

"I'm good. Umm. Good.", he said, sounding nervous.

Rico emerged from his office and witnessed me talking with Darren. He just smiled and disappeared back behind his door. Not wanting to interrupt what I'm sure he figured was my *smoozing* of a celebrity for the benefit of the club. Plus, he was a fan of Darren.

"Hi, I'm Darren.", he said, *gentlemanly* extending his hand, palm-upward, ready to receive my hand.

"I'm Raven."

"Raven, that's a very pretty name!"

"Thanks."

"You from Atlanta?"

"No."

"I could tell."

"Whatta you mean, you could tell?"

"I'on't mean nothing bad by that. You're just real chill about things. Like you got everything under control. It's all good. Where 'bout you from?"

"Don't laugh."

"I won't."

"Iowa.", I said, expecting him not to keep his promise. Or at least, make some disparaging comment about my hometown.

Amazingly, he didn't. Instead, he simply asked, "How long you been here?".

I was very intrigued. He seemed very genuine and a bit shy. Out of the ordinary for such a well known athlete. And, that was the other thing. We'd talked for several minutes and he'd not even so much as mention who he was.

"About 10 months.", I responded to his question, about my tenure in the A-T-L.

"You like it?"

"Yeah, it's cool. I like it."

Darren appeared to have become more nervous. Like he'd depleted his *small-talk* reservoir. He took a sip of the orange juice he was drinking. Whistled a moment. Glanced around the club, tryin' to *play-it-cool*. Which was hard to do when there's only naked women as scenery. And he *wasn't* tryin' to send the wrong message. He was so cute!

"Raven. I'm so bad at this."

"Bad at what?", I played stupid.

"I wondered, if you were free Friday.....I've got a couple of tickets to the *Destiny's Child* concert.....I wondered if you'd like to go with me?", humbly he asked.

He was so cute, I knew I couldn't resist finding out more about him. If I declined, I knew I'd probably never see him again. The strip-clubs were not his type of spot. So, he'd most likely not be back again. Yet, I didn't wanna seem anxious like a *groopie*.

"Well...Hmmm...", I pretended to be undecided.

"I'm sorry. I guess I should've asked if you already have a boyfriend first. I don't wanna start no trouble, if you've gotta man. I told you, I stink at this! But, I do want you to go with me, if you can?"

This guy was like a dream. Humble and considerate! Decided I'd better not delay answering much longer, before this thoughtful guy backpeddles out of his invitation.

"No, I don't have a boyfriend. It's just that I've gotta work on Friday night ...."

"Well, maybe another time?", he prematurely interjected.

Think Darren may have thought, I was politely turning him down with a lame excuse. Really he'd not let me finish my sentence. And just as I'd predicted, started his invitation-retreat.

"Well actually, I think I can get off on Friday.", I said, trying to draw a renewal of his invitation.

"Great! I mean, are you sure it's no problem?"

"Yeah, it's no problem. It sounds like fun. I love Destiny's Child!"

"I do too."

"Yeah, I'll bet you do!", teasingly I said, with a wink and a playful elbow to his rock-hard mid-section.

I was referring to how guys loved the sexy trio's *Bootylicious* style more than their pro-women, lyric-laden music.

My comment made him blushingly laugh.

We exchanged phone numbers. Having accomplished his goal, Darren left shortly thereafter.

It'd been so long since I'd been on a date. Besides Rico, this was my first one since moving to Atlanta.

I was definitely excited. Took the entire day off on Friday. Didn't even go into the club to pick-up the deposits I made daily at the bank. I just told Rico that I was burnt-out and needed a day off.

Friday morning, I went to Sergio's salon to get my hair done. Or as they say in Atlanta, 'my *hurr-did*'.

Shortly after arriving in the A-T-L, I abandoned my previous style, of a *wash-n-go* look. Nia and Tyanna, told me that it looked too *white-girlish*. Too frizzy. They'd convinced me to get it braided. And I liked it. Got many compliments with it braided. Even was told I resembled singer, Alicia Keys.

I had Sergio take out my braids. Tonight, I wanted my hair to be long and curly. Lotsa long-hanging, thick curls.

Went next door to the nails salon. Got both, my hands and my feet done.

Next, I visited Greenbrier Mall to find a *bootylicious* outfit. Having been clued-in by Darren's blushing, I wanted to look even more *bootylicious* than Beyonce', the lead singer for *Destiny's Child*.

Found an ensemble that oughta do the trick. A red, shiny-spandex, short-sleeve top, with a U-shaped neck line, adequate enough to accommodate my cleavage. Bought a flashing-light naval ring, similar to the one Tyanna had. A waist-line chain. Brown open-toed sandals. And, cream-colored shorts that fit snug enough to make even a *hard-brotha*, grin. Didn't want Darren not to notice my best *assets*, my butt and thighs.

Got home around 3 PM. Had enough time to *shave-the-land-down-under*, just in case it turned into a very-good night. And to get a little bit of rest so I could be upbeat without bags under my eyes.

Around 7pm as I was getting dressed, Nia was preparing to go to work at the club.

I *hipped* Nia to the deal, so she wouldn't accidentally *spill-the-beans* to Rico.

Nia was always impressed by how I attracted the *big-ballers*. Almost, living through me.

Nia also attracted *ballers* too. But, she just wasn't able to navigate her way in that world as well as me. They pressed her faster than they did me, because I'd learned, *the best defense is a good offense*. I'd keep them off-balance. Make 'em unsure of their next move with me until I'd gained some respect.

Nia's mistake was she became easily hypnotized. And, that's all a *baller* needs to see. Like they say, a dog can smell fear, a *baller* can sense cheers. Once they know you're just happy to be in their presence, it's all over. It's *put-up* or *shut-up* time. More like, *put-out* or get shut-out. Even if you do *put-out*, they're gone anyway, 'cause there's no mystery left about you.

"How do I look?", I asked Nia, who's opinion about fashion I definitely trusted.

Nia took her fashion-critic role seriously. Her eyes gave me the top-to-bottom stare. Had me spin around, not wanting to overlook a thing.

Nodding her head she said, "You look good, Rave. Those shorts make your butt look good. The top looks good, except, hmmm...."

"Except what? What?", I questioned.

It was no time for her to be silent.

"Well, I was just goin' say. If I were wearing that top? I wouldn't wear a bra underneath. I mean, it ain't bad. You can see the hook in the back, a little. That's it. It ain't *real* bad or nothing. But, that's what I would do."

I knew she believed in what she was saying. But I had to consider, Nia was blessed with self-supporting full breasts. Mine were not saggy or nothing. Just had to recognize that *there was* a difference between me and her before I made a final decision.

Went back upstairs and tried it without a bra. *Not too bad!*, I thought.

Came back downstairs, and before I could ask Nia's opinion she gave it.

"Now that's much better!"

I wasn't accustomed to going bra-less. The fabric rubbing against my bare skin, was already making me perky.

Seeing me becoming sensitive to that, Nia injected, "Girl, don't worry about that. A hint of nipples is sexy. You ain't nude, it's just a lil' bit of a tease. You look good!"

I've seen bra-less women with a little perkiness, including Nia, and it didn't look bad. But, I wasn't fortunate enough to have the kinda peaks that'd only get slightly perky. When mine got stimulated, they stood out. I mean, all the way out! And unlike Nia, I didn't have shorter peaks. Mine were much longer.

True, I *was* trying to get noticed. But I did not want *that* kind of attention.

Never mind me, I'm sure it'd even be embarrassing to Darren. Could imagine him walking with me as everyone's eyes were glued to my chest.

Made me think I should've chosen a top with writing on the front. At least then, maybe my peaks may've fallen behind one of the letters and been successfully disguised. But it was too late for hind-sight.

"Girl, stop worrying about it. You look good!", Nia again tried to convince me.

"Okay.", I said, as I started back up the stairs.

"Raven!", Nia stopped me. "Gurll, I know you!", she added with a smile. "You goin' go put back on that county-lookin' bra or change your top and spoil the whole look. I know you girl!"

"What?", I said, trying not to give away, that she'd just read my mind like *Miss Cleo*.

"Seeing as you ain't goin' trust me on this anyway. I'ma give you a secret I learned from modeling. Why don't you put some *Band-Aids* on, over your nipples. That'll keep them from showing through. Try that first before you do anything else."

It worked. The *Band-Aids* didn't even show through.

Darren arrived right on time, at 8 o'clock. Came up to my unit, flowers in hand. Met Nia, who gave me the secret *girl-he's-cute* eye, before taking the flowers for me, to put in water.

The concert was at Phillips Arena in downtown Atlanta, about six blocks from my building. Though we had time enough to have dinner before the concert, we decided to wait until after the show. Which was cool with me, because a meal may've made my already snug shorts unbearable.

I'd expected that Darren would have a limo waiting for us. But, he drove his own car. A new Ford Expedition.

We went to *Club 404* for appetizers and a pre-concert drink.

404 wasn't far, only about two miles north of my loft on Peachtree Street.

When I got *'carded'* it was no problem, 'cause I'd already parlayed the favors I provided to Sgt. Fillmore into a fake *ID* for me. Now, I was glad I'd met Sgt. Fillmore, 'cause I wasn't sure how Darren would've felt about dating a girl who was *still* several months away from being of legal-drinking age.

"Did I tell you, you look really good tonight?", Darren questioned.

He already had. Twice in fact. Inside my house and when he opened my car door.

"Yes, you have. But I don't get tired of hearing it!", I flirted.

Darren was lookin' mighty-fine himself. Wearing a tight shirt that complimented his contoured physique. And a pair of Tommy Hilfiger jeans that didn't hide the nice butt he has.

If I hadn't already known who Darren was, I'd never have guessed he was a heavyweight boxer. Had no facial scars. His nose wasn't flattened from punches. No collar-flower ears. Nothing. Just clear, blemish-free dark-caramel skin. I see why he's nicknamed, 'The Baby-faced Assassin'.

With his pure skin, strong jaw-line and his chiseled build, I'd've probably thought he was a model or an actor. Reminds me of a slightly darker Shemar Moore.

Darren was six-foot-two and 225 pounds, but he didn't look it. Didn't have a build that was so large, it made people turn around and stare.

Though Rico was only two-inches taller and about twenty-five pounds heavier, he looked *much* larger than Darren. I guess Darren was much leaner. Less body fat.

Anyway, he was sexy as hell! His broad, bold, beautiful chest water-falled into his *ripped* stomach. Looked like there was a xylophone underneath his shirt. My fingers wanted to become the mallets that played his abdominal instrument.

I could tell, he was *diggin'* me too. I caught him sneaking peaks at me. At my butt, as I stepped up into his 4x4. At my chest, over the top of his appetizer menu.

Likewise, he'd caught me watching his chest and abs, as he turned in his seat, searching for a waitress to summon.

After consuming the two glasses of merlot wine, I was feeling a nice buzz.

Was further intoxicated when I learned Darren was not the typical boxer. He was a college graduate from Morehouse. Had a degree in Business.

His goal was to become the second heavyweight champion who had a college degree.

I didn't even know there was a first!

"Well, the first fighter was James 'Bonecrusher' Smith. But, he never held all three belts: the WBA,WBC and IBF, at the same time. And, he lost the title not too long after he'd won it. I plan to take it a step further than 'Bonecrusher' Smith.", he said, confidently.

It was really hard, not to fall for this guy.

It was a lethal combination. Darren's sexy body and gentlemanly-nature, mixed with two glasses of good wine and my hormones, soon made my *Band-Aids* more important than I'd ever imagined.

We drove back to my building. Parked in my lot. Darren said he enjoyed talking with me so much, he hated to get to the concert too fast. So, he suggested that we walk there, that way we could talk some more.

He was so charming and I was already hooked. I thought to myself, *Okay, damn the concert, why don't you just fuck me now?!*

My secret thoughts surfaced in the form of a failed attempt to hold in my laugh.

As we walked hand-in-hand down Philips Avenue towards Philips Arena, I could now see the confidence that must be present in a championship fighter.

Spontaneously, Darren stopped walking. He firmly pulled me to him and delivered a kiss on me that tingled my toes.

I wasn't the public-affection type. And, I don't think he was either. But, his kiss felt like he'd wanted to do that for a long time and couldn't wait 'til after the concert.

It was the kinda kiss you don't want to end. That's why even when he'd figured that he should pull-back, I continued kissing him. Our first kiss lasted about 20 seconds. And, made us both blush.

"I'm really likin' you!", he declared. Having a *knack* for saying just the right thing at the right time.

His sense of timing was more stimulating than the wine. Darren was the natural version of the drug-*X* Tyanna attempted to get me to sample.

"Well, good. 'Cause I'm liking you too!", I said, folding my lips in, out of caution. Yet, wrapping my arms around his waist as we two-stepped to the arena.

The concert was great! Though, I'd never know it. My mind was busy thinking all sorts of thoughts about Darren. *From sex to marriage. From what our children would look like to what state we'd live in.*

Darren was constantly being asked for his autograph. *Hoochie-mamas* bogarding in front of me and everything. Darren was polite with each of them. Telling them he wasn't signing autographs tonight because he was on a date. But, they could come by his training camp on Sunday from 1-2 in the afternoon and get an autograph.

Even when the *hoochie-parade* had managed to push me several feet away from Darren, he used his muscular arm to part the sea of people, sternly telling them, "Hey. Excuse me. Let my lady through please!"

His lady? Hmmm?, I began thinking.

The *hoochie's* witnessing his intensity, cleared a path for me to return to my appropriate position, by his side.

From that moment on, Darren made sure not to lose me again by wrapping his arm around my waist with his hand on my hip.

After the concert, we picked up some Thai-food and returned to my place around midnight.

I placed the food in the kitchen and told him to make himself comfortable on the leather sofa while I grabbed us some plates and *real* utensils.

Returning with a plate I'd fixed for him, I also gave him the remote for the television.

Then I went upstairs to discreetly remove the *Band-Aids*, just in case we got into something. I didn't want him knowing my little secret. And if something did get started, I couldn't have him thinking my titties tasted like *Band-Aid* adhesive.

We ate, watched TV, and talk like old friends.

"You've gotta a very nice place!", Darren said, looking around.

I know he must've been wondering how I could afford this luxury, working at a strip-club. But he wasn't curious enough to ask. Nor did I volunteer any information.

"Thanks.", I plainly responded. "I've been wondering, why don't you have a wife or a girlfriend? Or do you have a girlfriend?"

"No, I don't have a girlfriend. How come you don't have a man, witchyo fine self?", he rebutted in a Denzel Washington style.

"I'on't know? Ain't been asked by the right guy I guess?"

I wasn't lying. Technically, Rico and I weren't together. We had no *formal* commitment.

Gently, I made myself comfortable on him. Laid my head on his chest, as he played with my new curls. It wasn't long before we were kissing again. Short ones. Long ones. Tongue ones.

I wanted to get it on. He seemed hesitant. Maybe he didn't wanna *go for it* on the first date, 'cause he thought I'd look at him differently.

I *wanted* him to go for it! Tried to give subtle hints, to no avail. Finally, I took matters in my own hands. Rubbed my hand over his chest. Pinched his nipples, hoping for some reciprocity.

I pinched them a second time, this time even harder and with my hand under his shirt. Thankfully, he began returning the favor. Swirled one finger around my peaks. They'd been dying to erect themselves all night.

Timidly, with his thumb and index fingers, he twisted them, like he was fine-tuning a delicate radio.

"Harder.", I softly, repeatedly whispered.

He increased the pressure of his squeeze in such small increments, that I had to tell him, "Harder. It doesn't hurt."

He never did go as hard as I liked it.

I decided to show him what I wanted. Lifted his shirt, swirled my tongue around his nipples. Bit down, softly. Sometimes, harder. He pulled my head away. Raised my shirt. Admired me for a moment, then got it *just* right. Squeezing one and sucking the other. Dividing the attention equally between them. Surprising me with the pressure. Starting soft, and dramatically switching to biting.

Then Darren started something that sent me absolutely crazy. Fit as much of my tittie in his mouth, as was possible. Slid his mouth towards the peak like my tittie was an ice cream cone. Reaching the peak, he continuously sucked hard on the nipple only. Sucked hard, like my nipple was a straw and he was trying to get a thick milk shake through it.

Repeatedly sucking. I felt a flutter in my tummy. Relentlessly sucking. My eyes squinted tightly, trying to ease the sensation. Continuously sucking. My mouth, starting to moan. Unforgiving sucking like he owned them. Sucked 'em so hard, it'd be hours before they'd returned to a normal state.

Darren's *straw technique* created a full-fledge yearning between my legs that didn't wanna be ignored.

I didn't want to, but I had to pull him off them. I couldn't take anymore.

I started to unbuckle his pants. Wanted to give him my version of the *straw technique.*

"Wait. Wait.", Darren urged.

"What's wrong?", I said, not wanting to delay.

"I gotta fight next weekend. I can't do this."

I'd seen the *Rocky* movies. And, knew that fighters weren't s'pose to have sex before a fight because it supposedly weakened them. But, I wasn't going away that easily.

"C'mon baby. We don't have to go all the way!", I lied.

I knew if he let me get hold of his *thang*, that it'd be all over.

"I'm sorry baby. I just can't. I shouldn't have started this. Maybe, I should just go?"

Definitely I didn't want him to go. And now I knew how guys felt when we teased them, 'cause I had an orgasm in me just waiting to be released. Hoped he'd at least take care of it for me. I didn't care how. With his hands. With his mouth. It didn't matter to me.

But, he didn't. He couldn't risk it leading to more.

Damn!, I thought.

Hadn't been this stimulated, ever! Wanted to go upstairs, grab my *lonely-night rod* out of my panty-dresser-drawer and take care of business myself.

Instead, we just rested in each others arms and fell asleep to the sounds of the television.

I was awakened around 3:30am when I heard Nia using her key in the door. She was just coming home from dancing at the club.

Nia, exhausted, perked up a bit at the sight of Darren lying with me on the sofa. She smiled and winked at me before using the remote to turn the television off for us and tip-toe-ing up the stairs.

The night hadn't ended as I would've preferred. Yet, I felt more comfortable than I had in months, sleeping in Darren's arms.

◆ ◆

Darren woke up the next morning early to the smell of me preparing him some breakfast.

"Good mornin' Raven.", he sang so sweetly.

"Mornin'.", I hummed back at him.

Walking into the kitchen, he stood right behind me and wrapped his big ol' arms around my waist, as I was scrambling the eggs.

"Is that for me?", he asked.

"Mmm-hmm."

"Now I know I can't let you get away. The girl is fine and can cook, too!", he complimented.

Just then, Nia shocked me. Not just by the fact that she was awake. More by what she had on. Shamelessly, coming down the steps wearing a white-satin spaghetti-strap nighty that barely made it down to mid-thigh.

Though, Nia normally wore this type of sleep-wear. Truthfully, she didn't have anything else. But I didn't *think* I had to tell her *not* to wear that stuff when I had a man in the house. Was putting on some sweatpants and a T-shirt really that difficult? Anyway, she should've already known better.

I could tell her debut had naturally caught Darren's eye, as his hands temporarily ceased from caressing my waist.

"Oh, good morning.", Nia said, bouncing her way down each step.

"Good morning Nia.", Darren said, obviously remembering her name from their one-time meeting.

Though Darren was behind me, from my peripheral vision I could tell his head was aimed at her. Watching Nia's unrestrained bosom, freely-bounce along with each step.

Had ignored that his hands stopped caressing when Nia first appeared. But, this was too much. I elbowed him in the stomach to send him a message which ignited his hands to resume on me.

Finished fixing Darren's plate that he took over to the sofa, where he turned on the TV and began eating.

My patience for Nia was shortening. Obviously she was looking for *something*. But I was getting tired of seeing her figure swaying in the satin.

Nia, in true model-stereotyping, could be a bit air-headed at times. Just not thinking. Which was most-likely the case here.

However, when she searched for *whatever* she was looking for in a chair next to Darren, she unconsciously without regard for what she had on, bent over in front of him, giving him a good look at her *melons* through the front of her nighty, I *had* to intervene.

"Umm, Nia! Can I speak to you, for a moment.", I said sharply.

"Yeah, what's up?", Nia innocently said, now in the kitchen.

"Girl, did you know you just *flashed* your titties when you bent over?"

Mentally recapping her movements, innocent-embarrassment grew on her face. She clutched the front of her *nighty* with one hand and put the other hand over her mouth.

"No-oh. Did I Raven?", she whispered. Now, too embarrassed to turn around. Almost hoping for me to say that I was just kidding. "No, Raven. Tell me I didn't do that? He didn't see anything, did he?"

I nodded my head that she *indeed* had done it. And, that he *definitely* saw them completely.

Nia's eyes rolled to the ceiling before closing. Exhaled a sigh of disgust for herself, as her whole body contracted from the embarrassment. She aborted her search and walked as *far* around Darren as she could. She didn't even dare to look in his direction on her way towards going back upstairs.

I knew she'd not done it on purpose. Nia, could be freaky, but *only* under the right circumstances. The right guy. Alcohol-induced. Girls-night-out. That sorta stuff. But truly, she was not the type who enjoyed giving guys she didn't know free shows. That was Tyanna. Heck, Nia didn't even like working at the club. And that was for money!

During our conversation, Darren stared at the television. P*layed-it-off* like he wasn't aware of the subject being discussed in the kitchen. Helped make Nia's exit easier by keeping his eyes glued to the TV.

"Hey babe. Breakfast was delicious!", Darren said, bringing his plate into the kitchen. Had a little bit of breakfast on the corner of his lip, accompanied by another *left-over,* a grin from Nia's early-morning entertainment.

I wiped off the piece of breakfast on his lip with a napkin. Could do nothing with the grin.

"What time you flying to Vegas today?"

His fight was next Saturday, a week from today. But it was customary for boxers to get to the site at least one-week before the fight. Gives them a chance to get acclimated.

"4:30 p.m. I'm telling you, you should come?", he invited me again as he had last night.

"I can't this time?", I said, not wanting to disappoint him.

Really, there were two reasons.

One was Rico, obviously. Though, I no longer cared *personally* about his feelings. Cared more about how *I'd* be impacted *if* I went to Vegas. Would he kick me to the curb like he'd done Nia? Plus, I didn't know where I was with Darren yet. Besides, how was I gonna explain it? Couldn't tell Rico that I was sick for a week. Knew he watched boxing. What if he saw me?

The second reason was, I wasn't ready for that yet. Didn't wanna become Darren's cheerleader. Even as nice as Darren is, if you show these guys you're only wit'em because of who they are, even nice-guys will put you into the *Hit-It-Only* category.

I wanted much more than just that. So it was a calculated risk on my part.

Darren gave me a big affection-filled hug at the door. Then left to go home so he could shower and pack for Las Vegas.

Hearing the door close, Nia immediately came back downstairs.

"Raven, I'm so-oh sorry! I wasn't trying to do that!", she apologized.

I knew she wasn't. But it was nice to know that she respected me enough to know she owed an apology.

"Gurrl, don't *even* trip! It ain't no thing!", I assured her.

Having sufficiently cleared-up the situation, Nia started her nosy-ness.

"So-oh, what's up Raven? What'd y'all do?", she said, fishing for hot and steamy details.

"We had some wine, went to the concert and came back here. That's it."

"Annnnd?", Nia sang with inquisitive eyes.

"And nothing. That's it."

"Y'all didn't do nothing?", she pressed, finding it hard to believe.

"Naw, for real!"

"But you likin' him, aren't you?", Nia said, trying to detect *any* little gleam in my eyes.

"Yeah, I am!", I couldn't resist sharing.

"I ain't mad at ya. He's fine as hell! Gurll, you know you better hang on to that!", Nia said complimentarily. Confident that I knew she wasn't interested in going after my man.

"Yeah, he is cute.", I thought out-loud.

"So, whatta 'bout Rico?"

"What'dya mean, what about Rico?", I said suspiciously.

Knew he wasn't ever gonna get back with her. But I also knew Nia must still have a thing for him having stayed in her dancing position this long.

"How you gonna work this?"

Then I thought, *Maybe she's just concerned, the way I was? Worried about what might happen to her living arrangement, if Rico and I were to fall-out?*

"Don't worry about it. Rico'll never know.", I tried to put her at ease.

It wasn't working.

"Okay, I'm just saying. Be careful. That's all.", Nia *veteranly* warned.

◆◆◆◆◆◆◆◆◆◆◆◆◆◆◆◆◆◆◆◆◆◆◆◆◆◆◆◆◆◆◆◆◆◆◆◆◆◆

On fight weekend, I was at Rico's house in Alpharetta, as usual.

Rico enjoyed throwing sporting-event parties for his boys. Lotsa music, booze and plenty of girls from the clubs to provide the pre-fight during-fight and post-fight entertainment.

The girls loved being asked to attend a Rico party. Even, in the capacity of the entertainment. Made 'em feel like they were important to Rico.

Plus, the money wasn't bad either. Definitely better than at the club. And more fun. All of Rico's friends were *ballers* too. Spread cash around like *Monopoly*-money.

Plus, they'd hoped to *hook-up* with a *baller*. But, they didn't understand that they'd never have a chance at that. Not when the *baller's* friends treat them like a *ho* at the party. Now how's that *baller* goin' bring her around his boys later as his women? Just ain't gonna happen. Reputation is too important to them.

Sometimes, Rico selected the girls to suit the tastes of his boys. Other times, he left it up to me.

Girls at the club, around Superbowl, Final Four, NBA Finals, World Series or big fight time, would suck-up to me. Hoping that I'd select them.

It wasn't all that uncommon for a girl to leave one of Rico's parties with a thousand dollars for just dancing. Even more if they set-up a private thing.

Couldn't get Nia in on these deals because she was still a distraction to Rico. Didn't wanna spoil his night, as he'd be sure to be surveying her every move.

Tyanna would've been perfect for this venue, but it was kinda the same deal as Nia.

Passion was just too cute! I wanted to keep my finger on her. And I knew that might not be possible, if I brought her to one of these parties.

As cute as she was, she just might be able to catch the eye of one of Rico's *well-to-do* buddies. Then, she wouldn't need *me* anymore.

I was playing hostess. Being shown-off by Rico.

Always dressed extra-sexy. I knew what he wanted. These were *Band-Aids*-free events. The more I teased, the more his pals envied him. And Rico loved it.

He'd ask me to get them some more beer. As I'd get up, he'd spank my backside in thanks. Loud enough to attract attention to my jiggling derriere as I went to the kitchen.

I spent alot of time in the kitchen during this fight. Having started something with Darren, I was now too nervous to watch it. Yet, I didn't want Rico to become aware of that.

This fight didn't last long. Darren gained his 27th knockout victory in the 3rd round.

"I told you. Give me my money!", Rico exclaimed. Collecting his money from the bets he'd made.

"Yo boy got lucky!"

"Lucky my ass! That'sa A-T-L boy! That boy can punch!", cheered Rico.

Unknown to Rico, his comments were solidifying my attraction to Darren.

"Bet he don't beat Lennox Lewis?", chanted one of tonight's losing-betters.

"Lennox won't fight him! Lennox has been *ducking* that boy since he turned pro!", charged Rico. "Only way Lennox is gonna fight 'em is *if* they threaten to take his titles away!"

"Yeah, whatever.", the loser dismissed Rico's comments.

After the party, Coco, one of the dancers that Rico'd selected remained at the house in the role of the clean-up girl.

Rico and I, had gotten out of her way. Gone into the bedroom and sat on the bed, watching TV.

"How'd you like that fight tonight?", Rico asked.

"It was good.", I purposely said blandly.

"Darren's goin' be champ if they give 'em a shot at the title."

"Think so?"

"Know so. Fo' sure."

Then Rico began fondling my breasts.

"Stop Rico. Coco's still out there!"

"So what. You want me to tell her to come in here?"

"What?!"

"Yeah. The three of us could have some fun!", Rico smiled at me like I was one the *ordinary* girls. "Yeah. I should call the youngster-rookie in here!", he continued.

Rico called Coco, *youngster-rookie* because she was barely eighteen. Having *just* graduated from high school in May.

"Why you trippin' Rico?", I said, making it clear it wasn't going down like that.

"I'm trippin'?"

"Yeah. You're trippin'."

"If I'm the one who's trippin', how come, one of my boys saw you at the *Destiny's Child* concert with Darren Sharper last week?", he sprung on me.

I was shocked.

"Oh, now you all quiet, huh? Didn't think I knew that?", Rico added.

"Rico, it ain't even like that.......", I started to begin lying.

"Yeah it is. But, it's cool. It ain't no *thang*, as long as we *both* know the deal. And, as long as everything's even."

"Rico, we just went to the concert and that was it."

"Why you nervous? Ain't no *thang*. I'ma 'bout to even it up right now.", Rico informed me. "If you don't like it, then you can make it on your own. Just like Nia! Or, we'll see *just* how cool you are with Darren. You think he goin' take care of you like I do?"

I didn't answer. Didn't wanna encourage his already escalating tones.

"Coco! Coco! Come in here for a minute!", Rico summoned her.

Though he'd called her, she still respectfully knocked on the door before opening it.

"Rico, did you call me?", she said, in her *late-teens sounding* voice.

"Yeah, come in Coco.", he invited. Then demanded to me, "Raven, sit down!".

He proceeded to have Coco strip for him. Caressing her dark-chocolate skin. Knew he didn't even need to ask her. Just did it. Sucked on her tiny titties like they were *Hershey's Kisses* candy.

Coco had no idea what was going on. But she did as he'd instructed.

"Raven! Keep your eyes on us!", he demanded. Knowing how painful it was for me to watch.

Coco wasn't very good. Not even close to me. Easily brought to moaning and shaking by any little thing Rico did.

But that *wasn't* the point. The tears that were streaming down my cheeks *was*.

Rico made me sit through everything. Coco sucking his *thang*. Him, licking the slender girl to vibrations. *Doggie-styled* her little-behind. Purposely adding insult to injury, using a finger where it *wasn't* s'pose to go, that had the petite girl noisily conceding.

"Okay. Okay, Rico. Ooo-woo, Rico, baby. Please, baby, please.", she groaned, reaching her hand back, begging him to abort.

Without regard to Coco, he continued with his finger, sending the message to me via the pained expression on her face.

The message was clear, he was in control. And, I'd better not forget it. Or, I'd be, metaphorically speaking, *painfully fucked*!

Rico seeing the pain that was contagiously transferred to my face by witnessing Coco's discomfort, decided to release his finger from her. Then released me as well. Telling me to go home.

Immediately, I did.

Rico had embarrassed me to Coco. Guess that's what he'd meant by, *as long as it's even.* I'd embarrassed him to his boy. Now I guess we were even.

Knew Coco *wasn't* gonna spread *anything* about tonight around the club. Fearful of Rico's and my wrath. Besides, she was young. Most certainly, she'd've been too embarrassed about her having been a *booty-ring* on Rico's finger.

Didn't feel much sympathy for Coco either. Other than during that brief moment. She'd fucked my man. In my face. Some things were unforgivable.

I needed to release some steam. Told Nia what had happened.

Two days later, I relieved Coco from her duties at the club. Had her in the same position as Passion. Working for me on the side as a bachelor party dancer.

That night made me realize even more, that I needed to find a way to become independent of Rico. Totally free. No more sneaking around, doing bachelor parties. I wanted the same total freedom that Rico enjoyed.

Too Hot To Hold CHAPTER SEVEN

When I got home, I had a message from Darren. He'd called me right after his fight and left his telephone number at the Las Vegas MGM Grand Hotel where he was staying.

I called him back. We talked for several hours. He wanted to take me out to celebrate his victory. Told me he'd be back in Atlanta on Monday morning and wanted to do breakfast.

Ignoring Rico's warning, I agreed. I figured Rico would do nothing because he needed me. I was making him too much money. That's why he hadn't dismissed me like he'd done to Nia.

After breakfast with Darren on Monday, I started working on my plan to free myself from Rico. Couldn't and didn't wanna rely on things working out between me and Darren.

So, I called Tyanna. Asked her to set-up a meeting for me with the porn-producer she'd told me about who'd offered her money, before I came to Atlanta. She did.

He wasn't as successful as he'd been before. Big budget porn-companies had made it difficult for him to compete. They simply could pay the girls more. But I had a plan.

Met him at his seedy office on Metropolitan Avenue in the East Point section of Atlanta. The building was located between an old automotive repair shop and a junkyard. It looked like it'd been a warehouse at some point. The old company's name, *Jensen's Mattress Factory*, had been covered-over with white paint, but was bleeding through.

"Hi, I'm Raven Klein. I have an appointment with Troy Reams.", I said to the bubble gum chewing receptionists.

"Wait just a minute.", she said, walking just inside a door that led to the back. Then she yelled down the corridor, "Troy, a girl is here to see you. Says her name's Raven or something like that?"

Heard a muffled response.

"You can go on back.", the receptionist informed me.

Walking through the door down the dimly lit hallway, I passed several rooms that were obviously *make-shift* video-taping studios. Each room had studio lights, a bed and different sets of street-corner-cheap furniture in it.

The early-40's, slightly-overweight white man, that watched me walking the whole way without making a step towards me, I assumed was Troy.

"Troy?"

"Yeah?"

"I'm Raven. Raven Klein. My friend Tyanna told you about me?"

"Oh, yeah. Tyanna. How's she doing?"

"Good. She's doing good. I wanted to talk with you about making movies?"

"Well, take your clothes off. Let me see what you got, then we'll talk."

"Oh, no. Not me being in the movies. I think I can help *you* find black girls to star in them."

"Black girls *are* hard to find.", Troy said, rubbing his goatee on his chin in thought. "And movies with black girls in-'em do sell very well. Keep talking."

"Well listen, if you'll sign a deal with me, I think you can get back to where Tyanna said you used to be?"

My last comment made Troy turn *somewhat* aggressive.

"You've ever been in the video-media before?"

"No."

"What you said sounds good. And, I am interested in shooting more scenes with black girls. But it's not that simple. The movie has gotta be of good quality too. Right now, I'm reduced to shooting with these old cameras. No matter how good and sexy the girls look, it just doesn't come across in the final product with this old equipment."

"I've got that solved too. What if I told you you'd be shooting with latest equipment? The same equipment used to make music videos."

"If you can pull that off, I'd be willing to talk!"

"I can do it. Let's talk money. I'll take no less than 70% of the net profits from sales in the US and North America. I retain all rights to the videos, and a 75% share of net profits from overseas markets."

"Whoa. Whoa. You asking an awful lot for just providing the bitches!"

"Not bitches. Women. According to my research, your company has not made a single sale overseas in 13 months. Your US-sales have steadily decreased by an average of 5.7% monthly. Not too mention, sales have dropped 42% in the past month alone."

"How do you know that?"

"Don't worry about how I know this. It's my job to know this. The way I see it, you're on a sinking ship Troy. The Titanic. The S.S. Minow. Whatever you wanna call it. At this rate, you'll be gone completely in the next 4-6 months. I'm sure you've done the numbers, so let's not play games with each other. Your ship is sinking. Here I come along on the Love Boat. Get on board Troy. Get on board."

"Alright. 50-50 on US Sales. 60% for you and 40% for me on international sales. Plus, we split the copyrights."

"Troy? Troy? I hear some more water in the boat. This is my last offer, and then I'm going elsewhere. US-Sales, 60% me, 40% you. International Sales, 75% me and 25% you. Your sources are gone overseas. And, I retain the copyrights. Take it or leave it, Troy. Tick-tock Troy. Time's a wasting. Whatzit gonna be? Sink or swim?"

"Alright. Deal."

"I need you to sign this paperwork. Make our partnership official and I'll get back with you by Wednesday. Be ready for the first shoot on Friday!"

Left directly from Troy's office to a meeting with Clive Sparks, the Grammy Award-winning music video producer that had gotten Nia into trouble with Rico.

Worked out a deal that paid Clive $200 per shoot and 20% of US-Sales, just for him to allow us to use the state-of-the-art video equipment of the video production company he worked for, Peachtree Music Live (PML). And, he'd do the final editing of each movie.

In addition, gave Clive $4,000 advance bonus in hush-money. Keep things quiet from Rico. He barely knew Rico. But, I wanted the added protection until things got rolling.

Clive was alot like me. He too was looking for some security and tired of kissing butt. Clive knew, all he needed was *one* baby-ass entertainer to say that they didn't like working with him and PML would fire him. Plus, he wasn't making a killing there. Even with a *Grammy* on the shelf, he pulled down about 42-grand a year.

On Tuesday, I went by Clark College, Morehouse College and Morris Brown College. Found the top IT-majors at each school.

Paid each of these *egg-head nerdy* guys $200 plus a little *booty* to design for me one of the best websites. Which'd be my vehicle to the overseas market.

Didn't mind trading a *little ass*, when it was for my benefit. Unlike when Rico had tried to *ho-me-out* to Sgt. Fillmore, simply for the sake of the club.

Plus, with these nearly-virgin academies, I think the *booty* not the money sealed the deal.

Now I had everything set.

I'd provide the girls for the shoot and front the money to pay them. Clive would provide the quality cameras for Troy. Troy would provide the lighting, set, shoot-location and the crew. Clive would pick-up the equipment and the unedited scenes. Clive would then edit and reproduce it on the VHS tapes I provided. VHS tapes that cost only 27¢ each that I'd purchased via the internet from Taiwan.

The *nerds* would do the desktop publishing for the video tape box-covers and update the website as we finished another film.

I'd market the final product in the United States through distribution companies. Already had several contacts with distribution companies. These same companies also advertised on the bathroom walls at *Slick-N-Thick* and *The Carmel Club*. Everything was set except for one thing. I had no girls.

Before getting girls, I met with Troy to discuss what was actually needed for the shoot.

"Generally in a movie, variety is the key. Guy-girl scenes. Girl-girl scenes. Three person scenes. Light-skinned and dark-skinned. Big butts and tiny butts. Big titties and little titties. Big dicks and well, more big dicks. Oral sex. Masturbation. Sex Toys. The more variety you're able to put together, the better the movie will sell!", Troy shared his expertise. "You even need variety within a particular scene. Multiple sex positions. And girls who'll do more than just regular sex is ideal. Need vocal girls. Gotta be able to hear them. They gotta be animated. Outgoing. Shy girls have no place in porn. If they need a drink or whatever to relax, get it for them."

"How many scenes do we need?"

"Four to five normally. Remember, a scene is 12-15 minutes of actual final-edit sex time."

"Okay, I got it. Do you have some guys?"

Yeah, but they're quick-cummers. With them you gotta shoot over several days to get a scene finished."

"Well, that won't work. We'll have the equipment for only one-day on each movie. So we gotta get it all taped the same day."

"Well, I do have one guy that can hold his own pretty well. But, he's a white boy and you know sistas. Especially their first time on camera, they ain't hardly tryin' to be fuckin a white boy. Trust me, I know.", he enlightened me.

Troy did have a point. But, I wanted options.

"Well, bring him anyway. We'll see if we use him? Hey, have you come up with a name for our movies yet?", I asked.

"Yeah, I have. What's big now are the series titles. *Dirty Debutantes* movies. *Up and Cummers* movies. *My Baby Got Back* movies. What do you think about, Atlanta Amateur Brown Sugar?"

"Sounds sweet!", I said with a laugh.

Having gotten all the information, I thought about which girls I'd ask to be in the movie.

Knew I had to be real careful if I was gonna use a girl from the club. Decided to choose some of the girls who weren't making very much money. True, there's a direct relationship in beauty and financial success at the club. But, it wasn't always true. Look at Nia.

Besides, any girl that worked at the club was probably the prettiest girl in her high school. The ones who weren't making much money, were either like Nia, not enthused about doing it, therefore the guys figured they'd not get their moneys-worth. Or, they were just competing against the *major-leagues* of beautiful women that also worked at the club.

Either way, they'd be cute enough for the movie.

◆ ◆

Just when I didn't need it, one-day before our first porn-shoot, there were complications at the clubs.

Went in early on Thursday. Sat down in a three-way meeting with Rico and Sgt. Fillmore.

When I arrived, they were already discussing the matter.

"You're late!", Rico negatively greeted me.

"There was an accident on I-85. I got caught in traffic.", I explained.

"Save it! Sit down!", Rico shouted.

"Hey Raven.", Sgt. Fillmore addressed me, more politely.

"Hi."

"All I'm saying Rico is it's gonna cost a measly $1000 more a week."

"You're trying to rip me off. You know that don't you?", Rico charged.

"$1000 more for what?", I jumped in.

"For the same old shit. Keep the mayor's task-force on nude bars from reaching us.", Rico clarified.

"Rico, you're not looking at the big picture here ....", Sgt. Fillmore attempted.

"Oh yes I am. I'm looking at paying *you* $78,000 a year instead of the $26,000 a year we've already agreed on! That's the big picture to me!", Rico sharply returned.

"Without my services Rico, each time one of your girls even brushes her butt up against a customers leg, you'd be fined what?...umm...$5,000. Not to mention, they might shut you down for one to three days while they conduct some bullshit interviews of your girls. Best case scenario, that's another 20-grand, minimum. Plus, your girls ain't making money while you're closed. They'll probably find work somewhere else. Not to mention, if the Atlanta-PD files charges, you'll spend another 15-grand just to defend it. Do the math Rico. That's like what?, 40-grand for each time. Then, they'll really try to shut you down, PERMANENTLY! Just look what they did to *The Gold Club*.", Sgt Fillmore asserted like an insurance salesman.

"Damn Stan!", Rico sounded like a rapper. "I don't know? 1500-a-week is a little steep."

"Hey, I gotta get paid for the risk I'm taking. I gotta a wife and kids to feed too, you know! There's alot people lookin' over my shoulder. And now, I gotta deal with the mayor's hot-shot homicide detective, Devin Lorenz, who's just been appointed over the task-force. He ain't even in this division and they appoint him over the task-force, 'cause he's the mayor's boy! Look, I got my police-force pension I'm putting on the line here! So, what's it gonna be?"

Looking to me, Rico responded, "I'ma have to think about it?".

"Well think fast! You've got 'til Monday, Rico! Monday!", Sgt. Fillmore said with a deliberate tone.

And with that he stood up, kissed *me* on the cheek and left.

"Can you believe that motherfucka? And what he's tryin' to do to me? He's a lucky man. He don't know. I'm from the A-T-L. I could have a couple of the street-brothas pay his wife and kids a visit!"

I was shocked by what I was hearing. Actually, scared. Maybe Rico was just pissed. You know, talkin' out the side of his neck. But it didn't seem so. Sounded like he meant it. Like he was seriously contemplating killing a cop. And I was hearing it.

"Rico, listen baby. You know you can't kill a cop. You'll go to jail. And what will that solve? Nothing."

"Yeah, but I ain't gonna let that, *piece-of-shit-son-of-a-bitch*, fuck with me like that. I gotta do something. Otherwise, what's to stop him from saying he wants $250,000? Huh?"

"Calm down baby.", I whispered, rubbing the back of his neck as he paced back and forth.

"It ain't time to be calm. It's time to take care of business!"

I sensed he'd made a decision to kill Sgt. Fillmore.

"Okay, listen. Baby, give me a chance to talk to him. You know, I'ma women. He might listen to me?"

"Raven, titties and ass ain't got nothing to do with this shit! It's about greed. You think he'll change his mind, 'cause you goin' give him some more ass?"

It was clear he was still in the dark about my *not* fucking Sgt. Fillmore.

"Give me until Sunday? That's all I'm asking. Ain't got nothing to lose? Just 'til Sunday?"

"Yeah, okay. Whatever. If I don't hear from him by Sunday, I'm handling this shit my way! You hear me?"

"I hear you. But you *gotta* promise me you ain't gonna do nothing until after Sunday, okay?"

"Yeah."

"Rico, if I *do* pull this off, save you 52-grand. What do *I* get out of the deal?"

"Ain't that a bitch! What? You tryin' to *shake-me-down*, too?!"

"No Rico. It ain't even like that! You know I've got your back. Haven't I always?"

"Yeah. I'm sorry Raven. I'm just pissed-off right now. I'm sorry. What you want? A Rolex? New furniture? A vacation? What?"

"I wanna be paid on the books. At least 30-grand's worth."

"Raven, we've already had this discussion haven't we?"

"I know. But I'ma save you fitty-grand. I'm only asking for thirty on the books. Now that's fair!"

"Okay Raven. Seeing as I don't *think* you got pussy good enough to convince a man to forget about 52-grand anyway. If by some miracle you are able to pull this off, I'll do you one better. I'll give you 5% ownership, in one of the clubs. That's worth, way more than 30-grand."

"Deal. I want my 5% in *Slick-N-Thick*!"

"Fine.", Rico agreed. Confident I wouldn't achieve my goal.

Couldn't believe it. Partial ownership. I chose *Slick-N-Thick* over *The Carmel Club* because I'd seen the books. Though *The Carmel Club* catered to the more affluent customer, it had more overhead and a higher mortgage. That made it less profitable than the less fancy *Slick-N-Thick* club that catered more to ordinary *suit-and-tie* corporate-class and the occasional street *baller*.

I'd figured that *Slick-N-Thick* made about 1.8 million per year after expenses and taxes. 5% ownership could equate to about 90-grand.

◆ ◆

On Friday morning, I was at the studio watching Troy prepare for today's shoot. Wanted to be there so I'd be able to learn the process.

Knowledge is power, I remember reading somewhere. I wanted to be knowledgeable of every aspect of this business. That way I'd control my own destiny.

Watched Troy and his crew set up monitors, test equipment and arrange lights.

The shoot was scheduled to begin at 12:00-noon.

I'd decided to play-it-safe on this first shoot. Choose girls I knew I could trust. Or, girls that I had something hanging over their head.

The stars of this first video would be, Passion, Coco, Tyanna, one of Tyanna's friends, and Nia.

Convincing Nia, I'd had to use my *aces*. Hated to do it, but I had to. Otherwise, I'd be one scene short. I reminded Nia of how I'd helped her meet the music-producer. About my patching things up between her and Rico. Even about that she was staying in, what was now, *my* loft. And the fact that I'd bought a car for her to drive from an auction.

It took everything I had on her for her to finally agree to do a masturbation-only scene. And it meant that we'd be even.

Once the *stars* had arrived, I began seeing the benefit of Troy's experience.

He assembled the girls in one dressing room as he began giving them instructions.

"Okay. Listen up. It's very important that we stay on schedule. So I need each of you to be ready when it's you turn, okay?", Troy spoke with much energy. "Now there are a few simple rules I need you to follow:

1. No chewing gum during the scene.
2. Those of you doing intercourse scenes, you'll find a script next to your locker. It's an order of positions. Don't worry about sticking to the script. If you find a position that feels better, then go with it!
3. Do not stop! No matter what! If the sensation is feeling too good, which I've never heard of such a thing, but if it is, just keep going anyway.

4. If you're sitting in the studio during a taping of a scene you're not in, ABSOLUTELY no giggling.
5. Keep the hair out of your face. We need to be able to see your face. And try to keep your eyes open as much as possible. Especially during initial penetration. It's okay, if you close them. Just don't keep 'em closed during the entire scene.
6. Always make sure we can see your head.
7. ALWAYS acknowledge any orgasms. I need to hear *your* words. *'I'm cumming or I'm gonna cum'*, is what I need to hear you say.
8. Just know, you WILL have cum on you today. Do not, I repeat, do not wipe it off of you. We will give you a towel at the end of the scene. But allow the guy to do his ejaculation where-ever is most stimulating for him, please. It ain't poison!

And finally, most importantly, RELAX & HAVE FUN! We're gonna start in about 45 minutes. Those of you who need a little *liquid-courage*, help yourself to the bar!", Troy finished his pep-talk.

Like a man on a mission, Troy called each girl into a room to shoot still-pictures of them in bikinis. These photos would be used for the front of the box cover.

We were almost ready to begin. Troy's crew consisted of 6 people. Three cameramen, a sound *boom-mike* guy, a lighting guy and a production assistant a.k.a. *gopher*. *Gopher* means, they *go-for* and get, anything the director needs.

It was time for our first scene.

"Okay, I need Passion in here, pronto!", Troy yelled, from his director's chair.

Passion appeared a little nervous being the first one up. But she wasn't as nervous as I think I'd've been. Maybe not as nervous as I was just watching the production, hoping all the equipment would work properly.

All of the other girls had lined the edge of the wall inside the studio out of curiosity. Troy turned to them with a stern look, reminding them to be quiet.

"Okay Passion. You look great today!"

"Thank you!", she said, looking around to see who she'd be sharing the scene with.

"Wow! What a perfect body you have!", Troy complimented her, trying to make her less nervous.

Instinctively she repeated thanks as she awaited her co-star.

Her co-star was a *ringer*. A professional I'd hired.

"Passion, honey, your guy's gonna come in, in just a minute. Listen, what I need is for you to kneel on the floor with your hands over your eyes. I'll bring him in, stand him in front of you, then we'll start with you removing your hands from your eyes, okay?"

"Okay.", Passion said, as she did what Troy directed.

To the gasp of the girls lined against the wall, Passion's co-star entered the room. It was King Kong.

Thinking about what Troy had said about the guys he had who were quick-cummers, I'd hired him to make sure we had someone, who'd be able to handle it.

Tyanna and Nia had grins that reached both ears. Even Tyanna's friend, Heather, at the sight of Kong's *dangaling* had to cover her mouth, so not to break Troy's rule #4.

"Okay Passion, you can take your hands down."

Passion's head jerked back as her eyebrows rose in disbelief. Her eyes widened, like her face was too close to *it* and she couldn't focus.

"Damn!", she said, her eyes darting to Troy. Back to Kong's *thang*. Up to Kong's face. Back to Troy again.

"Go, Passion!", Troy whispered and motioned with his hands.

Finally she did. Grabbing his *monster* with two hands and opening her mouth to yawning-proportions to fit him in.

As she moistened him, he untied her bikini-top. Pulled her away from her *kneeling-duties*. Laid her back to the bed. And with his mouth, started in on her *already* fully-elevated peaks.

Passion was really feeling her namesake, as Kong slid his hands inside her bikini-bottoms and strummed her like an acoustic guitar. To which, Passion was now humming along to the *music* with her intense moaning.

Then Kong, in one smooth, quick motion, slipped her bottoms off her. Definitely the move of a veteran. Firmly pushed her legs back and wide, grabbing behind her knees. Like he'd planned to really *put-it* on her.

Passion, sensing it too, immediately went into a defensive mode. Holding her hands above her *kitty*, ready to push against Kong's stomach in an effort to control the depth.

As he entered, Passion's back arched to gymnastic-flexibility. Her eyebrows furrowed tremendous sensation. Face squinted ecstasy as her nostrils flared.

Her head would shake quickly from side-to-side as Kong pummeled her. The song they were creating together soon gained lyrics.

"Oh my gaa...ooo-woo...oh my gaa...ooo-woo...oh my gaa", Passion uncontrollably sung as her toes curled into a *foot-fist*.

Tremors had begun in her legs harnessed only by Kong's grip of her thighs. Her toned, abdominal muscles were constantly contracting. And she struggled to periodically open her eyes.

For the first time, Passion didn't seem so perfect. She was being handled.

When Kong released his grip from the back of her legs, the tremors had grown into an earthquake. The quake made her voice sound like she was stuttering.

"Oh-oh shee-ee-it. Oh-oh my-yi gaa-ah. I-I'm gon-na-ah cuh-umm!", Passion shrieked.

Not quite satisfied with a single ecstasy-claim, Kong turned her over. Passion's hair was all over the place. She bought herself some time, by positioning herself for *doggie*, *very* slowly. Appearing very spent, she took a couple of deep breaths before raising her backside up, ready to resume.

Kong grabbed her hair, in an effort to give it some order and to keep her face in camera-view. Used her hair the way an equestrian used a reign.

His never-ending motions were beginning to wear her down. Her head would slump. And no longer was she supporting herself with her hands. Instead, resting forward on her forearms.

Undeterred, Kong bounced back-and-forth causing her cute lil' derriere to harmoniously dance in sync to his rhythm. Her peaks were also swaying to the back-and-forth beat.

Then without warning, Kong started making the song a duet!

"Oh, shit! Oh, Shit! You gonna make me cum! Oh, shit!", Kong warned, as the cameramen scurried into position to capture the moment.

Kong's vocals had given life back to Passion. Now she was back on the palms of her hands, sacrificing additional depth in hopes of a *jackpot* reward.

"Oh-shit Passion! I'm gonna cum, Passion!", Kong grunted her name.

Then he pulled out. Rested his *monster* on her backside *groove*, before erupting. Released a *jackpot* so large, almost enough to *lotion* her entire back!

Troy looked over at me with a *huge* smile. Gave me a *thumbs-up*, signaling that we *definitely* had a *keeper-scene*.

Passion took a huge breath. A sigh of relief that immediately turned into a pride-filled smile for what she'd been able to do.

"Nice job Passion!", Troy cheered.

The crew applauded both of them as they were cleaning up with towels.

Though we had a great scene, one that'd be *sure* to help sales, I was *still* a little jealous. Passion, by herself was able to do what me, Nia *and* Tyanna, could not.

The rest of the girls, deftly silent, knew Passion would be tough to follow.

It'd be about 15 minutes before we'd be ready for our next scene. The crew had to change rooms so that the set would be different. That way, the movie wouldn't seem like it was shot all in the same day.

As part of the crew moved equipment, Passion and Kong were busy recreating their scene for still-pictures. Troy placed them into positions they'd just been in. Penetration and everything. Had them put-on their best sensual faces so he could get good, clear, 35mm photos for the cover.

Apparently, that's how it's done. *During the scene taking a still photo, you'd most likely end-up with a blurry picture. Besides, it's just easier that way.*, Troy later explained to me.

The next scene matched a very-nervous and *sensitive-to-touch*, Coco with Troy's *too-experienced-for-Coco* white boy named Chad. This scene would be best described as a 1st-round knockout. But, we kept the scene anyway, despite the fact that Chad was forced to make *himself* jackpot at the end.

The third scene rivaled our first scene. Tyanna and her, I assumed-to-be lesbian friend, Heather, also put on quite a show.

Heather was a dark-skinned *Serena Williams-like brickhouse*. Built like the track-sprinter she was at the University of Georgia.

During their noisy, passion-filled moments, they'd done *69*, double-penetrated and used sex toys on each other. Climaxing, with a facing-each-other-seated, dual-headed dildo, masturbation scene.

This *booty-jiggling, thigh-shaking* affair earned them the second *thumbs-up* of the day from Troy.

The final scene with Nia, was not at all, what we'd hoped for. At least, not in the beginning. And certainly not worth the *we're-even* promise, she'd made me declare.

Nia had the easiest scene of all. Just masturbation. Alone. But Nia wasn't being sensual. She was just going through the motions. Rubbing here. Pinching there. But it lacked genuineness. And just like at the club, it showed here too.

"Cut!", Troy yelled, as he walked over to the bed. "Nia baby. You've gotta give me a little more feeling, okay? Can you do that?"

"Okay, I'll try?", she said, noncommittally.

"Babe. I don't need you to try. I need you to do it!", Troy tried to inspire.

"I'm trying?", Nia said, embarrassed to have been the *only* scene to require coaching.

"Can someone tell Chad and K.K. I need them in here.", he directed to his production assistant.

A naked Nia just sat back against the headboard with her eyes rolling to the ceiling. Partially out of embarrassment, as all of the girls who'd *successfully* finished their scenes were looking-on. But mainly because she knew her failure to be sensual was about to lead to a scene change.

Both Chad and Kong, arrived fully-clothed. They took their shirts off and stood on opposite sides of Nia who was resting with her back to the bed.

At the same time, Chad and Kong leaned over her to begin nibbling each of Nia's peaks. They made room enough for a camera to get in close, to capture her peaks' firmness.

Nia had her legs closed as they both reached down that way.

Troy, using sign-language, signaled Coco to come to him. She did. He whispered something in her ear. And she entered the scene.

The veteran guys could read Troy's mind. Each of them grabbed one leg, opening Nia to Coco.

Coco used a combination of fingers and tongue to save the scene from being cut.

Nia, almost being restrained like a patient at *Bellevue Psychiatric Hospital*, finally fell prey to the shear, unimpeded stimulation.

From my angle behind Coco, I could only see the back of Coco's head bobbing and her elbow quickly churning in and out.

Even without a clear view, I could hear that we were getting a good scene.

"Okay, okay, okay.", Nia begged, like she was negotiating a deal. Her negotiating soon gave way to an affirmation of Coco's achievement, "Oh-shit! I'm cumming! I'm cumming! I'm cumming!", Nia claimed, having now gotten into the *swing-of-things*. And her legs doing the *butterfly-kick* swim move.

Coco *showed-off* her fingers to the camera. Nia'd given more *glazing* to Coco's fingers than there was on most *Krispy-Kreme* doughnuts!

Though Coco in her *own* scene had not done *real-well* either, her new playfulness proved to me that it was obviously easier for her to have fun when she *wasn't* the main subject of the scene.

Gained some bonus footage when Heather couldn't resist a shot at the *King*. Which was typical according to Troy. *On just about every shoot, there'll be two people who are attracted to each other and don't wanna wait to go home to do it. Besides, they were already doing the movie, so they don't mind it being filmed.*

A thickly-stacked and fully-packed Heather, sat Kong on the bed. His back against the headboard. Then, stroked him to *ready*.

Facing him, with her hands on his muscular chest, Heather eased her way on-board the love train. Kong's hands couldn't resist grabbing a handful of her ample, round backside. Swirled them around. Heather *rowed* her hips in a scooping, circular motion. Kong pushed her hips down for more depth. Then, dug his heels into the bed and began giving it *to her*.

Tyanna's *freaky* self jumped in the action. Pouring oil, all over Heather's backside. Watching it cascading down her *bubble*, before rubbing it in. Spread it all over. Up her back. Down her meaty legs and thighs. Around her butt. Even in the seam. Heather's dark-chocolate skin now glistened like shiny black-gold.

Then Tyanna lubed a *mini-rubber-version* of Kong. Teased it up and down Heather's *crease*, as Kong was making her *kitty* purr. Tyanna teased her no more, giving it to her.

Then this *brickhouse* inhaled deeply with her eyes rolling to the ceiling in enjoyment. She placed one hand on Kong's heavenly chest and wrapped the other around Tyanna's wrist to *slow her roll*. Tyanna had been *going-to-town* on her. Thought her grasp of Tyanna's wrist, would help her contain the sensation she was feeling. Did minimize her jerking for a moment. But it was of no use. Too much sensation had already made it down.

Then I saw firsthand what Tyanna had described as the *'best type of orgasm'*! *Cream* flowed from Heather and onto Kong like a waitress back in Iowa missing the coffee cup completely.

It wasn't a *real-long* scene, but it was definitely attention-grabbing!

So, there it was. I had my first porn movie, as they call it in the business. *In-the-can*. Meaning, it was done, ready to be edited and distributed.

◆◆◆◆◆◆◆◆◆◆◆◆◆◆◆◆◆◆◆◆◆◆◆◆◆◆◆◆◆◆◆◆◆◆

Friday's shoot was just the beginning of a very long weekend.

I still had to talk to Sgt. Fillmore before Sunday. And, Darren was becoming confused as to why I didn't have any time for him. Gave him an excuse that I'd told the employees to not have personal visits at work and that I didn't wanna set a bad example, that's why he could not come by the club to see me. The excuse probably wasn't necessary, 'cause that really wasn't Darren's type of place anyway. But I wanted the added insurance.

The good news was, I didn't have to work until Sunday night. Which meant I'd be able to see Darren on Saturday night. Didn't wanna do anything at any places where Rico'd be sure to have friends. So I made a cozy date to watch movies with Darren at his 6-bedroom home in Roswell, GA.

Friday night, I called Sgt. Fillmore. Made a *date* to meet him at a motel on Saturday afternoon. Didn't go into details. Just told him I *needed* to see him.

Knew Sgt. Fillmore had taken my sensually-vague bait.

When he arrived, he greeted me with a behind-squeezing hug. Looked around the room to see that we were alone and started speaking in third-person.

"Aw, I see. You wanna try Stan out for yourself, huh?", Stan said, like he was Harrison Ford.

Not even close! Not with your little-ass dick!, I thought to myself.

Stan wasn't ugly. Physically fit. Clean cut. Just reminded me of the dads of some of my Iowa-friends. Plus, half the excitement is not knowing what's in the *package*. I already knew he had a *very* small gift.

Besides, I was here on business. Serious business!

"Have a seat Stan, please?!"

"Okay.", he said, still interested in other things.

We sat next to each other on the edge of the bed.

"Stan. I need to talk with you about the extra grand a week."

"Whatta 'bout it?", Stan replied, feeling on my breast.

Wanted him to stop it. But I didn't make him right then. Maybe, he'd be more receptive in hearing me out and not forcing me to do what I didn't wanna do.

"Listen. We can't afford that. Honest-LEE!", my voice cracked, as he'd pinched my peak a little too hard.

"So, what you want me to do about it?"

I pulled his hand away from my breast until I finished my reply, subtly teasing that he'd might get more if he complied.

"Can we just stay at the $500-a-week? Huh baby?"

"Let's talk about it when we're done.", Stan said, implying that we were going to have sex.

"No. I need to know now.", I said, not dispelling his *incorrect* notion.

Tired of playing *fore-play karate* with me, as he tried to resume caressing, while I blocked every move. Stan sat-up more erect.

"Raven. I wish there was something I could do. But, I don't think you guys understand the tremendous risk I'm taking. Cops who get caught, *definitely* go to jail! You see what I'm saying?"

"Yeah, but I just thought you ...."

"Raven. You can quit wasting your time and mine. I'm *not* gonna change my mind and that's that!", Sgt. Fillmore stood firmly. "Now, are we gonna do this or what?"

I paused for a moment. Knew what I was about to do would put me in the *big leagues* where it's dangerous. Needed a moment to think some more about it. But, I didn't have one.

"Raven! Are we gonna fuck or what?"

"No! No, we're not Stan!", I decided to turn aggressive. "And you wanna know *why* we're not gonna fuck Stan?! Huh?! It's because you've already been fucked!"

I threw a copy of the tape of him and Passion on the bed.

"What's this?", Stan questioned.

"Well, let's see?", I said, snatching it out of his hand and placing it in the hotel VCR.

When his image with Passion came up, it infuriated Stan. He stood up, cocked his arm back like he was planning to hit me. I covered my head with my arms, as Stan stopped short of actually striking me.

"You bitch! You fuckin'-little bitch! I can't believe this shit!", Stan yelled at me. Then paced around the room, shaking his head.

With Stan now a safe distance away, I lowered my arms so that I could see his every move. He turned around towards me with even more intensity in his eyes. Stomped his way in my direction with his finger pointing at me the whole way.

"You have no idea who you are playing with! I could fuckin' kill you right now and who'd care? It'd be just another nigger-stripper dead.", Stan said, with his hand around my throat.

He was squeezing my throat so tightly, I was beginning to feel light-headed. And his forceful grasp had me on my *tip-toes*.

"I should kill you right now!", he said, like he meant it. Then he pulled his gun from his holster and pointed it to the side of my head.

I was scared as hell. Water just burst from my eyes.

Sgt. Fillmore surveyed the room.

"You know, I could kill you right now. Just tell everyone you're a prostitute I was trying to arrest. Things got oughtta hand and I shot you. Who you think they gonna believe? A cop? Or, a stripper turned hooker? So Raven, tell me, why *shouldn't* I just kill you right now?!", he whispered, now conscious of his volume.

Instincts told me to beg for my life. But then I realized something. Had been clued in by Stan's comments.

He wouldn't kill me, until he knew all the facts!, I thought.

"That tape is just a copy. If I die, there are copies that'll be sent to your wife, first! Then, to Internal Affairs at the police department. Oh yeah, did I mention, the media? Now, TAKE YOUR DAMN HANDS OFF ME!", I strongly yelled.

Stan did.

I used my hand to rub feeling back into my neck, as Stan, still with the gun in his hand, was pondering his next move.

Having successfully bluffed my way out of a bad situation that I failed to predict. I knew the first thing I'd do upon getting home would be to give a copy of the tape to Nia. Just in case something did happen to me.

"Stan, can you put the gun away please?", I asked firmly. Now that I'd gotten his respect.

He did. Then folded his arms across his chest.

"Raven. You know this is a dangerous game Rico's got you playing?"

"Rico ain't got shit to do with this! This is my deal. He don't even know about these tapes!"

Sgt. Fillmore squinted his eyes in confusion.

"So, what you trying to do then Raven. Huh? What do you want?"

"For now, I want you to back-off of the extra-grand a week! Call Rico tomorrow. Just tell him Raven made you change your mind. That's it!", I said, calmly walking to him.

"That's it?"

"For now, that's it.", I continued, as I softened him by seductively rubbing my hands down his chest.

"And when do I get all copies, of these tapes. And, how will I know I have all the copies?"

Unbuttoning my shirt, I responded, "You'll *never* get the copies."

"What kinda shit you tryin' to pull here?!"

"Like you said, Stan. I'm just a stripper girl. Who'd care if I ended up dead? You said it yourself. As long as I have these tapes, I'm assured that won't happen. But don't frown Stan. I'ma make you a rich man! It's just time to make a new plan Stan.", I said, borrowing lyrics from an old 70's song. "But, you gotta play with me too.", I added, tossing my shirt on the floor. "Play along with my plan and we'll all be rich!"

Intrigued by my mystery, Stan inquired, "What plan? What are you talking about? You gotta let me know so it doesn't get all fouled-up, okay?"

"I'll let you know in time Stan!", I said, removing my own bra before passionately kissing him.

By the time I left the motel, I had *rocked his world*. Was easy to do. Especially, with me on top and Stan not having much of a *weapon*. Made Stan submit two or three times. Made sure to. Was part of the plan.

Even after leaving, I was still on top of Stan. And again, he didn't have much of a weapon. Not while I had custody of the tape.

Had three *hooks* into my cop-fish. Made him fall in love that afternoon. I was *that* white-man's dream. I already knew I was. Even when he was fucking perfect-bodied Passion, I knew he really wanted me. A mixed-girl with a big butt. When I finished slapping my big booty up and down on him, psst, it was over! Just like in Iowa. He'd've left his wife right after if I told him to. That was hook #1. The tapes were hook #2. And, his greed was #3.

From the hotel I went home.

"Hey Raven.", Nia greeted me, as she was preparing to go to work at the strip club.

"What's up girl?"

"Nothin. Darren called."

"Cool. Thanks."

"Hey Rave. I wanted to talk to you about something."

"You know how you were saying, you needed me at the shoot because you had to have at least four scenes?"

"Yeah?"

"Well, I was thinking last night. With that extra scene you got of Heather and King Kong, I was thinking, maybe you don't need my scene in the movie?"

"Naw, it's cool girl. Your scene looked good. It'll come out fine after it's edited!"

"Well, that's not what I'm saying. I guess I'm saying I've changed my mind. I don't wanna be in the movie.", Nia confessed.

"Aw Nee. I need your scene! Even with Heather and Kong's extra scene the movie would still be a little short in length.", I tried to explain.

"I know our deal would be off. And, I'd still owe you for everything else. It's just that I got this music thing going now. And I know that's because of you! But if it takes off, I wouldn't want anything like that out there that could mess up any recording-deals."

"Damn Nee! I'on't know."

"Please Rave! Do this for me as a friend! Do it, and I'll owe you even more!"

Knew I didn't have to do a damn thing! She had signed a release like everybody else. But I had a soft spot for Nia. I'd never be where I was if I'd not met her at the bus station.

"Okay Nee. But you owe me big time!"

"No problem! Anything you need, I'll do it!", she said, relieved that I'd agreed.

I called Clive to let him know to cut Nia's scene out of the film. Clive did as told. However, Troy was pissed. He didn't understand what I was doing. But how could he?

◆◆◆◆◆◆◆◆◆◆◆◆◆◆◆◆◆◆◆◆◆◆◆◆◆◆◆◆◆◆◆◆◆◆

Saturday evening, I drove to Darren's house in Roswell, GA. I was very impressed as I parked in his horseshoe-shaped driveway.

Darren greeted me at the door with one of his customary, *feet-lifting-off-the-ground* bear hugs. He'd already made popcorn as we sat down in his entertainment-room to watch the DVD movies I'd rented from Blockbuster.

The room felt like an *actual* theatre. Mainly because it had an 80-inch flat-screen television with surround sound. There was even a small kitchen and bar in the room. And a remote that controlled the TV, DVD, stereo, fireplace and dimmed the lights. This was the shit!

"You want some wine Raven?", Darren offered.

"Sure!", I said, feeling like Princess Diana.

He returned to the sofa with two wine-filled glasses. Handed one to me. Rested his arm behind me and proposed a toast.

Raising his glass, he spoke.

"To Raven. The most beautiful woman I've ever known. Just seeing your eyes gives me reason to pause. The brightness of your smile makes the sun obsolete. Your wavy hair causes thoughts of a rolling sea. The color of your skin is a perfect copper-tone. Here's to hoping my queen never leaves me alone."

"Aw, that's so pretty. Thank you Darren!", I said, placing a peck on his cheek.

We clicked our glasses together and drank.

I'd never had anyone do poetry or anything like that for me. It sounded rehearsed, but, it didn't matter. It was still sweet.

This was the type of date that I only heard white-girls in Iowa describe. You know, having a picnic while the guy reads poetry to you under a tree. Never came true for me. Until now.

I can get with this!, I thought to myself. *A sweet guy. And he's rich! And, fine as hell!*

"So Raven, I've been meaning to ask you, why do you work at a strip-club?"

"Why not there?", I defended my occupation.

"That's true.   But why there?", Darren countered without being judgmental.

"Honestly?"

"Yeah, of course honestly."

"The money."

"The money?"

"Yeah, the money. I mean, I was a waitress back in Iowa. Tell me what kinda job I'd get here in Atlanta that'd pay me more than the club?"

"Is it just about the money with you? Whatta 'bout enjoying your job?"

"How do you know I don't enjoy my job?"

"Your face. Can see it in your eyes. Tension. Whenever you're away from there, like before the concert, you seemed real relaxed."

"Well, I guess I did like it more when I first started there. That's true."

"Why don't you work somewhere else? Or, is it all about the money?"

"I told you, I can't find a job that'd pay me the same. And no, it's not all about the money, but money is important."

"Have you looked?"

"Well, um,.........."

"Then how do you know? Girl, I can tell that you are very smart. Ever think about going to college?"

"Yeah, I thought about it."

"You should go. I know you'd do well!"

"Think so?"

"I know it!"

"Maybe I'll think about it seriously."

"Do that. For real. If you decide to go, I'll have your back! You're too smart to be just managing a club. You're smart enough to own your own business!"

I knew he was right. He was confirming my own thoughts.

That night was my best night in Atlanta. Darren made me feel special. Important. Worthy. And it wasn't because he had the usual-guy ulterior motives. Darren made me feel like I could do anything. Felt cleansed in his presence. Like I could declare a new start anytime and it not be too late.

I *ended-up* spending the night. Slept in the same bed. But we didn't fool-around.

Atlanta had hardened my soul. I'd forgotten what love felt like. Not that I ever really knew. But Darren was definitely rubbing the feeling back into my heart.

Big Pimpin' CHAPTER EIGHT

In September of the next year, I was busy preparing to move into my new 3-bedroom loft in the ritzy yuppy neighborhood of Buckhead.

It'd been two months since I'd kept my end of the bargain, keeping Sgt. Fillmore from charging an extra-grand to Rico. Unfortunately, Rico hadn't kept his end of our deal. Well, sort-of.

Our agreement was that I'd be a 5% owner of *Slick-N-Thick*. He did pay me the money, 5% of the week's profit in cash. But, he'd not signed the official paperwork making it legal. That was gonna happen later today. But he'd said that before.

I wasn't worried about it though. I had the *cards* in my hand. And this time Rico couldn't deny it.

Was still dating Darren. Now openly. Rico knew he'd better not piss me off or he'd lose his protection at the clubs from Sgt. Fillmore.

Though I was with the man I wanted, Darren, still I was hurt a bit by the fact that Rico wasn't real upset that I was dating Darren. Never showed any signs. After all we'd been through. It'd've been nice to know that he'd cared enough to be *a little* hurt, jealous or sumthin'.

The only sign of bitterness was when Rico mentioned that if I intended on staying in his loft, I'd have to pay him rent now that I was getting 5% of the profits from *Slick-N-Thick*. That's why I decided to move into a place of my own. Wanted to break that tie completely with Rico.

After that brief conversation, Rico seemed only concerned about whether or not I was taking care of business at the clubs.

Shortly after making the deal with Sgt. Fillmore, he brought by a very handsome, young-looking, Atlanta Police Detective. Devin Lorenz. Didn't look any older than Rico. I'd say about 27 or 28.

Sgt. Fillmore previously had described Devin as the *Mayor's boy*.

I could tell Sgt. Fillmore didn't like having to answer to such a young man. Or, a young black man.

Devin Lorenz' visit wasn't a problem. Since taking over the Mayor's Task Force, Devin had been visiting different nude-dancing clubs. Just making his presence known.

Sgt. Fillmore assured me that we had nothing to worry about. This was just a formality. He'd made Det. Lorenz aware that our clubs were not violating any Georgia laws.

Devin, for such a young man, had a confident demeanor of a man twice his age. Spoke confidently without being too aggressive.

"Rico, Raven, I wanna introduce you to my boss, Detective Devin Lorenz. Detective Lorenz heads-up the Mayor's Task Force.", Sgt. Fillmore introduced us.

Both Rico and I took turns shaking his hand.

"Sgt. Fillmore tells me you guys keep your noses clean here! That's good!", Devin said authoritatively while looking around.

"Yeah, we do. I can't have that crazy stuff going-on in my club. I ain't gonna lose *my* liquor license!", Rico returned.

"Well, as long as you guys play by the rules, you'll have no problems from me. Some people think my job is to shut-down every nude-club.

It's not. I don't really care about the morality. Hell, I don't see nothing wrong. Dancers are adults. Customers are adults. As long as there ain't nothing illegal going-on, I could care less!"

Placing his hand on my back, trying to indicate that we had a good working-relationship, Rico drew attention to me by saying, "Well Raven makes sure of that for me!".

"Good, good. Well as long as I'm here, would you mind if I took a tour of your place?", Devin asked looking directly at me.

"No, not at all. Raven will be happy to show you around!", Rico suggested tapping me on the back.

I took the hint. Began showing this very handsome brother around. The changing rooms. The VIP rooms. The kitchen. The stock rooms. The bars.

During my tour, I'd noticed he *didn't* have on a wedding ring. This was kinda surprising for such a handsome and career-oriented man. Thought for sure he'd've chosen someone gorgeous for his arm by now. But what did I know, he could be engaged?

"So Raven. Can I call you Raven?"

"Sure."

"How long have you been running the club?"

"About ten months!"

"You like it?"

"Yeah, it's okay. It ain't bad. So, Det. Lorenz, how long have you been a detective?", I began my interrogation of him.

Devin turned his head around. Surprised that I felt comfortable enough to ask *him* questions. I thought I might've even seen a slight blush seep out his professional-smiling face.

"Well, about 3-years, why?"

"You don't look old enough to be a detective.", I said candidly.

"I get that all the time. I was 25 when I first made detective. And not a single day has gone by where I didn't hear that."

After doing the quick math in my head to determine that he was 28, I returned serve.

"Det. Lorenz, I didn't mean it negatively......"

"Oh, Raven. I know you didn't! And by the way, call me Devin."

"Okay, Dev-vv-in", I played with his name while flirtatiously twisting my hips.

"I was just saying that I get it all the time. I'm not offended by it. Actually, it's a compliment. I'm sure you're not offended when people tell you how beautiful you are."

Now he was making me blush. The way he'd inserted the compliment caught me off-guard. Though it wasn't a direct compliment, I acknowledged it like it was.

"Thank you.", I smiled back to him.

Before we made our way back to the office where Rico and Sgt. Fillmore were standing, Devin gave me his card.

"If you ever have any problems or anything, feel free to give me a call!", he said to me.

"Thanks. Call *only* if I have problems?", I smirked seductively.

"No. You can call me anytime. For anything.", coyly he responded.

Devin had to be conscious of his role. Was toe-ing the line very well. Trying to read my reaction to his every move. Yet, making sure he wasn't crossing the line. Therefore, I knew it'd be up to me to move things along.

Couldn't resist seeing if he was interested. And apparently he was. So was I. Out of curiosity. Well, maybe out of physical curiosity.

I was already *diggin'* Darren. Had a good thing going with him. But the *Denzel Washington*-style of Devin Lorenz was definitely intriguing as well. He was extremely attractive. Knew I'd be hanging onto his card!

♦ ♦

Sitting in my new loft, surrounded by unopened boxes, I was on the phone with Nia, who'd been in New York City the past three weeks.

Nia'd gotten *hooked-up*, in more than one way, with the music producer she'd met in the club. They were now a couple.

Miles Vincent had taken her to New York to try to get a record deal for her.

Ever since he took an interest in her, things were beginning to happen.

While performing at *Hairston's*, a local nightclub in Stone Mountain, Atlanta's premier radio DJ's, Frank Ski, Porsche Foxx and Wanda Smith were in attendance. They'd heard her singing a song she used on her demo-CD. They were so impressed, they played her song on V-103.

Floods of calls came into the station. People were asking where they could buy the CD. Of course they couldn't. It was only a demo.

However, Miles seizing a business opportunity had his small company, Dirty South Records, produce 2,000 CD's of the single. That way, they could give them away where-ever she was performing.

Miles was most known for discovering rap talent. Nia's style was more in the newly-named category of Neo-Soul. Currently dominated by artists, Jill Scott, Musiq and Erykah Badu.

Nia had a three-fold style. Sultry, hip-hop and jazzy. None of these styles dominated over the others. Well-balanced. Very unique. If Toni Braxton, Queen Latifah, and Etta James were blended together, that'd make Nia's style.

"What's up girl? How you likin' New York?", I asked Nia, holding the phone to my ear with my shoulder, as I looked through moving boxes.

"Oh, it's cool! We're just trying to set-up some meetings to see about a deal."

"Gurrl, I'm so proud of you. Making it, big time!", I cheered her.

"Oh, I ain't big time yet. I ain't even got a record deal."

"You'll get one! I just know it!", I reassured her.

"Well, I do have some good news."

"What?"

"My single's been getting alot of airtime around the country. Miles just looked it up on the Billboard website. It's number 63 on the charts!"

"Whaaaat? Girl you bad! I know you goin' get a record deal!"

"I'm trippin'! Miles says, if that single can move like that without it even having an album or any promotion, he thinks I can blow-up right away like Alicia Keys if I get a deal."

"Dammnn, girl! I'm really happy for you! Make sure I get tickets to all your concerts. And I don't want the cheap ones. Make mine front row!"

"You crazy! Raven you know I'll never forget my girls. You or Tyanna!"

"So, when you coming back?"

"I'm not sure. It depends on what we get worked-out at the record companies. I might have to go on tour, opening for other groups, so my name will be known when my CD drops. Rave, how's the new loft?"

"Very nice. I love it! Just gotta get all these boxes unpacked. Darren's gonna come over later to help me. Nee, you know no matter what happens, you always gotta place to stay, with me!"

"Thanks Raven. 'Ppreciate it! But Miles and I are cool right now. I'ma keep staying with him in the A-T-L. But it's nice to know that. Thanks!"

Turned out that Nia was right about her career. And a good thing that we'd cut her out of the porn video.

That video, *Atlanta Amateur Brown Sugar - Volume 1*, was doing modest store sales in the US. However, it was doing very well over the internet. Not to mention, in the Atlanta area.

Though sales of our first film were not excellent, I did make $3,000.

A.A.B.S.-Vol. 2 was being edited. And I was busy finding new girls for Vol. 3. The only return performers in Vol. 2 were Tyanna and Kong, who shared an incredible scene. Even better than their first encounter at *Pleasers* in St. Louis.

Troy warned that we needed to have a majority of new girls for each new video. Some repeats were okay, but only if they'd been good in the earlier films.

Tyanna was getting offers from other porn producers that'd seen her in our movie. And, she'd done three other films for other porn companies.

Passion also had done one other film. She was a bit more selective than Tyanna. For Passion, it was all about how much they were paying. I couldn't blame her.

I was using girls from the club without worry. Now that I was financially-free of Rico. He knew it. Never said anything about it, 'cause there was nothing to be said.

Even achieved diversity in Vol. 2, using two-Latinos, one white girl, and three black girls.

Still had not found any real quality guys that could appear regularly. Had plenty that volunteered. However, when it came time to shoot, they either didn't have big-dicks as they'd bragged. Or, if they did they were QC's, quick-cummers. Either way, it forced me to keep flying in Kong and using the white-boy, Chad.

◆ ◆

After running up my Bellsouth long-distance bill talking to Nia for almost an hour, I'd fallen asleep on the sofa, waiting for Darren to come over.

Was awaken by a knock at my door. It was Rico. Had purposely not given him my new address. His actions had shown me that we were just business partners. So I saw no reason to be more than that to him.

"Hey Rave!", Rico said, holding an African-art piece he offered as a house-warming gift."

"Umm...Rico...Hi.", I said surprised.

"Just thought I'd bring you a little house warming gift."

I just stood there at the door, mouth opened. Wondering, how Rico knew where I lived?

There was an awkward moment of silence.

"Well, Rave. You gonna invite me in?", Rico asked.

Didn't want to. I was not dressed very well. Head-wrap on my head. Cut-off sweatpants. Fluffy house-slippers. And bra-less in an old Atlanta Braves t-shirt.

"Well, actually Rico, I'm expecting company."

"I'll only be a minute?"

By my hesitancy to respond, Rico took that as a yes, as he slid past me inside my loft.

"This is a nice place you have!", Rico commented, handing me the house-warming gift.

"Thanks. Listen, Rico. I really am expecting company soon."

"Who, Darren?"

"I don't think I really owe you an explanation, do I?"

"It's Darren. Anyway, I also brought you the papers legally conveying the 5% ownership in Slick-N-Thick. I signed them. All you have to do is sign them as well and it's done.", Rico informed me, as he was giving himself a tour of my place.

"Okay. Thanks. I'll have my attorney look them over and get them back to you later.", I said, as I followed Rico around trying to shorten his uninvited visit.

He was busy picking up my belongings, looking at them like he was at a garage sale or something. I'd take them out of his hands and place them back where they were.

"Look Rave. I know you got this little thing going with Darren. But I wanna talk to you about us."

"I can't deal with this right now. Rico, you gotta go!"

"Rave, you know yourself we make a good team. And I admit, maybe I wasn't all that I could've been for you. But you gotta admit that I've done alot for you. I'm just saying, maybe we can give it another try? I'm ready to get serious, now. I mean it! How about it? Can we try it again?"

Three months ago, I'd've been in tears. Ready to give my heart away.

But Rico was simply too late. I was happy where I was in my life. Enjoyed my freedom.

"Rico, I can't."

"Why not?"

"I just can't. Rico, you've gotta go! Now!"

"Alright, I'ma go. Just think about it. I know I mean more to you than Darren or who-ever. And in your heart, you know it too! I'll see you later Rave.", Rico said, placing a kiss on my cheek.

As I shut the door, I turned around with my back against it. Had to pause for a moment. Take a big sigh with my eyes closed.

Rico had upset my internal peace. He'd planted a seed that had me thinking.

Darren was the *somewhat* clear choice while Rico was not wanting to be serious. But Rico was more exciting. A bit of a bad boy.

At the same time, I'd felt an exuberance to remaining free. Free to meet new people like Devin Lorenz.

Ten minutes ago I knew what I wanted. Now, I wasn't so sure.

Felt like something was wrong with me. Had too many men in my life. Rico. Darren. And, wanted to get to know Devin.

Then again, I was just 20. *Maybe there's nothing wrong with, being attracted to several different guys, at the same time*, I thought.

◆◆◆◆◆◆◆◆◆◆◆◆◆◆◆◆◆◆◆◆◆◆◆◆◆◆◆◆◆◆◆◆◆◆◆◆

On Monday, I took the contract Rico had given me to Darren's attorney for review. He told me it was a good deal. So I signed it.

Then I took the legal documents into Rico.

"What's up Rave?"

"Nothing. I just brought back the paperwork. Here you go.", I said handing them to him.

"How was your weekend?"

"Good."

"That's good. Did you think about what we talked about?", Rico jumped right into that subject again.

"What's that?", I played dumb.

"About me and you."

"Well, like I said Rico. I dunno. I mean, you're rushing me. I ain't saying never. I'm just saying, right now, I'on't know? Give me some time. I just moved and everything. Got alotta things on my mind right now!"

"Rave, I'm not trying to *sweat* you. Nothing like that. I just wanted to know if you thought about it. And I can see that you have. That's all I wanted. We'll see how it goes? Fair enough?"

"Cool."

I was glad Rico didn't push anymore. Needed to find out for myself what he really meant to me. The only way I knew how to do that, was by seeing other guys. And if I still kept thinking about Rico, then it must be meant for us to be together.

I figured during our time apart, he could do the same. Cut-off who-ever it was he'd been seeing. I still didn't know who *that* girl(s) was. But I knew it was his turn to prove his loyalty to me. Before meeting Darren, I'd been loyal to Rico even while he wasn't.

On Tuesday morning, I pulled out Devin's business card. Stared at it. Smelled it. Had thought about him more often than I'd care to admit.

I was thinking about calling him. But I had to figure out a way to not seem obvious. A way that though I'd be making the first contact with him, would also allow *him* to make the first move on me.

Couldn't think of any real good way to do it. So, I decided to go for it anyway.

"Atlanta Police, Homicide Department, this is Sgt. Lorenz speaking."

"Wow. That's a mouthful.", I nervously said.

"I'm sorry, who am I speaking to?"

"Oh, I'm sorry. This is Raven Klein. Raven, the manager of *Slick-N-Thick* and *The Carmel Club*."

"Ohhhh. Hey, Raven! How you doing?"

"Fine."

"What's up?"

"Nothing. I was just going through my wallet. Found your card. Thought I'd give you a call. You know, just keeping in touch.", I tried to be subtle.

"Well that's nice. I appreciate it. Most times when I get a call, it's normally bad news."

"Well, I didn't really want nothing, I was just calling.", I said backpedaling, as I was beginning to *chicken-out*.

"Hey, hey. Don't hang up. I'm really glad you called. I normally don't do this. And, don't feel any pressure to say yes. But I was wondering if you were available tomorrow? I get tired of eating alone. Maybe we could get something to eat together. If you don't have any plans."

"No, I don't have any plans?", I quickly respond, even faster than I planned to.

"Well can I call you tonight to set things up?"

"Sure."

Mission accomplished. I gave Devin my number and as promised, he called me that evening on my cell phone while I was at work.

The next day, I met Devin downtown at The UnderGround Mall.

The entire mall was built underground. Hence, the name. Inside the mall, it had a feel like you were outside. A red, cobblestone walkway with sidewalks. Along the sidewalks were shops like The Gap. Street carts filled with merchandise were on the cobblestone street walkway. T-shirts, souvenirs, art work, and jewelry was the type of merchandise you could buy from the street carts.

It was more of a tourist-mall than anything. But it's below-ground architectural design and cotton-candy atmosphere made it also a romantic mall. A tunnel-of-love of sorts.

Devin and I ate at the food court, while listening to an outstanding, one-man-band, jazz musician, *Saxxyy*, who was definitely too good to be there. Had talent equal to Kenny G and Najee. I figured, anyone who could hold an audience at a food court mall was *definitely* too good to be there!

Atlanta was definitely the place to get discovered for a musician. Seemed like all the top acts were from the A-T-L. Ludacris, Jagged Edge, 112, Sunshine Anderson, India Arie, Musiq, Blue Cantrell, Kelly Price, TLC, Toni Braxton, and of course, J.D. (Jermaine Dupri) over at So So Def Records.

After he finished his set, Devin went up to the musician to talk with him. Then returned to our table with Saxxyy's CD he'd purchased for me.

We finished our date at the UnderGround, sharing some ice cream at an old-fashioned parlor and getting a hand-painted drawing of the two of us made.

Both of us were having such a good time, we didn't want it to end.

So I followed Devin back to his house in Conyers, an Atlanta suburb.

We were both playing the game. Acting as though we weren't as horny as we both were.

Quaintly, we snuggled on the sofa. Soon, caressing and kissing began. After that, neither one-of-us were *that* interested in deferring our hormones any longer for the sake of just waiting.

Devin proceeded to *rock-my-world*. Better than it'd ever been rocked before.

Duration. Style. Technique. Variety. All of it was the best.

And, not to brag, but I know I had *put it on him*, too!

I'd met my sexual perfect-match. Every touch had a tingle to it. Every move was fulfilling.

And timing was impeccable. When a certain part of my body needed touching, he was already there. Before the time had expired on a certain position, he'd already changed it.

Though Devin was straight-laced, he had sexual flare.

We'd done a vertical-*69*. Him holding me in the air upside down. Me *taking care of* him, while he did the same for me.

We'd done *doggy* with him holding my arms out behind my back, in both of his hands. Used my arms to *sling-shot* himself in me.

Done *it* with him standing up carrying me in the air. My legs, wrapped around his waist. My arms around his neck. His hands underneath my booty. Purposely letting go, at times so that gravity would give me unbelievably enjoyable depth.

It'd been a while since I'd out-orgasm'd a man. By the time Devin *lotioned* me with his love juice, I was more than ready for it.

Both of us, sweaty and winded, slept very good that night.

The next morning, like good detectives, we decided to reenact the scene of our passion. Another heat-filled encounter. We were addicted.

Upon leaving Devin's house, he was definitely a *front-runner* of the guys I was dating. Though, the other guys had their own good points too.

Almost wished guys were made of clay. Then, I could compile the best of each guy into one. A *masterpiece-of-a-man* sculpture.

Darren had wealth and was a gentleman. But, he was a little slow-moving. We hadn't even had sex yet. Wanted to tell him to forget the door-opening. Focus on the leg-opening.

Rico had a mysterious, bad-boy style. And I always knew where I stood with him. But, he could be a little *too* dangerous for me.

Devin had sexual prowess. But he was a *by-the-book* police detective. It'd be like being a preacher's wife. Not enough excitement *outside* of the bedroom.

All three of them were cute. Though Devin had an edge.

All three of them had great bodies. Darren's ripped stomach gained him the nod here.

All three of them were intriguing. Guess Rico with his mystery would be the winner in this category.

As far as money, it'd be Rico and Darren. Though Devin was doing very well! As a Lead Homicide Detective, made about 65-70K a year. Just not in the league of professional athletes. But damn, could that man screw! Made me forget about the money.

Over the next three months, I dated all three. Shuffled them according to my needs.

Wanted to feel special, like a queen. I dated Darren.

Need some hot, butt-naked sex. Devin got the call.

Felt like a little spice, it'd be Rico, who knew I wasn't being exclusive. He didn't like it. But, he settled for it.

Besides, I knew he hadn't gotten the player totally out of his system. He'd get calls in the office. Try to talk in code, like I couldn't tell that it was a woman on the phone.

Darren was busy trying to get his title shot.

Don King had called once while I was over his house. Offered him a 4-fight contract that included his title shot. But Darren was feeling guilty about leaving his trainer that he'd been with since his amateur boxing days.

Darren was loyal. To a fault!

I didn't understand why he'd give up a chance at his dream! For what? To say that he'd stayed loyal?

His trainer should've understood. *If not, then that's too bad!*, was the way I saw it. Besides, how could he blame Darren for leaving, when it was his trainer who wasn't able to get *him* a title shot.

But, that was Darren. Love him or leave him.

◆◆◆◆◆◆◆◆◆◆◆◆◆◆◆◆◆◆◆◆◆◆◆◆◆◆◆◆◆◆◆

In December of the next year, I was preparing for another *Shake It Fast* Amateur Dance Contest at the clubs, that'd take place on New Year's Eve.

As I walked-in, I was shocked when I passed Tyanna hurriedly leaving Rico's office.

I turned and yelled, "Tyanna! Tyanna!"

But she sped out of the club, crying.

As I walked into Rico's office, he was noticeably upset. Pacing around his desk.

"I just saw Tyanna crying. What's going on?", I asked.

"Nothing! It's nothing. I need you to take the deposits to the bank.", Rico said, still pacing.

"Rico, I just wanted to know ...."

"Just take the damn deposits to the bank, OKAY?!!", Rico shouted.

"Damn! Okay Rico, shit!"

I did as he'd said.

On my way to Wachovia Bank, I tried to call Tyanna on her cell phone. But she must've not had her phone turned-on, because her voice-mail picked-up immediately.

"Tyanna, it's Raven, girl. Give me a call. I'on't know what's going on, but give me a call. I wanna talk to you. Call me Tee, okay? Bye.", I left a message.

About five minutes later my cell phone rang. Thinking it was Tyanna, I'd answered it so fast that I didn't even look at the incoming phone number.

"Hello!"

"Damn Rave. How could you do that to me?"

"Do what?"

It was Nia on the phone.

"You know what! I thought we were cool. Then I find out you stabbing me in back!"

"Nee! Calm down! Tell me what you're talking about!"

"Oh, you don't know?!"

"No!"

"You don't know?!"

"No. What are you talking about?"

"You saying you don't know about ATL Celeb Babes.com?"

"No. What's that?"

"A website of nude celebrities. Pictures of me are on that site. It says the video will be available for sale starting December 20th. Hell, there's already an on-line video clips preview of me having sex. The same video that *you* promised was cut out of the film!"

"Nee, I promise. You are not in the video!"

"I know that. But how did the footage end up on the internet?"

"I don't know Nee? I swear, I don't know?"

"Well, you do have the original footage, don't you?"

"Oh, shit!"

It had just dawned on me, that I had not gotten the original footage from *Atlanta Amateur Brown Sugar-Volume 1*.

"Oh shit, what?! Rave, tell me that you still have the original tape?"

"Uhmm...."

"Aw shit, Raven!"

"Don't worry! I'ma take care of it. It can only be one of two people. Either, Troy or Clive. I'll handle it, I promise!"

"Fuck, Rave! You better get it done! I mean, real fast! Remember, I've got your tape of *that* police officer and Passion. Two can play that game. We'll see how you like it if that tape ends up on the internet. Or, we'll see what the police officer does to you?", Nia threatened.

It was an honest accident. But I understood what she saying.

She'd just gotten a record deal. Finished her debut CD that'd just been released and was making its way up the charts. The AABS-Vol. 1 footage of her threatened it all.

Knew I *had* to get the tape back. And, get it off the internet. If I didn't, it could mean my death.

My safety was in *having* the tape of Sgt. Fillmore, not in *using* it. Once it was out there, I'd be dead for sure. There'd be no reason for him *not* to kill me, out of revenge.

Plus I knew Nia wasn't playing around. She'd use the tape if her career got ruined for the same reason. Revenge.

First, I had to find out who was behind it.

Asked Troy. He said, he knew nothing about it. I believed him. Though, it wasn't beyond the realm of possibility.

But he didn't know Nia. Or that she was a singer. And had only seen her once. Besides, with Troy's country-music-listening-self, he'd never have recognized Nia, even if she'd become as famous as Mariah Carey.

Figured, it must be Clive. He had motive. Nia and he had a bad history, dating back to the MC Krush video shoot incident. And, he had the original tape last while he was doing the editing.

He must've held on to it just in case Nia got famous, I thought.

And I knew Clive was interested in profits by any means.

I went directly to Peachtree Music Live Studios.

When I entered Clive's office, I could tell he knew the reason for my visit.

"Hello Raven. Have a seat."

"No thank you. I won't be here long! What did you do with the footage from AABS-Vol. 1?!"

"Edited it, why?", Clive said.

I knew *he knew* what I meant. But just like a kid not wanting to tell on himself before making sure whether or not their parents already know, Clive didn't give anything away.

"You know what I'm talking about! There's some footage of Nia on the internet!"

"Yeah?"

"Yeah my ass! What the fuck is wrong with you?! You just can't go around doing that shit without her permission!"

Clive just smiled at me.

"Is this shit funny to you?!", I yelled.

He shrugged his shoulders.

"You are so fucked up! Give me the damn tape. And I want you to take that shit off the internet, right now!"

"I can't do that."

"What?! No, you are gonna do that! Or I'm gonna talk to your boss and tell them what you've done and that you've been using their equipment for the porn films."

"You won't do that."

"Yes I will!"

"No you won't.", Clive said confidently. "If you do, you'll be admitting to a felony. I won't even get fired. I'll just tell them I was helping a friend and didn't know what you used the film equipment for. You, on the other hand will be facing a law suit and jail time. Even if you don't go to jail, your porn film business will be over without my equipment."

Clive did have a point. I didn't have any proof that he'd edited our films. His name wasn't listed in the credits. And payment to him had been made in cash.

At this point, I didn't care about losing the use of his equipment. I just knew I had to get the tape back somehow. And the photos off the internet. So, I decided to try a softer approach.

"Clive, I'm sorry. You know I wouldn't snitch on you. Nia is a good friend of mine. I promised her she wouldn't be in the film, that's all."

"Yeah, I know Nia. She's a spoiled little bitch! I don't even know how she got a record deal! She ain't talented. Probably fucking someone!"

He was pissing me off talking about Nia like that. But I had to remain calm.

"I know you and Nia don't get along. But as a favor to me, can you take it off of the internet and give me the tape? For me?", I asked with a smoldering look I'd perfected.

Clive leaned back in his chair in thought.

"Why should I?", he asked, forcing me to venture further than innuendo.

"I'll owe you.", I said, as sweet as I could.

"Yeah. But I stand to make alot of money. Looks like Nia's gonna be a big star. Nude pictures can bring alot of money. Nude video, oh my goodness, the sky's the limit! Just think about the Pamela Anderson-Tommy Lee video. Or, the Tanya Harding wedding night video."

"C'mon Clive, this is my friend!"

"That's right. Your friend. Not mine."

Felt I was losing him. So I stood right next to him and began to turn up the heat.

"Isn't there something I could do that'll convince you to do this favor for me?", I said, rubbing the back of his neck.

"Ummm? Uhn-uhn."

"You sure?", I continued. Now, with my butt in his crotch and my hair in his face.

"Uhn-uhn.", his mouth said. But his dick on the rise was saying hell yes.

Facing him, seductively I slid down him. Stopped at his bulging zipper. Unharnessed him. Clive inhaled heavily at my unzipping of his monster and the wrapping of my hand around it.

Gave him what he wanted. Had him making the *ugly face*. Tickled his tip with my tongue. When all of a sudden, without notice, that *son-of-a-bitch*, released *his joy* in my mouth. Like I was a *'ho'* or sumthin'.

I jumped up and brushed my tongue off a couple of times with my hands before going to the bathroom to wash out my mouth.

After making sure I'd gotten off even the slightest *salty* residue of *his joy* out of my mouth, I returned to his office to get the tape that surely he'd give to me now.

To my unbelievable surprise, he wouldn't give it to me. Said we'd made no deal. Thanked me for the blow job and told me that I had to leave now.

I was pissed! That day marked the first time my best weapon, my body, had failed to seal a deal.

Out of anger, I knocked over a few things on Clive's desk before I stormed out of his office.

I'd never been as angry as I was right then.   Actually, had thoughts of killing him.

Built on a solid foundation of anger, I was also embarrassed. Embarrassed to myself.

He'd used me like a prostitute. A free one!, I couldn't get that thought out of my head. *The hell if I'm gonna let Clive get away with having me sucking on his dick, for nothing in return. That was for sure!*

But, I hadn't quite figured out how.   And, I was *under-the-gun*. December 20th, the day Nia's stolen film would be sold, was only ten days away.

Frying Pan CHAPTER NINE

"**G**et on your knees.......Right now!...........Open your safe..........Give 'em to me. And these better be the only copies or we'll be back!", Rico shouted wielding a gun and flanked by two bouncers from the club, in gangsta-rapper-producer style.

We were in Clive's office retrieving Nia's film footage.

With Rico's gun taped to his temple, Clive, sweating at his computer was nervously removing Nia from his website.

It was the night of December 19th. I had no choice but to enlist the help of Rico. Didn't know what the cost of his help would be, but I knew it was gonna be expensive.

To gain Rico's help, I had to confess to him how I'd achieved getting Sgt. Fillmore to drop his request for the extra money. That way, he'd understand why I *needed* him to get back the tape of Nia. Otherwise, Rico wouldn't've cared about Nia's reputation. At least not enough to do what we were doing.

Rico knew that if we didn't stop the release of Nia's sex tapes, she'd in-revenge release the tape of Sgt. Fillmore, then he'd faces charges of bribing a police officer. So he had to stop *that* from happening. Which meant getting Nia's porn tape back.

Neither Rico nor I enjoyed what we were doing, but we had no choice. There was too much at stake for both of us. My life. His business and possibly his life too.

"Rave, let's go!", Rico said, grabbing me by the arm after making sure Nia was erased from the internet site.

The two bouncers remained at Clive's office after we left. Busy giving Clive a *beat-down*.

In the car, I recognized that we'd crossed a horrible line. Into the world of a real crime.

"Rico, what if Clive calls the police?", I said worried.

"He won't!", Rico confidently responded, like he'd done this sort-of thing before.

"How can you be so sure?"

"What's he gonna say? That we stole a porn film that he stole from you? Think about it. He'd be bringing trouble on himself. And with nuttin' to gain. Why would he do that? It'd be different if he still had the tape."

"You don't think he will?"

"Hell no! He ain't stupid. He'd have to be willing to give up his job and have his name in the newspapers as a guy who'd stolen a porn film. He'd be sued fo' sure by his company for all the bad publicity he'd be bringing to them. So he ain't gonna do shit! Plus, the *beat-down* he's getting right now, will make him know not to *fuck* with us."

Made sense. But it seemed as though Rico was just saying what I wanted to hear. What did I know. I'd never been involved in *anything* close to this before.

Rico pulled up to the curb at my loft to drop me off.

As I reached back into the backseat to get the tape, Rico stopped me. Placed his hand on top of mine.

"Uhn-uhn. This tape stays with me until Nia gives us the Sgt. Fillmore tape.", Rico said suspiciously. "That's why you should've told me what you were doing! We could've gotten fucked by this mistake. If Nia had sent the Sgt. Fillmore tape to the police, it'd've been over. All of us could've gone to jail. Rave, I've gotta know what you're doing! That way, we don't have any more problems. You hurrd?"

"Yeah."

"Cool. I ain't goin' lecture you, seeing as it all worked out. But, call Nee, right away! Let her know you got her tapes. And, that you want yours. Then, *hit me up* later. Oh yeah! Don't call Clive anymore! But, you should already know that! Don't call him for nothing! I'm serious, Rave! You hurrd me?"

"Yeah. I got it."

My control was unraveling.

Had no more leverage with Rico once he knew what I *had* on Sgt. Fillmore. It was a good thing that I'd already signed my 5% ownership contract, or he'd've never given it to me, not after this.

Though I'd corrected the situation, Nia and I might *never* be as good of friends. At best I figured it'd be a long time before the wounds would heal. Especially after this kind of a mistake. And, after all her threats.

Didn't have a clue as to what was gonna happen with the porn-film business I'd begun. No longer had access to quality film equipment. And I even wondered if Rico would *still* be silent on my using girls from the club. Doubted it.

◆◆◆◆◆◆◆◆◆◆◆◆◆◆◆◆◆◆◆◆◆◆◆◆◆◆◆◆◆◆◆◆◆

The next morning, I was having breakfast with Devin in the food-court of the Hartsfield International Airport.

My flight back to Iowa didn't depart until 9:30 AM. After the World Trade Center attacks on Sept. 11th, it'd been reported that passengers should arrive about 3 hours prior to departure.

Hartsfield was one of the busiest and largest airports in the world. It was so large, you had to take a train just to get to your gate.

Devin had long-ago offered to take me to the airport and keep me company while I waited for my flight's departure.

Even though we'd planned this far in advance of last night's events in Clive's office, I felt nervous.

Wondered if Devin's police instincts would be able to detect something different in my behavior.

Felt like a fugitive fleeing from the scene of the crime, which was actually true.

Luckily, Devin didn't suspect a thing. Just talked about how he was gonna miss me.

Before kissing me goodbye at my departure gate, Devin surprised me with a gold bracelet as a Christmas gift. It was the kind-of gift that symbolized that he *was* getting serious about me.

Now I felt a different type of guilt because I hadn't gotten him anything. We'd never talked about exchanging gifts. And, he seemed understanding. But I told him I'd bring him something back when I returned from Iowa.

Arriving the afternoon of December 20th marked my first time back in Des Moines in about 15 months.

I'd scheduled my return flight to Atlanta on December 30th, so that I'd be able to oversee the *Shake It Fast* Contest at the clubs on New Year's Eve.

I'd decided to come home because I wanted to reach an understanding with my foster mom. We hadn't talked at all since I left Iowa.

I'd left because she didn't *understand where I was coming from* as a black women. The problems and the frustration I faced everyday in Des Moines.

Think she thought I was just using race as an excuse.

The popular term in Iowa was coined by the prosecution team in the OJ Simpson trial. The *race-card*.

When my mom would tell me that I was trying to play the *race-card*, I'd be infuriated.

'Playing the race-card' insinuated that *it's* a game. Prejudice, is not a game!

In addition, the phrase indicates that there are other cards that could've been played.

I don't know about other people, but my skin is the same color all day! Everyday! It ain't a tan. I can't remove it. So there ain't no other cards in my deck I'm black everyday!

That phrase had become a white person's secret code for dismissing any claim of racism.

Guess I was hurt hearing *my own* mom using it.

Homosexuals and Jewish people also are victims of prejudice. However, unlike these other groups, my skin color is a visual *bulls-eye* for these unwarranted attacks. You can't see sexual-preference or religious-affiliation. Skin-color, you can.

I often wondered, *How could she be taking the side of the racially offensive people of Iowa? Why would she wanna be a foster parent to a black child if she wasn't gonna try to understand me?*

Felt like when it came down to it, ethnic-loyalty was more important to her than family-loyalty.

I never considered that she just might not understand. Or possibly, embarrassed by her race and not know how to explain it. Even maybe, she didn't realize people treated me differently when she wasn't around.

My mom had grown up in Des Moines. Never lived anywhere else. So, how could she understand. Yet, I still felt that she hadn't *really* tried to.

This miscommunication had been one of the many arguments cited by black leaders as to why black kids *need* black parents.

Didn't view my mom as a bad person. And, I appreciated her helping me escape the *foster-care-shuffle* at the age 15.

Prior to her, I'd averaged living in 2-3 different homes every year.

I didn't know what I was feeling towards my foster mom. Didn't know if it was love or not. All I knew is that it was *something* strong enough to bring me back to Iowa. And it involved her.

Though I didn't feel that she was my *real* mom. I'd always addressed her by her first name, Sue, rather than *'mom'*. But I have to admit, she'd been the closest thing to a *motherly-figure* I'd ever known. And, I wasn't ready to close the door on that yet.

My attempt to make amends with my foster mom wasn't going as I'd planned. It was met with *some* resentment, which I understood. I'd embarrassed her by leaving.

I'm sure people asked her about me over the past 15 months. And, having not spoken with me, she'd probably been forced to lie about how I was doing. Not wanting them to know we weren't in contact with each other.

Thinking about this pain that I'd caused her, I wanted to do something special for her.

The day after my arrival, while she was hard at work at the diner, I went to Target to buy some holiday lights to decorate the house. On my mom's salary that was something we never had.

While at the store, I ran into Rick Matthews, an old high school friend.

Rick had always been cool to me. One of the rare, *good* white boys at my school.

"Raven? Is that you?"

"How are you doing Rick?!", I said, volunteering a hug.

"Wow! You look great!", he said, stepping back to get a full-view of how much I'd changed.

Rick was referring to my new, sexier style. Had forgotten about it until that moment. My hair wasn't *ratty* like it'd been all those years in high school. It was in braids. My clothing was semi-sexy, despite it being cold. Had on a pair of tight blue jeans and a form-fitting, ribbed, multi-colored sweater.

Hanging with girls like Nia, I discovered *working-out*. My body was very toned. Had a waist to be proud of. Muscular arms and toned legs. Still had the big butt. That was genetics. And now I knew my big butt was a good thing.

Through my entire high school era, I'd not viewed myself as attractive. Atlanta made me realize that I *was* cute. Walked like I was. Talked like I was. And, acted like I was.

Rick had changed as well since joining the marines. And not just because of his short military-issued haircut.

He'd been slender in high school. But wasn't anymore. The increased size of his arms and chest was clearly evident, even through his bulky sweater.

I'd never been attracted to Rick. Though, he *was* so sweet and kind. I guess I thought of him more like a brother. But, he was definitely looking fine today.

It'd been a while since I'd seen a white man, other than Sgt. Fillmore. Let alone being attracted to one.

"You look good too Rick!", I returned his compliment.

"Wow! I just can't get over how different you look!", Rick said.

His *conversation-subject* was stuck, like a needle on an old, scratched, vinyl record.

Having received that *encore-compliment*, I thought it deserved a slow, 360-degree spin. So he could get the full view I *knew* he wanted.

As I spun, I knew Rick was *checking-out* my butt. Could tell by the way his eyes attempted to quickly elevate to at least *neck-level* by the time I'd finished my spin. And by the mischievous grin painted on his face that'd given away what he'd must've been thinking.

"So Rick, how's the military?"

"It's cool. I don't know if I'm gonna re-enlist or not, yet. I'm thinking about going to Iowa State. Whatta 'bout you? What you doing these days?"

"I'm part owner of a nightclub in Atlanta.", I relayed proudly.

"Get out! No shit!...oh, um, excuse me.", Rick said. Embarrassed that he'd let his military-lingo slip out.

"Oh please. I'ma big girl. You can curse.", I gave him relief. "You worried about having to go to Afghanistan?"

"Not really. I mean, if I gotta go, I gotta go. I'm ready!", Rick said courageously.

My cell phone rang. I looked at the display screen. Seeing it was Rico, I decided not to answer it. I'd told him before I left that I didn't want *any* calls while I was in Iowa.

"Go ahead. Don't let me stop you from answering your phone.", Rick bowed out.

"No, it's okay. It's not important. I'ma let it go to voice mail. I'll call them back."

"Well...um...how long you gonna be in town?", Rick said, struggling for a subject other than my physical transformation.

"Until the 30th. Whatta 'bout you?"

"January 2nd........Hey Raven, we should get together sometime. If you're not gonna be too busy.", Rick offered.

"Yeah, that sounds nice!", I accepted.

We exchanged phone numbers and parted.

That afternoon, I called Rick. Needed some help hanging the lights outside the house. Plus it made for a good excuse to call.

Rick came over and quickly hung the lights in the frigid weather.

When he'd finished, I had a cup of hot chocolate already prepared for him.

We sat on the sofa reminiscing while paging through our high school yearbook. Talked about old times. Who was doing what now. Just enjoying each other's company.

After finishing the *remember-when* stories, we both leaned back and relaxed to the sounds of the television.

Rick gently rested his hand on my thigh. Gentle enough for ambiguity.

Didn't know if this was the start of a *pass* or not. Though his hand was palm-down with spread fingers, it could've been just a friendly touch.

Nevertheless, my peaks had already gone *'boing!'*, in anticipation. Wasn't *real* concerned because I had on a bra and a sweater. So I knew Rick couldn't see it.

I placed my hand over his, just as ambiguously as Rick had done. Didn't squeeze his hand. Nor attempt to interlock fingers.

We were playing a *cat-&-mouse* game. Which I found *very* sensual. Hadn't done that at all in Atlanta. This was refreshing. The shear mystery of wondering was almost too much. My body was nervous, like I was thirteen again. Had to concentrate to keep the nervousness from turning into a shivering hand.

Now this is fun!, I thought to myself.

Even the fact that my mom was at work added to the butterflies that'd developed in my tummy. Though I was grown, *this was still* my momma's house.

It was just 3 o'clock. Mom's shift at the diner didn't end until 6:00.

I was excited just thinking about the possibility of having adventurous-sex at my mom's house. Trying to enjoy pleasure, while listening for a key-turning noise.

Made me realize just how much romance was missing from my soul. Sex had become simply the act of doing it. Or, a way to get things.

My secret thoughts about Rick unknowingly had made it down to my hand. I was now rubbing my hand against the back of his.

Before drifting in thought, I'd not planned to do that. Instead, I'd planned to continue our *cat-&-mouse* game until *his* desires forced him to make the first move.

However, my brief daydreaming had ruined that plan.

Rick's hand did reply. Stroking up and down my denim-covered thigh. Felt a *virgin's-tingle*. He massaged my leg *just* right. Just enough to lazily shut my eyes. Caressed like a masseuse trying to get the blood flowing. And he was certainly getting me flowing all right!

With his hand never losing contact with my thigh, Rick got up and knelt between my legs. Leaned in and started kissing me confidently.

Loved the way he did it. No words he *thought* I might wanna hear. No words period. His swirling tongue talked for him. And, spoke very well. If his tongue ever enrolled at Iowa State, it'd be a communication-major for sure!

Rick raised my sweater with military-confidence and precision. Then, slid the bottom of my bra up to expose me. Felt a quick shiver.

From Rick, there was no long gaze in wonderment of how black titties looked, like the guys back in high school. But that wasn't surprising. See, Rick wasn't one of those guys who notched his belt after each conquest.

As he glided my bra up, I was a little embarrassed by my peaks being already firm before even a *single* hand caress. But mostly by the way they'd flung-out from underneath the under-wire bra fabric, as it passed over them.

Rick's mouth immediately *zeroed-in* on my nipples. The way *US Patriot-missiles* did to Saddam Hussein's *Scud-missiles* during the Gulf War. His tongue-flicking was pleasurable torture. My body *was already* well-ahead of where we were.

When his mouth returned to nibble my ear, it resurrected the butterfly-feelings.

Resting one hand on the back of the sofa and the other now between my legs, Rick was circular-stroking me through the jean-material. My body had already been waiting for that. With his hands' *around-the-world* technique, I was about to *prematurely* explode.

It was as though he'd had some *military-intelligence* on the location of my spot. Accurate information he had. I fought hard to *at least* limit my body's vibrations and maintain a *cool* face.

Then Rick unbuttoned my jeans. Tugged hard, as I wiggled to get out of them. Took the panties next. Could've done them both at the same time, but he purposely didn't. Unveiled me in layers. Nice move.

Swirled his tongue in my navel for a while. Then raised my legs and moistly kissed the inside of each thigh. Alternated sides with each *thigh-kiss* as he descended to my *garden*.

Unbelievable anticipation had grown as my explosion premonition was reached only moments after his talented-tongue had begun cultivating my *garden*.

Rick gripped my shaking thighs, keeping them from instinctively closing towards each other like magnets.

I had hoped to make him work a little harder. But if there's one thing I knew about white boys, it was that they gave excellent *mouth-love*! Rick was no exception!

His tongue traced me around and around, like a game of *musical-chairs*. My moaning was the music, whenever the *music* would stop. Rick sucked on the start *button*.

Didn't know the cause for this incredible stimulation. Was it a sentimental reunion with the snow and cold I'd been missing? Or, reuniting with my past that I'd spent over a year running from? Better still, maybe it was the reunion with an old friend? One I was sure of. Unlike any *friends* I had in Atlanta.

Felt totally safe with Rick. Knew this escapade wouldn't be on a verbal *highlight-reel* in some bar. It was between us. Two good friends.

I returned the *mouth-loving* favor. Out of courtesy. More as a formality than anything. I wasn't as confident in my *mouth-loving* ability. Even more self-conscious about it with a white boy.

I'd learned, white girls had the *patent* on this. They had the most experience, not to mention the *true desire* to do it.

I remember groups of girls as early as age twelve, getting together after school so they could practice *deep-throating* carrots. To a white girl, *dick-sucking* was an obligatory item on the sex-menu. Just as much so as a restaurant designated a *soul-food* restaurant, would *have to* serve collard greens.

All of the black women I knew were *sucking thangs* out of necessity. Not 'cause they enjoyed it. They figured, *brothers* were goin' get a little of that *somewhere*. So, they'd give their man a *half-hearted* effort. Just enough, to keep 'em home. But nowhere near the intensity of the *head-bobbing,-tongue-swirling,-Hoover-Vacuum-love-juice-extracting* approach of white girls.

Knowing this, I didn't wanna pale by comparison. So I cut that part short. Just gave the *payback* I owed him and that was it.

I knew my strength lied in my *droppin'-it-on-'em*. This is where I had my advantage over the narrow-butt white girls he'd experienced. Had much more to *drop*! I knew that when I *dropped-it-like-it's-hot*, I'd get his *jackpot*!

Rick was larger than I expected. He wasn't Mandingo or anything. But, better than Sgt. Fillmore, who I silently nicknamed *Sgt. Fill-less*.

I guess Rick's decent size was surprising to me, 'cause he didn't act like a guy who had a *good-size* dick. You know, brash, arrogant and cocky.

We took turns, giving each other a ride. First, me on top of him. Then, him, *doggying* me.

In Tyanna-style, I became impromptu. My body had been ahead of our actions all this time. So I changed the script. Had always, secretly desired to try something *new*. Something *different*. Something *exotic*. And right now just seemed like the time to go for it.

I reached behind me. Slid Rick's hand from my hip to my crease. Encouraged his thumb to tickling *my fancy*.

As I continued bouncing back on him, Rick took the hint. Gave me about a *fingernails-worth* of thumb.

"Whew-www", I exhaled.

My eyes couldn't help but close, with the initiation of his thumb's inaugural entrance. And from my first, *dual*-experience.

By the time I'd gotten a *knuckle's-worth*, I could personally attest to Tyanna's revelation about the best kind of orgasm.

My hands went numb. Vision blurred and faded to black as my eyes rolled upward in my head. Noise was temporarily muted. And my body was unable to harness its jitters.

Rick's joyous declaration wasn't far behind mine. His *jackpot* glistened my backside as bright as the lights he'd hung outside.

Rick and I had shared firsts. And there was something *special* about that.

What made it even more special was after we'd finished, we didn't lie to each other. Act as though it meant more than it did. We were *too* good of friends to reduce it to that.

We laid there together, knowing each of us would have a special place in the heart of the other. Always happens when you're someone's first. In this case, we were each other's.

I was his first black girl! I was sure of it. And his pioneering thumb, was the first to explore my *fancy*. Not to mention, Rick had become my first *TCW, Triple Crown Winner*.

TCW was a Tyanna-ism, for a guy that was able to cause *three* separate and distinct orgasms using his fingers, mouth and *thang*. To gain the honor of a *TCW*, it all had to occur during the same sexcapade.

Later, Tyanna added the baseball inspired term, *Grand-Slammer*, to her raunchy *sex-cabulary*. In baseball, a *Grand-Slammer* scored four runs. Hence the name, to describe a four-orgasm creator. Everything was the same as a TCW, with the fourth being created from, whatelse, his *thang* in her booty.

Normally after sex I'd be exhausted. However, Rick and I had shared the kind that actually makes you horny for the rest of the day. The kind, where you can't wait to do it again. Do the things we'd not gotten to the first time around.

It was nearly 5:00 o'clock when Rick left. Gave me time enough to spray the room with *Lysol* in an effort to disperse the romance-scent in the air before my mom got home. Despite the frigid temperature, I'd even opened the door for a while to keep our scent from being trapped inside.

Picking up my cell phone to check the time, I noticed that Rico had called, two more times.

Didn't have a clue as to what was so important. But whatever it was, I figured he could handle it.

Part of the reason for this trip back home was to get away from the craziness I'd been experiencing in Atlanta of late.

I was determined to *not* spoil my holiday vacation. And didn't *even* wanna think about any of those situations while I was in Iowa. That's why I never called him back.

◆ ◆

Later that evening, I saw the headlights of my mom's car pull into the driveway of our newly decorated, holiday-spirited house.

"Raven, did you put the lights on the house?", mom said with excitement, entering through the garage door.

"Uhm-hmm", modestly I chimed.

"Ohhh, baby, that's so nice! You didn't have to do that!", she said, giving me a warm hug of reconciliation that made my trip worth-while. "Let me give you the money for that.", mom added reaching in her purse.

"No. It's my gift to you.... mom!", I said.

We both paused for moment. It was the first time, the word 'mom', had come out of my mouth. I didn't plan it. It just happened.

Mom stoically fought back the tears. Didn't make a big-deal out of it. Instead, she turned her back to me, continuing our conversation as she walked into the kitchen.

From behind her, I saw both of her hands wipe her face clean before spinning back around to face me.

"You hungry?", she asked, attempting to ignore her feelings.

"A little.", I said, though I wasn't.

Figured it'd help my mom control her emotions by giving her something to do. And, it helped me too. My eyelids were blinking rapidly to control my own tears.

We sat at the kitchen table the way we'd done every night throughout my late teen years. Same small octagon-shaped table that wobbled on the left side. Same seat-assignments. Mom on my right. Me, facing the TV. Same dishes. Same *dollar-store* centerpiece. Everything was the same.

Found there was comfort in predictability.

We talked for hours. Long after the dishes were washed and the meatloaf had been plastic-wrapped and placed on the middle shelf of the refrigerator that was designated for *leftover* food.

I was trying to get in 15-months worth of conversation all in one night.

Told mom how well I was doing managing a nightclub. Didn't mention that it was a strip-club. And bragged about my friend Nia whose music video was debuting tonight on BET.

Really, I wanted to call Nia to congratulate her. But I knew she was still mad after the tape fiasco.

I sat up tall and pressed the record button on the VCR as the start of Nia's video to her song, *Fo' Real For Real*, began airing.

"That's your friend?! Oh, she's gorgeous!", my mom said impressed.

"I know!", proudly I responded, like I had sumthin' to do with *that*.

I knew my mom wasn't into R&B music. And had I not told her about Nia, she'd've gone to bed long ago. But still, it was nice hanging out with her.

It felt like a mother-daughter slumber-party.

After Nia's video went off, I flipped around the channels. Stopped on CNN to brag some more about Atlanta.

"Mom, did you know CNN is located in Atlanta?"

"Really?!"

Mom wasn't a TV-watcher. But, she knew of CNN.

Caused me to wonder why mom hadn't disconnected cable service after my departure.

It was nearly 11:00pm. Mom was working a double-shift the next morning and had to be at the diner by 5am to prepare for the Saturday-morning, last-minute-Christmas-shopping, breakfast crowd.

I could tell she was staying-up for me. I was just about to let her know that she didn't have to stay-up for me, when a familiar picture flashed across CNN.

I turned up the volume so that I could hear the news-anchor's report:

"In other news, Grammy-Award winning music-producer, Clive Sparks died today, after being viscously attacked Wednesday night, at his Atlanta studio. The 37-year old Sparks, was taken to Emory Medical Center late Wednesday night, where he remained in a coma, Thursday, until his death, early Friday morning. Reasons for the attack are still unclear, according to Atlanta Police Department Lead Homicide Detective, Devin Lorenz, who released this brief statement at a press conference today:

'In the attack that preceded Mr. Sparks' death. There were no signs of forced entry. To our knowledge, no witnesses. And, nothing of significant value was stolen. The Rolex watch Mr. Sparks was wearing, was not removed. Which leads us to believe, this was a Personal-Attack rather than a robbery.

We're asking for the public's help on this one. Anyone who has information about this murder, please call the APD crime hotline number. Although currently, we don't have much to go on, I can assure the public, we will find Mr. Sparks' killers! And, seek maximum prosecution of these cowards! Thank you.'

Sparks was in high-demand and best known for his controversial use of nude-women dancers in rap-music videos. His latest video, produced for rapper MC Krush, originally was banned from MTV, VH1 and BET, and had to be re-edited before music-station executives would agree to airing it.....Sparks was just 37.", the news anchor concluded.

"What's the matter Raven?", mom surprised me by speaking.

I'd been lost in that CNN-story and had forgotten mom was still here.

"Oh nothing. Nothing.", I said, trying not to appear as scared as I was.

"Okay. Well, I think I'm gonna *hit-the-sack*. Good-night, baby.", mom said, giving me a hug.

"Good-night mom."

That must've been why Rico was *blowing-up* my cell phone.

Despite it being after midnight in Atlanta, I called Rico anyway.

Stepped into the cold garage for privacy's sake and used my cell phone.

With me gone, my guess was, Rico was probably at one of the clubs. He wasn't.

Finally I reached him on his cell phone.

"Hello?", Rico answered.

"Rico?"

"Raven! Damn, I've been trying to reach you!"

"I know, I just saw Clive on the news ....."

"Raven, shut up! Don't talk on the phone! I need to talk with you, in person, right away! I'll book you a flight back, tomorrow!"

I decided against coming back early. Heck, thought about not coming back to Atlanta at all. But, I *needed* to know what was going on. What to do. Not to mention, though I *was* enjoying my Iowa-visit, that's all Iowa meant to me now-- a place to visit.

Rico didn't like it, but he had no choice. I *was* gonna stay in Iowa with my mother until December 30th.

It was tough trying to conceal my uneasiness from someone who knew me so well. Though there were moments on Christmas day when I was *actually* able to *temporarily* put my situation out of my mind.

Over my last nine days in Des Moines, I'd foregone any additional sexual rendezvous' with Rick. No longer in the mood for that. Too worried about the situation back in Atlanta. Plus, I didn't wanna taint the one moment we shared, by reverting back to my Atlanta sex-habits. Doing it just for the sake of doing it.

Wasn't sure what Rick made of my sudden coldness. But, we still went to the movies and bowling. And later, exchanged phone numbers.

Even though Rick's military base was far away, in Oklahoma, he promised he'd visit me in Atlanta when he got a chance. Truth be known, he'd be a welcomed change.

Still, I couldn't see myself seriously dating or marrying a white-boy. It was the main reason for me leaving Iowa. But I guess if it was possible that I ever *could* fall in love with a white-boy, it'd be one like Rick.

My Iowa visit had been a bitter-sweet one. Glad that I'd made the re-connection with my mom. Longed for a simpler life that I knew I really didn't want. Felt renewed, just by a single love-making session to a good-old friend. And sorrow knowing I had to return to the A-T-L.

It wasn't the city. I loved it there. Warm-weather. Trees. The unique combination of southern hospitality and a metropolitan city. Lotsa successful black people.

However, I knew I'd not yet tapped into *all* the promise that Atlanta offered.

Knew I'd be returning to a life in the seedy fast lane. And, I wasn't looking forward to it. But I knew no other way of holding on to the things I'd become accustomed to, while trying to break-away from negative influences that were now clearly visible to me, after returning to Iowa.

Have your cake and eat it too, is how my mom would've described it.

Only in my case, it was not that simple. For me, I was playing the dangerous game, where the *cake* might eat me!

Back In The Saddle CHAPTER TEN

On Sunday, December 30th of that year, as promised Devin picked me up from Hartsfield Airport. Flowers in hand.

Felt guilty, accepting them from him. Especially him.

I was certain, Devin was extremely busy trying to find Clive's killers. Yet, he was so interested in me, he took time that he *really* didn't have to buy me a gift and pick me up. All the while, unaware that his search might lead him to me.

Though I didn't kill Clive, personally. I knew that I was guilty by association. I had been there during a crime. Not during the murder. But during the crime that eventually led to the murder.

'What's wrong, baby?", Devin questioned.

"Nothing?", I said, wondering what would happen if he ever found out that I was at the scene of the murder.

'Are you sure? You seem sort-of nervous."

"Naw, I'm cool. Just tired, I guess.", I tried to cover.

"I've been working on this big case. I'on know if you saw me on CNN or not. But, I'm kinda stressin' about it. Maybe we can get together later, I really need to relax and just forget about the case for a while."

"Yeah. Sure. Just call me.", I said, dodging whether or not I knew about the case.

By the time Devin had dropped me off in Buckhead, my blood-pressure rivaled that of an overweight black man running a marathon while smoking a cigarette and eating a bucket of chicken. Very high.

Thought about confiding in Devin. Just tell him the real deal. *Maybe, just maybe, he'd understand and help me out of this situation?*, I thought. But I chickened-out.

As I exited the elevator to my 3rd floor loft, I saw Rico standing by my door. He scared the hell out of me!

Quickly I peered out the hallway window to make sure Devin was not coming up to give me a bag I might've *accidentally* forgotten to take out of his car. Thankfully, his car was gone from the parking lot.

"Rico, what are you doing here?", I said sternly.

"I needed to talk to you."

"Well I told you I'd come by the club when I got back in town!", I said, deliberately waiting to open my door.

"I didn't wanna talk there."

I opened my door with my key, slid my bags inside and used my body to block the entrance to my loft.

"Rico. Let me get a shower and I'll meet you somewhere."

Annoyed by my suggestion, Rico looked down the hallway in both directions before grabbing me around the throat and pushing me into my loft.

"Is this a fuckin' game to you Raven?! You stupid bitch! This shit is fo' real!", Rico shouted at me, as he backed me all the way in. Taking time to close and lock the door.

With his hand still around my neck, he pushed me on the sofa.

"Rave, I swear. You better stop fucking with me!", Rico said with his finger pointing at me.

Remembering who I was dealing with, I didn't give any more resistance. Even when Rico's hand was wrapped around my throat, I didn't attempt to remove it or put-up a fight. Instead, I allowed him to forcefully guide me about my loft.

"Rico, I ain't fucking with you baby. I was just saying, I wanted to take a shower. That's it.", I said with puppy-dog eyes. Hoping to calm him down.

Ignoring my apology, Rico bantered, "Rave, remember that guy who came by the club? His name is Sgt. Lorenz?"

"Umm, yeah?", I said, acting as though I had to struggle to remember.

"He's been assigned to the Sparks murder case."

"Whatever happened that night?", genuinely curious, I asked.

"Whatchya mean, what happened? The motherfucka's dead! That's what happened!", Rico shouted.

"No, I mean.....umm.....never-mind.", I said.

It had just dawned on me that Clive's murder was no accident. The two bouncers didn't remain behind to give him *just* a *beat-down*. They'd intended to kill Clive all along.

"Rave, I'm worried. Sparks is too good! Stan says he's never had a case he hasn't solved. He's got a perfect record, fourteen for fourteen. Shit, Rave. You know what they call him down at the police station?"

"Uhn-un."

"The Solution! The Solution, Rave. That's got me worried. I know he's gonna be asking alot of questions. So I gotta make sure we're all on the same page. You know what I'm saying? I ain't worried about the bouncers. Shit, they actually did the killing. I know they don't wanna go to jail! Besides, I already told them to say they were at the club, in my office counting money, if they're ever questioned about it. Raven, you just say you were in my office too, okay?", Rico said pacing back and forth.

"Okay."

"We'll all be each other's alibi. My only worry now is Nia."

"Nia?"

"Yeah, Nia! What if the police start talking with all the girls, *you* had doing those damn porn movies. Nia's chicken-hearted! And chicken-headed! You know that!"

"Oh, Nia won't say shit.", I tried to reassure.

"I don't think she would either. Not with her singing-career going so well. But, seeing as she's the only person who knows *why* we'd've gone to see Clive, I think I should talk with her just in case. Do you know how I can get in-touch with her?", Rico said charmingly.

Maybe he should talk with her?, I wondered what that meant. *Talk with her, the way he'd talked with Clive?*

"I'on't know where she is now, Rico. Think she's going on tour or something? I'on't know?", I responded, attempting to be very vague.

"Whatta 'bout her cell phone. Can you call her for me?"

"Her record company just got her a new cell phone and I don't have the number. Nee said she'd give it to me. But, she hasn't called me yet. She's probably *still* pissed at me, about the movie."

Rico seemed to *somewhat* believe me. Or at least wasn't certain that I was lying.

"Okay, Rave. WHEN you get Nee's new number, give me a call right-away, okay?", Rico said with raised eyebrows. Making sure I understood, just how serious he was.

"Yeah. No problem."

"Oh yeah, there's one more thing.", Rico said, reaching into the pocket of his warm-up jacket.

Made me uneasy, as he walked directly in front of me.

What's he getting ready to do? Was he planning to get rid of me?, I nervously wondered in rapid, warp-speed, as I prepared to defend myself in the only way I knew how.

I filled my lungs to capacity with air, just in case I needed to scream.

Also, slid my right foot backward for leverage, ready to deliver the hardest nut-crushing *Tae-Bo*-taught kick of my life.

Desperately, I tried to quickly read Rico's intentions. Looked him up and down. Glanced at his eyes, then back to his hand that was still in his pocket.

Now standing very close to me, Rico's towering frame caused my head to choose to focus on either his eyes or his hand. Chose his hand.

With one hand squeezing my hip and the other mysteriously still in his warm-up jacket pocket, Rico slid down to one knee. His face, just above crotch-level.

I exhaled the pent-up tension, as I rolled my eyes to the ceiling, figuring Rico was *just* planning some *freaky* shit.

Thought he was planning to pull my jeans down, so that he could have a *sex-meal*. After all, this was one of his *favorite* positions. Me, standing and him, kneeling. Rico enjoyed watching me struggle to remain standing, as his tongue would lick all the strength from my legs.

Under normal circumstances, I loved this technique just as much as Rico did. Actually, more than Rico.

However, at this particular moment, I was in no mood for that. But like always, I was prepared to concede if pressured.

Also at that moment, I realized that I was no longer attracted to him. His bad-boy, unpredictable aura, was what originally made him sexy to me. But with proof that his image was more than a facade, I was scared terribly.

For me, the only redeemable quality left about Rico, were the checks he wrote.

This time, sex was not at all what was on Rico's mind.

"Raven, baby. We've been through alot together. Through the good and the bad times, we've always made it. I've never had someone like you in my corner before. Guess, what I'm trying to say is, will you marry me, Raven?"

Shocked doesn't begin to describe my reaction. Discombobulated and utterly confused, before I knew it, I'd said *Yes* to his second offering of a nuptial invitation.

During his repeat attempt, Rico had mixed in the question of whether or not I loved him. Followed by a duplicate request for my hand in marriage.

My *Yes*, was actually to the first question -- that I did love him. Hoping to delay him. But as usual, Rico took it the way he wanted it. Rearranged my *Yes* and applied it to his proposal.

Rising from his kneeling position, Rico stood up and gave me a tongue-kiss. Sealing our *engagement* by placing the ring he had in his warm-up jacket pocket on my finger.

Felt it was *too* late to try to clarify. Truthfully, feared the response I might get. Besides, I wasn't totally sure that Rico didn't already know what he was doing.

Not five minutes after Rico had gone, I was sitting on my sofa with my head in my hands wondering, *How I'd gotten myself into this situation?*

My phone rang. It was Darren.

Had only spoken to him sparingly over the past month. We were still cool. Actually, Darren was *really* diggin' me. However, for me, Darren was slipping more into the category of someone to admire. Especially, when I considered we'd not made love.

Maybe that makes me shallow. But that's how I felt.

I wanted..... No, I *needed* someone who was so physically attracted to me, they couldn't resist the temptation of having sex.

I guess, in actuality, I kinda knew Darren *was* tempted. But he'd become very religious and was trying not to engage in pre-marital sex. That's a perfect example of how he was someone to be admired. And I'd feel guilty trying to get him to break his religious code.

Sex for me, was my relationship-compass. I could tell where a relationship was heading by the way a guy made love to me. Without that *compass*, I was lost.

Maybe, I just didn't know how to date a really nice guy. And Darren, was certainly that.

Clouding my feelings further was the fact that Darren was an excellent kisser. And whenever he'd hold me, firm and genuine, it made me desperately long for him. It was double-edged torture.

When Darren would be standing behind me, arms wrapped around my torso, kissing my neck, he made me wanna un-peel his embrace and just *force* his hands to caress my breasts. But, I never did. It was the guilt I felt.

Though Darren never tried to make me feel that way, I felt too tainted for him. What I did for a living. And everything else that I was doing that he didn't know about.

Just being around him caused me to have to '*check myself*'. Evaluate who I'd become. Right now, I didn't like that person. So, I'd shy away from looking in the mirror—Darren.

In my conversation with Darren, I made up an excuse about having to work. That way I'd be able to get off the phone.

I was feeling *bad-enough*, already.

◆ ◆

The next day was New Year's Eve. I decided to go to the club early in the morning to make sure everything was prepared for the *Shake It Fast* Contest.

As I pulled into the parking lot, I caught a glimpse of what looked like Sgt. Fillmore's car exiting the other side of the parking lot.

Parked directly in front of the door was Rico's Escalade. I was surprised to see it, because from my first experience with Rico back in St. Louis, he'd never been an early-riser. And looking at my watch, it was just 7:45 in the morning.

I started walking toward the front door just as Rico was coming out. He looked surprised to see me.

"Hey Rave, whatchya doing here this early?", Rico addressed me. But his eyes were surveying the parking lot.

"Just wanna make sure, everything's set for *Shake It Fast*.", I responded, making no mention of Sgt. Fillmore's car I'd just seen leave.

"Well, don't stay too long!", Rico said, holding the door open for me, "I'ma need you rested for tonight. It's gonna be busy fo' sho'!"

"I won't!", I responded as I entered the building.

Rico seemed all too happy to allow me in, without trying to hold a longer conversation. Which wasn't typical for Rico.

With his keys, he locked the door from the outside for me after I'd gone inside. Then he left.

There we had been, just the two of us at the club, alone. The Rico I knew, would've certainly *hinted* at the possibility of having sex, before the rest of the staff starts wandering in around 9:30AM.

But he didn't say a word. Which I found very odd. Rico didn't even notice that I wasn't wearing the *engagement* ring he'd given. Not to mention, no kiss for the woman he'd planned to marry.

Something weird was going on?, I thought.

Because I didn't trust Rico as far as I could throw him, I snooped around his desk for about an hour. Looking for *anything* that would *clue-me-in* about what was going on.

In the trash bucket, I found a balled-up piece of paper with the company letterhead, that had everything written on it, *scribbled-out*.

I remembered a technique I'd learned as a child on how to find out what was written on it. I'd simply need the next sheet of paper off the pad and a pencil.

The pen that was used to write the original message on the discarded top sheet of paper, also created indentations on the next piece of paper on the pad.

All I had to do was lightly brush the pencil, back and forth against the second piece of paper, almost shadowing the entire page. That way, the writing would be revealed because it *wouldn't* be shadowed by the pencil.

It was a good plan, except we didn't have any pencils in the office.

I slipped both the original paper and the next sheet off the pad into my purse. I'd have to do it when I got home.

My curiosity having been fueled by the discovery of the *crossed-out* note, I used a letter-opener to gain entrance into Rico's locked desk drawer.

Once inside, I rummaged through the usual business documents, until I found Rico's personal checkbook.

Discovered two checks that concerned me. Both of them, dated December 26th, just five days ago.

The first was written to *Choices Inc* in the amount of $850. The second was for $5,000, made-out to Tyanna.

Seeing Tyanna's name on the second check, reminded me of a couple of weeks ago, when I'd seen her leaving Rico's office crying.

Immediately, I'd tried to call her. But she never *did* call me back. Then, all the stuff *went-down* about the tape-incident. After that, I was on vacation in Iowa. So, I never *did* find out the deal.

When the staff began to arrive around 9:30 AM, I placed everything back in the drawer and called Tyanna.

"Hello.", Tyanna struggled out, in a raspier than normal voice.

"Tyanna - you sleep?"

"Oh, hey Rave. No, I'm just laying down. I'ma 'bout to get up."

"I'm over here by the club, just wanted to see if you wanna get some breakfast?"

"Where you going?"

"I'on't know? Waffle House or maybe IHOP? You wanna go?"

"Yeah, if we go to IHOP."

"I can pick you up in about 20 minutes."

"I'll be ready!", Tyanna responded, sounding more awake.

Tyanna had moved into an apartment, almost exactly half-way, between the *Carmel Club* and my loft in Buckhead.

◆◆◆◆◆◆◆◆◆◆◆◆◆◆◆◆◆◆◆◆◆◆◆◆◆◆◆◆◆◆

At IHOP, Tyanna ordered the pigs-in-a-blanket, extra pancakes and a large chocolate milk. I had the assorted fruit bowl and a medium orange juice.

"Gurrll, you and Nia….unh-mmm-unh", Tyanna said smiling, shaking her head.

"What?"

"Y'all be eatin' so crazy!"

"Why? 'Cause I ordered fruit?"

"Yeah. That's why Nia ain't got no butt. And yours *dun* slimmed down a lot from the time I first met you!"

It was true. My butt wasn't as big. Partly from my diet. Mainly from my exercising. I'd toned it up.

To hear Tyanna tell it, you'd think I had a flat booty. Which was never gonna happen! I don't care how many squats I did or laps I ran. Nature had given me plenty of meat back there.

"Ty, you trippin'! I can't speak for Nee. But, I know, if there's one thing I got, it's plenty of ass!"

"Speaking of Nee, did you see how skinny she looked in her video?!", Tyanna said, squinting her nose.

"I thought she looked good!"

"Look who I'm asking? Miss Fruit-Bowl for breakfast. I'on't know what I expected you to say?"

"Well, you know it's different in the music business."

"I guess?", Tyanna conceded. "I always knew Nia'd make it big someday!"

"Me too! She is just so damn talented!"

"I know! Don't it make you sick?!", Tyanna giggled.

"For real."

"No. Fo' real, For Real!", Tyanna comically amended my response, using the title of Nia's hit song.

"You crazy!", I laughed.

"Hey, d'ya hear, Nee s'pose to be on-tour in Atlanta, in February?"

"Uhn-uhn?"

"You know she gonna *hook-us-up*, right? Back stage passes and the whole nine!"

"I'm there!", I said.

"Thought about surprising her at the hotel. Send her a 60-Finger massage from Cerino's. But, I'on't know? She's getting kinda serious with Miles. And, I don't wanna mess that up, you know?"

I was glad to hear that she was using judgment. A 60-Finger massage would not be cool should Miles hear about it.

Trust me, I know. Tyanna'd gotten me one for my birthday.

It was definitely the kinda gift for the *very* single women. For one-hour, six, sensually-muscular men, simultaneously massage their designated area of your body. Two, assigned to your legs and feet. Two more, delegated to your arms and upper torso. One allotted for your head, face and shoulders. And the last one, *teases* all the *special* places that are sure to have you chewing your lip!

◆ ◆

After breakfast, I drove Tyanna home and parked in the lot of her apartment.

"You wanna come in, Rave?", Tyanna offered.

"No, that's okay. I'm gonna go home."

"Okay. I'll see you later."

"Wait a minute, Ty. I need to ask you something and I don't know how? It ain't no big deal. But, I gotta know the truth?"

Closing the car door to avoid hearing the continuous door-ajar sound, Tyanna asked, "What is it Rave? What's wrong?"

"What's the deal between you and Rico?"

"What? Ain't nothing between me and Rico!"

"Ty, it ain't no big deal. I just need to know?"

"Rave, I'm tellin' you, there ain't nothin' going on!......", Tyanna said, with less convincing zeal.

I just paused. Watched her stare at my dash-board and shake her head like she was having an internal conversation with herself. She appeared as though she wanted to get something off her chest, but just needed to know that it was okay.

"Ty?", I said softly, as I saw tears for the first time from the usually rock-solid Tyanna.

"Ty? Tell me about it. I'm your friend, you know that right?", I hummed gently.

Tyanna nodded.

"Then tell me about it. I already know about the $5,000 check. What's up?"

Tyanna's head raised, surprised by my fiduciary awareness.

"Rico doesn't know that I know about the money. What's going on?"

"I never meant to hurt you, Rave. It started back when I was mad at you, 'cause I thought you sided with Rico against Nee.", she reluctantly spoke.

"Ah-humm?", I encouraged her to continue.

"I only did it to....well that don't matter now....that's how it started, anyway...and well, I never thought I'd get pregnant.", Tyanna finished by resuming her inspection of my dash-board.

"Ohhh, Ty. Are you alright?", I said, hugging her.

Though her tears interrupted her speech, I was able to piece the scenario together.

She was the one, who'd been *sexin'* Rico all along. Apparently, it was suppose to be a payback to me. And, it'd begun after Nia and Rico had *fallen-out* and I accepted Nia's car from Rico.

Now, it's all makes sense. The day she left Rico's office crying, she must've told him that she was pregnant. *Choices Inc.*, the name on the first check, turned out to be an abortion clinic. That's why that name sounded familiar to me. Rico must've paid Tyanna 5-grand to have an abortion and keep quiet about it.

As if the fact that Rico would have Clive killed wasn't enough proof! It was officially confirmed by Tyanna's story that he was an asshole too.

"I'm sorry Rave. I know I was wrong.", Tyanna sniffled out.

For all her toughness, Tyanna was absolutely afraid of Rico. Hell, so was I.

"Rave, please believe me. I'm really sorry!", Tyanna again begged.

"Don't worry about it. I'm just glad you're alright. Trust me, this ain't no thang!"

"Yes it is, Rave. I mean, Rico told me y'all gonna get married."

"That's what he thinks!", I confided in her. Felt like I had to.

Tyanna was carrying enough of a burden, having been forced to have an abortion that clearly she regretted. I didn't wanna add to it, by having her feel like she was *messing-up* a relationship that she was not.

I did *end-up* going inside of her apartment after hearing what she'd been through. Allowed her to talk and cry. Get out everything she'd kept a secret for too long. Held her in my arms with disregarded of her bisexuality. Did it, 'cause she was my friend. Not a perfect one. I know I wasn't one. But still, she *was* a friend.

Stayed at her house until it was nearly time for me to go to the club.

During that time, I made therapeutic confessions to her as well. Told her everything I'd done. Including about Clive, Sgt. Fillmore and Devin Lorenz.

I wanted to make sure that Tyanna didn't underestimate Rico. Or what he was capable of doing.

Preparing to leave her apartment, on my way to the door, I noticed a pencil on the dining room table. Asked to borrow it. Tyanna obliged.

Before I left, Tyanna thanked me, gave me a hug and a peck-kiss on the cheek.

I forced my mind to ignore the thought of the kiss being a lesbian-pass towards me.

◆ ◆

In the car, I began my childhood note-decoder trick using the pencil.

It worked. But, the message meant nothing to me.

It read, *1 / 2 – DL@G.Spkr@6@UG-423KHL*

Thought it might've been a website address. So when I got home, I logged on to the internet. But there was no such site.

Still, there was something familiar about the note. I just couldn't put my finger on it. And I didn't have time to dwell on it, 'cause I had to hurry to work for the *Shake It Fast* Contest.

Choices CHAPTER ELEVEN

I wandered into the *Carmel Club* around 10:30 PM. Only an hour-and-a-half before the *Shake It Fast* Contest was to begin.

Engulfed in the internet, I'd lost track of time. Then Devin called to ask me to lunch tomorrow, New Years Day.

I just knew Rico was gonna be pissed 'cause I was so late getting there.

The place was packed! Just like last year's successful contest.

I headed for the office to give my somber excuse. The door was cracked open and I could see Rico was in there, along with the two bouncers that killed Clive.

As I got closer to the door, one of the bouncers looked directly at me and shut the door.

What's that all about?, I wondered.

Didn't think it had anything to do with the murder, 'cause we'd not been contacted by the police at all.

And, even if that was the subject of their secret meeting, why would he shut the door on me?, I wondered.

I went back into the club to perform my normal club duties. Talked with the bartenders to make sure we had ample cash for change and that we weren't short on any booze. Talked with Bernice, the house-mom, to make sure there were no problems between dancers.

When the bouncers finally emerged from Rico's office, as they passed me, I noticed one of them had a piece of paper in his hand with part of our company letterhead on it. Visibly I could see there was a corner missing on it. Like it'd been ripped from the pad quickly.

It must've come off the same note pad as I'd seen earlier., I thought.

I walked into Rico's office.

"Hey Gurrl! When d'ya get here?", Rico said smiling.

I was happy that he wasn't mad. But, I wondered, *Why not?*

"Oh, I've been here a while. Just checking things out. Making sure everything's cool!"

"Another packed-house promotion of yours!", Rico bragged, as though there was more than *just* he and I in the room.

"Well, you know, what can I say!", I teased back to him, running my left hand through my hair.

Rico's eyes followed my hand. It was a good thing that I'd remembered to put *back-on* his ring before I left home.

Proud to see me displaying his ring, Rico walked over to the door and locked it. Then, romantically he wrapped his arms around me and swayed me side to side. Almost like we were dancing.

"Listen baby. This whole thing'll be over soon. I've got a good feeling. Soon, it'll just be us that we'll have to worry about. Trust me.", Rico softly spoke in my ear, while his hands slid from my waist to my butt.

"I know baby.", I replied, almost having trouble remembering that I was acting.

Rico *was* good-looking. And very charming, when he wanted to be. It could be difficult at times, especially at times like right now, to remember this was the same man who had someone murdered.

His tender embrace, made me wish he wasn't insane. Then maybe, this *could* work.

I'd come to notice, Rico's biggest aphrodisiac was money. Whenever he'd make a major-deal, he'd then really want sex!

Nibbling my ear, Rico pulled one hand away from my butt long enough to peak at his watch.

Then he whispered, "How 'bout you Shake It Fast for me?"

"Oh, Rico.", I *played-it-off* as though he *must* be joking, seeing as we were only an hour away from midnight. The start of the new year. And the beginning of the contest.

"Come on Rave!", sweetly he hummed, as his derriere-caressing was beginning to feel so-good.

"Uhn-un", I chirped the way a helpless bird would.

Sliding up the mini-skirt I was wearing, Rico's warm hands continued swirling my backside. Occasionally tugging at my thong.

From underneath my arms, Rico lifted me and sat me on the desk. Still facing me, both his hands cupped my breasts. The forcefulness of his grasp erected my nipples even before he'd reached them.

Using his knees, he widened my legs as his fingers were pinching my peaks with *just* the right amount of pressure.

Then he pushed me back, slid my butt to the edge of the desk. Didn't even bother to waste time, removing my thong. Instead, he just grabbed a handful of it and slid it over enough to expose me.

I raised my head to see what he was planning to do next.

He stuck two fingers in his mouth, then pressed them firmly on my clit. Rico rolled his fingers around my clit like it was cookie-dough and he was trying to make a perfect marble-shape that'd go in the oven.

I gritted my teeth and gripped the desk with my hands, but that aggressive technique had me shivering in no time.

"Aw, shit, Rico, I'm cumming!", I advised him, hoping he'd take it easier on me.

Rico wrapped his left arm around the outside of my thigh. With his other hand, he spread the skin and tongue-flicked my clit until my eyelids fluttered and my eyes rolled to the top of my head.

I folded my lips in, attempting to mute the sound. It wasn't like anyone would be able to hear us anyway over the blaring music in the club. But it was an instinctive reaction.

When he seamlessly slid his right hand's two fingers in, while *circumferencing* my *marble* with his tongue, I was in full-blown euphoria.

"Oooohh, SHIT! I'm cumm..mmm..ing!", I accidentally shouted, as my entire body was now quivering.

My hands were tightly gripped around Rico's ears.

If he didn't give me a reprieve soon, he might end-up earless!, I thought.

And that's just what he did.

Now I figured it was my turn to return the favor.

As I struggled to sit-up, still present were the residual jitters, accompanied by a flustered look on my face.

Rico smiled proudly at my battle to regain composure. I smiled too. Wasn't like I could *play-it-off* anyway. Hell, my legs were still shaking.

As I reached to unbuckle Rico's belt in an effort to even the score and to do what I was sure he wanted, Rico declined.

Despite being *rock-hard*, Rico refused any attention for himself. Choosing instead to make sure I knew that tonight was all about me.

Just when it was becoming *so easy* to despise him, Rico was making it hard.

Evident in tonight's sexcapade, Rico appeared to be serious about making it work between us. For the first time, he'd put me ahead of his ego.

While I was cleaning up in Rico's office bathroom, I again came to my senses. Realizing that no matter how sincere Rico was tonight, it didn't mean that he'd stay that way.

As I was leaving the bathroom, I glanced over to Rico's desk. Saw the note pad that had the torn piece of paper from the bouncer's note, still attached to it.

Rico had gone back into the club while I was in the bathroom. So, I was able to grab the next sheet off the pad with no problem.

Though, I was curious about what message he'd given to the bouncers and anxious to use my message-decoder trick again. It'd have to wait because I'd left the pencil that I borrowed from Tyanna at my house.

As I was busy passing out fake dollar bills, in preparation for the *Shake It Fast* Contest, Rico seemed in very good spirits. Occasionally, he'd make eye-contact and wink at me.

The fake dollar bills I was distributing would be used to determine the winner of the contest. The girl who'd been given the most dollar bills from customers was the winner.

With a plethora of barely-covered girls awaiting the start of the contest as a backdrop, Rico got on the stage. Leaning against one of the brass poles, he explained the rules of the contest.

Just before he finished, he addressed a comment towards me.

"I'd like to thank someone special for making *this* year, the best year of my life…", impulsively he added, pointing to me.

Raising his glass, he continued, "…without her, there'd never have been a Shake It Fast Contest…..".

Now the amateur *hoochies* behind Rico began to softly clap, scared they'd be disadvantaged in the contest if they did not clap.

"…..I just gotta stop and recognize, Raven, MY FIANCE'!"

Heard gasps from the club's regular dancers. And, I knew exactly what they were thinking. Shocked that I could *hook* someone like Rico.

Though, I didn't intend on *actually* marrying Rico. After his unexpected nuptial-announcement, my demeanor turned defensive. Looking around the club, almost daring any of the dancers to make a disparaging *under-their-breath* remark. As I did this, a sobering thought crossed my mind.

I wonder how many of the pussy's in this room has Rico had his dick in?, I thought.

I didn't even know about Tyanna. And she was *my* friend.

I don't know why, but I mentally began making a list of those dancers, he'd probably fucked. Coco, I'd witnessed. After Tyanna, I knew it was almost certain that Passion had. Thinking about how arrogant she'd been at the club calendar photo shoot. No one would've been that bold, unless...well, I'm sure he had fucked Passion.

My inkling was confirmed when I looked over to Passion. With her back to a customer she was servicing, busy doing *the Booty-Shake*, Passion forced a phony smile of congratulations across her face.

Now I was feeling like a fool.

All this time, I'd felt that I'd been a great manager. Thought I'd gotten respect from my employees because I got results.

Now I was realizing, maybe half the regular dancers here tonight, about forty or so, had most likely fucked Rico during the time I was suppose to be his special one.

It wasn't me they respected. It was him. They knew, they'd better not divulge to me that they'd slept with Rico, or they'd've had to pay a *helluva* price to Rico.

All this while, I'd viewed myself as *better* than the dancers. Smarter than them.

It hurt to think that they were *probably* laughing at me.

This internal, cerebral conversation that I was having with myself served to sour the moments we'd just shared in his office. Replaced instead by anger and thoughts of how I'd been shamed by Rico right under my nose.

Ironically, just as Tyanna had previously felt towards me, I wanted revenge. Ultimate revenge. And I vowed to myself, I'd get it!

◆◆◆◆◆◆◆◆◆◆◆◆◆◆◆◆◆◆◆◆◆◆◆◆◆◆◆◆◆◆◆◆◆◆◆◆

New Year's Day, I was at the Three Dollar Café on Peachtree Street, just five-blocks from my loft, having lunch with Devin.

Devin didn't seem to be in his usual, up-beat mood. And, he was more inquisitive than normal.

"So, how'd it go last night at the club?", Devin questioned.

"Okay, I guess?", I said humm-drumly, uncomfortable with the club as a conversation topic.

Devin had *never* asked about the club.

"Just okay?", he continued the subject.

"Yeah. I mean, we were busy and all. But nothing special."

Being extremely uncomfortable, I decided to change the subject. But, I didn't wanna talk about *his* job, 'cause I knew he was still working on solving Clive's murder.

"Howzit going for you?", I'd already said before thinking about it.

"Busy. I've got some new leads on the Sparks Murder Case that I gotta check out.", Devin said staring directly into my eyes.

I wanted to ask, *What leads?*, though I chose not to. Instead, I avoided eye-contact by lowering my head to my plate and filled my mouth with a fork-full of the seafood linguini I'd ordered.

"Rave, I was wondering what you're doing tomorrow?"

"Tomorrow? I dunno? What time?"

"'Round 6 PM."

"Six? Nothing, why?"

"Well, I'm giving a speech to D.A.R.E kids at the UnderGround Mall. Wanted to know if you'd come with me? Maybe we can see a movie after it?", Devin said staring so intently that I couldn't refuse.

"Yeah. Sure! I'd loved to!", I smiled back.

"Ohh. Ohh-kay. I mean, cool!", Devin said, seemingly surprised that I agreed.

"Do you wanna meet there?", I asked.

I was trying to be considerate, seeing as he lived east of downtown and I lived far north.

"No, don't worry about it. I'll pick you up at five!", Devin advised me.

We finished our meals and headed to my place.

◆ ◆

As Devin walked me to my loft door, I invited him in.

"You wanna stay for a while?", I romantically offered.

"I wish I could, but I can't right now.", Devin apologized, holding both of my hands.

I stood on my tip-toes to give him a warm hug. Then planted a long passionate tongue-kiss on him as I pulled his arms around my waist.

"Ohhh, Rave. I don't know about you?", Devin smiled on half of his face while shaking his head.

"What does that mean?"

"Nothing. I just don't know where we're going?", Devin said like cupid had done a *drive-by* on him.

Forcing his arms to tighten the embrace, I kissed him again and spoke.

"Devin, I really care about you. Alot! You have no idea how much!", I said, with my hands caressing his back. "I really do!"

After my comments, for the first time today, Devin initiated affection, placing a kiss on my lips.

"Alright, I'll see you tomorrow.", Devin confirmed again.

"Yeah baby! I can't wait!", I said, flirting with my eyes.

◆ ◆

Inside my loft, watching Devin drive-off from my window, reminded me that I'd not decoded the note from last night.

Strangely, the message Rico'd given to the bouncers was identical to the other message: *1 / 2 – DL@G.Spkr@6@UG-423KHL.*

It was then I put sense to what was familiar about the message. Having just watched Devin drive off, the *423 KHL* that was on the note, was Devin's license plate number. The letters, *DL*, were Devin Lorenz' initials. *UG*, must've stood for the UnderGround Mall. The *1 / 2* , originally I thought meant one-half, was actually the date, January 2nd. And *6*, was the time he'd be giving his speech to the D.A.R.E kids.

Oh my god! Rico's planning to have the bouncers murder Devin!, I thought with my hand over my mouth.

So that's what Rico must've meant when he said, *it'd all be over soon.*

My hand was being forced. I had to make a choice.

◆◆◆◆◆◆◆◆◆◆◆◆◆◆◆◆◆◆◆◆◆◆◆◆◆◆◆◆◆◆◆◆◆◆

"Oh, I'm glad I caught you!", I said.

"What's up, Rave?"

"Well, I was thinking about tomorrow."

"Yeah? Whatta 'bout tomorrow?"

"Umm. I was thinking, maybe we could go to dinner *and* a movie?"

"Fine Rave. Right after my speech.", Devin seemed annoyed at my suggestion.

"I was thinking we'd go to dinner around six. Then *hit* the 7:30 show."

"Rave, you know I got a speech to give at six."

"Do you have to give the speech? Can't someone else do it?"

"That's not the point Rave. It's prestigious to give the speech. The Mayor and the Police Chief are gonna be there."

Devin was intent on giving that speech. Yet, I had to warn him. But I didn't wanna lay all my cards on the table.

"C'mon Devin, do it for me?", I begged him.

"Why is it so important to you that I not give the speech? What's going on Rave?"

"I just feel like having a special night with you! A really special night!", I tried to entice him.

Devin cleared his throat.

"Does it mean that much to you Rave?"

"Yes."

"Well, I guess I could have my Deputy Lead Detective deliver my speech?"

"Thanks Devin. I'll call you later, bye.", I said faster than a cattle-auctioneer. Not wanting to give him an opportunity to change his mind.

My shoulders sank in relief, having convinced Devin to change his plans for tomorrow. Though I was well aware, it was only a *temporary* solution.

I knew it'd be up to me to gain the courage to impose a *permanent* solution!

Discovering Love CHAPTER TWELVE

On New Year's Day, with the exception of lunch with Devin, I'd not gone anywhere. Stayed at home. Pondered my next move. My options.

The revelation of Rico's note to the bouncers, combined with the fact that a showdown was inevitable, made me both hyper and tired.

It was now around 10:30 PM. I'd not moved off the sofa in about 9- hours, since figuring out the meaning of the note. Not even to eat.

After last night's contest, Rico told me that I could have tonight off. Ordinarily, I'd've taken advantage of it by hanging out with Tyanna. Or going on a date. But tonight, I simply had too much on my mind.

I slipped out of my jeans. Took a shower and proceeded to get comfortably dressed in just panties and bra-less in a Morehouse T-shirt that'd been given to me by one of the computer geeks that created my porn-movie website.

Though I'd been parked in front of the TV all afternoon, I couldn't remember a single show that'd come on.

I was the definition of conflicted. Weary, yet restless. Certain of what needed to be done, yet unsure of whether or not I could do it.

My stomach had been growling for several hours. Yet, I didn't have the mental energy to cook, nor the desire to order delivery food, knowing that I probably would not eat much anyway.

The shower I'd just taken, breathed *some* life back into me. So, I decided to make some popcorn.

I placed a bucket of popcorn that was a *left-over* from a Blockbuster movie-night in the microwave. Pushed the automatic setting and went into my bedroom.

I began transitioning from the living room to the bedroom. Turned off the lights and the television in the living room.

It was while I was in the bedroom turning on *that* TV and wrapping my hair up, that I heard the start of the familiar 5-beep sound of the microwave.

I started to stop wrapping my head and go get the popcorn, because I hate when popcorn tastes like it's burnt. But I chose to let the popcorn cool for a moment while I finished with my hair.

The fifth beep that normally signaled the microwave had finished was immediately followed by a loud, ear-piercing explosion sound!

I scurried around the corner to witness my kitchen had been blown to bits and was now, totally engulfed in flames. The flames had grown so fast from the explosion, my exit through the front door was blocked.

Frozen-stiff, it wasn't until black smoke began to fill my loft that I'd shaken out of my daze.

I struggled to slide open the bedroom window, that I'd recently complained to the management about it being difficult to open.

Desperately, I continued to try to open it as the choking smoke was making it's way into my bedroom.

Quickly, I closed the door to slow the smoke's path and used dirty clothes from the hamper to block the gap at the bottom of the door.

Coughing and my eyes beginning to burn, I tugged relentlessly at the window. Over and over again, I used every ounce of my 130 lbs. in an attempt to free myself.

Finally, I grabbed a tall lamp. Using the base of it as a batter-ram, I broke the glass and made my exit via the fire-escape.

Standing in the parking lot, watching the flames waving out of my bedroom window like a flag, I thought, *This was no accident!*

As I stood, shivering from the cold night-air, I couldn't believe that I had gotten myself into this situation.

Had to admit to myself that *my* actions were partly to blame. And that I was old enough to know better. My mom always said, *the choices you make, will determine the quality of your life.*

And, I'd just looked straight in the face at the possibility of losing mine.

Here I was in the middle of the night, scantily clad, sitting on a street curb, wrapped in a borrowed jacket with the letters APD (Atlanta Police Department) stenciled on the back, answering a detectives questions while trying to shield the blinding glare of a squad car's flashing lights.

"Mam, do you know anyone who'd want to harm you?", the detective asked, after the fire had been quenched by fire fighters.

"No.", I lied, not wanting to answer anymore questions.

"Are you sure, mam?"

"Yeah. I'm sure."

"Mam, we can't help *you*, unless you help *us*."

"What do you want from me?!", I shouted, out of confusion.

The detective's next question was interrupted by the head fire fighter.

"Excuse me Det. Greene?!", the fire-fighter broke into our conversation, holding a charred object.

"Yeah, what is it?"

"This is what caused the explosion.", he continued, showing the device to the detective. "It's a mercury-switch activated explosive device. Whoever did this, knew what they were doing!"

"Okay, okay, okay. Thank you. Give the evidence to Detective Williams.", Det. Greene said, pointing to an area near a row of police cars.

Reading my face, Det. Greene hurried the fire fighter away, out of fear that he might scare me into further silence.

"Mam, I'd suggest that you go to the hospital to get checked out. I can authorize police protection for you as well. At least until we get this straightened out."

"No. I'm okay."

"Look! I don't know *what* you're involved in. But whatever it is, someone obviously wants you dead. And they're certainly not gonna stop trying. We can help you. But you have to let us!"

"No. I'm okay.", I said, declining his offer.

"Well, I can't make you go to the hospital. And, I can't force you to let us help you. But I'm gonna give you my phone number, just in case you change your mind. And I hope you do change your mind. It'd be a shame if the next time they succeeded!", Det. Greene made one last effort to scare me into compliance, as he handed me his card.

"Do you have a safe place where you can stay for the night?", Det. Greene asked. "Do you need a ride somewhere?"

"No. Do you think I can go back in to get some clothes?", I said, realizing that at some point I'd have to give back the jacket that covered me.

"Absolutely not. This is now a crime scene. Plus, we don't know if the building is safe or not?"

"Well then, can I use someone's cell phone? I wanna have a friend pick me up."

"Sure. Use mine.", he offered.

I called Tyanna because my car keys were still in the loft. And besides, I was concerned that there might be a bomb in my car, as well.

Within fifteen minutes, Tyanna'd made it to the scene to pick me up.

I had no choice but to spend the night at Tyanna's.

I didn't call, Devin. Though I knew he'd hear about it soon through the law enforcement grapevine.

I knew he'd be worried when he learned of tonight's astonishing event. And be frustrated, because he'd not be able to reach me, as my cell phone was also in the burnt loft.

But right now, what I needed was peace.

That's why I for damn sure, didn't call Rico! Was very suspicious of him. He knew where I lived. And I wondered why he'd decided to give me the night off? *Was his proposal a ploy to get me to relax, so that he could set me up?,* I wondered.

Tyanna had planned to stay at home with me, even though she had a video-shoot scheduled for tonight. After almost an hour of my urging and pleading, Tyanna did go to her shoot.

◆ ◆

The next morning around 10 AM, I called Devin on his personal cell phone.

"Raven, we've been looking for you!", Devin said.

We've?, I thought.

"Did you hear about last night?"

"Yes, I need to talk to you about it. Why don't you come by the station."

"Why at the station?"

"Rave, just come by. Don't let anyone know that you know me, okay? Well, don't let 'em know we've been kickin' it.", Devin whispered.

"What's going on?"

"It's no big deal. I can explain more, but I don't wanna keep-on talking over this cell phone. I'll meet you at the place where we first ate in one hour. Don't say the name of it, just in case someone's listening. One-hour, Rave! Don't be late!"

He was referring to the UnderGround Mall food-court area.

When I arrived, I saw Devin across the food-court making eye contact with me and motioning with his head for me to follow him.

He didn't wait for me to catch-up to him. Clearly, he didn't want anyone who might be watching to know that we were together.

We ducked out of public-view through some metal industrial doors that led to a mechanical room.

"What's going on Devin?"

"You don't know?"

"No.", I said raising my voice.

"Last night Rico was murdered. The department is looking for you, because they uncovered an ownership contract that conveys full-ownership of both clubs to the surviving owner in the event of one owner's death."

"What?! I didn't even know there was a clause like that......."

"Listen, I know you didn't kill Rico."

"I didn't!"

"The department, just wants to ask you some questions. It's just procedure. If you're innocent, it shouldn't be any big deal?"

"I am innocent! You don't think that I'm innocent?!"

"Yes! I know you are! I miss-spoke. Anyway, I'm gonna help you. But, no one can know that we date. Or I'll be banished from the case. Then I won't be able to tell you what to do."

"Okay. What should I do?"

"Just go to the club. Act shocked at the news of Rico's death. Then voluntarily come to the station with the police officer. Don't worry, they're not gonna arrest you. They ain't got no evidence for that. But, they might ask for some voluntary samples from you. You know, hair, blood, finger prints, and stuff like that. Give it to them."

"What? Why? If I don't have to, why should I give it to them?"

"'Cause it shows, you have nothing to hide! They won't pursue you beyond a cursory investigation."

"I'on't know. Maybe I should get an attorney?"

"Rave, if you show up at the station, having already called a lawyer, it's gonna look like you'd planned this. And believe me, there's a way to link *anyone* to *any* murder. Trust me on this one?"

I just stared at him. Devin was asking me to do something, I'd not done ever in Atlanta. Truly trust someone.

My pause, drew more comments from Devin.

"Rave, I care about you, alot. Hell, I could lose my job for what I'm doing right now—advising a potential suspect in a murder case. I'm just trying to help you....because I...I love you."

My eyes watered, hearing his heart-felt plea and declaration.

"But, I'm scared.", I admitted, falling into his arms.

Finally, at last, I was trusting someone.

"I know. But it's gonna be alright! Everything's gonna be okay! You just gotta do what I say!"

"I know. But there's some things I need to tell you."

"Don't worry about it. I know more than you think. Let's not talk about it, until after you talk with the department. I don't want you to sound rehearsed! Here's a room key to the Super-8 Hotel on Luckie Street. It's room 412. Take a cab to the hotel. Don't use the main entrance. Go through the parking ramp-side, instead. I'll meet you there tonight, after you're finished with the police department. Why don't we say around 8:30, okay?"

"Okay."

"Oh yeah, don't call me anymore on my cell phone. Not until this is over."

◆ ◆

I did just as Devin had advised. Went to the club, where police officers were waiting for me to show up.

My visit at police headquarters was uneventful. The most eye-raising response I received was when they asked about my whereabouts during the murder.

They easily were able to verify that my loft had burned the same night. But, because Tyanna had gone to her shoot, there was no one to corroborate that I was indeed at her apartment the entire night.

Once I volunteered the samples, even that, seemed not to be as big of an issue to them.

◆ ◆

That night at the Super-8, Devin was already inside the room. I jumped, startled by his presence. My nerves were just that bad.

"I'm sorry Rave. Did I scare you?"

"Yeah. I'm just so nervous."

"That's understandable. You've been through a lot!"

"Devin, I've got so much I need to tell you. I don't know how you're gonna feel about me, after you hear it? But, I gotta get it off of my chest.", I said, ready to confess everything before I chickened-out.

"We can talk about all that later. I don't wanna waste the night, 'cause this might be the last night we can have together for a while. We don't wanna raise suspicion.", Devin urged.

"Devin, I gotta tell you this!"

"It doesn't matter. I already know what I need to know. The rest is unimportant. I know, you were producing porn-films with the help of Clive Sparks. You didn't think I knew that, huh? Your number showed up, when I did a phone record search. So did Troy's. I put two and two together."

"Well why didn't you arrest me?"

"Arrest you for what? I know you didn't kill Clive."

"How did you know that?"

"Well, unless you've been wrestling in the WWF, there's no way, you could've inflicted the punishment that he received. Plus, it doesn't fit the profile of a woman murderer."

"Well then, how'd you know that I didn't hire someone to kill him?", I said, almost daring him to arrest me.

"I didn't know. At least not for sure. I wasn't certain until after lunch on New Year's Day."

"Huh?"

"It's a long story. One I'll share later. I don't wanna waste our time together on this stuff."

"Okay, okay. Just answer this? Rico planted the bomb in my microwave, didn't he?"

"No. It was another acquaintance of yours. Stan. You might know him by, Sgt. Fillmore."

"Sgt. Fillmore tried to kill me?"

"Yeah. But you don't have to worry. He's already in police-custody. We've known that he was taking *kick-backs* for quite some time now. But I didn't know about the Nia tapes until last night, when your friend Tyanna came by to see me. She thought you could use my help......"

I just shook my head and smiled.

"..... You were very lucky to not have died in the bomb blast! Once Tyanna had come by and I heard about the type of device, it was easy to figure out who'd done it. Stan had worked for eight years in the bomb-division."

"Man! I can't believe it!"

"Believe it. It's true."

"But, I still don't get it? How come the police didn't come after me, when they'd seen that I'd made calls to Clive's office?"

"They never saw those records. Rave, I'm the Lead Detective on the case. I did the phone record search. I just kept that information to myself."

"Why? I mean, why would you do that for me, when you said at that time you weren't 100% sure, that I *wasn't* involved? Why would you risk yourself for me?"

"I had a hunch. Actually, had two of them. Somehow, I just knew you didn't do it. And my hunches are usually right."

"You said, you had two?"

"The other was that you and I were meant to be together."

My eyes *watered* from his tender comments, as he continued.

"New Year's Eve, I thought my hunch might've failed me. See Rave, I had a private company install surveillance cameras and microphones into the club and Rico's office."

"Let me explain!", I started to beg. Realizing the reason he'd been uncharacteristically cold to me during our lunch on New Year's Day. He'd seen me and Rico's final sexcapade on tape. And, heard Rico announce our 'engagement' on stage.

It was a good thing, Devin had hired the company privately. Instead of using police department equipment and staff. Then, there'd be no way to keep everything I'd done quiet.

"Devin, let me explain what that was about?", I again attempted.

"No need. Plus, I'd rather you not. You were in a tough spot, with no one to help you. You did what you had to do. Let's just leave it at that, okay?"

I still wanted to explain it, but I just said, "Okay."

"The important part is that you cared enough about me, to warn me about Rico's plan to kill me. I'd already known about the plan. I'd watched the live conversation between Rico and his boys, as Rico directed them to kill me, the way they'd done to Clive Sparks."

"Why didn't you arrest them right then?"

"Well, think about it. First of all, I had gotten this information from an illegal surveillance. Which wouldn't be admissible in court. And, I'd be suspended from the force, not to mention, facing charges myself. But most importantly, I needed to know where *we* stood! And I found out. Though, you didn't tell me directly—you still wanted to keep me from going to the UnderGround to be killed. That's when I knew, my second-hunch was right!"

"What about the bouncers? Won't they still try to kill you?"

"It's all being taken care of!", Devin assured, as he warmly embraced me.

In his arms, I felt as loved and as safe as I ever experienced.

I kissed him with passion. Not because he'd saved me. But, because he truly loved me. And was willing to risk himself for me before he knew he had something to gain.

This was true love. And love was exhilarating. Liberating.

This night I'd planned to make love to every inch of him. Wanted every part of him to experience the joy he'd brought to my soul. And I could tell, he felt the same way.

I unbuttoned his shirt, revealing his police-academy, well-developed, semi-hairy chest. Rubbed my hands through his chest hair, as though my fingers were the teeth on a comb.

Swirled my index fingers around his nipples, while adoring the sensation-brewing look on his face. Began pinching him, the way I imagined he'd be doing to me soon.

He interrupted me, by kissing me while firmly hugging me like he planned to never let me go.

I broke free of his grip, not because it didn't feel good. It did! Felt great, to be held in love. But, I was on a mission. One that would not be deterred.

I renewed my finger-flicking of his nipples until they'd become erected. Placed my mouth on them. Swirled my tongue the way I'd experienced from men. Bit them with light pressure until he could take no more.

Devin pulled my shirt over my head. Determined to not be out-done by me, he immediately bit my nipples to firmness. Then eased the tortuous pleasure, by swirling his tongue around my peaks. Followed by a massaging, man-handling of my breasts. Squeezing tightly at the base of my *mountains*, he succeeded in gaining my nipples' perkiest, most-erected state possible.

Using his hands, Devin pushed my breasts together, creating better cleavage than the most expensive *Victoria's Secrets* bra.

His tongue alternated a routine on each nipple. First, a long, slow lick, starting at the base of the nipple, over the peak, to the top. Next, a *'round-the-world* swirl. Followed by a brief *ice-cream-cone-like* suck. Then, a series of *machine-gun fast*, up & down and side-to-side tongue flicks. Ending with a teasing bite and an encore suck.

After he'd repeated this process, two or three times, then negotiated both peaks in his mouth at the same time, flicking both of them on opposite sides of his tongue, I'd already orgasmed at least once.

Amazingly, during his mountain-adventure, I'd been able to unbuckle his pants. I turned him around. Pushed him to sitting, and pulled his pants completely off.

Devin's *thang* stretched his navy blue *Calvin Klein* briefs like he'd shoplifted a banana and hid it in his underwear. I peeled down his navy blues and moistened him with my mouth. Glided my tongue, up and down him. Supported his balls in one hand, as I stroked him with the other.

Took him in my mouth deeply. The way I'd witnessed girls practicing on carrots in Iowa.

"Oh, baby! Oooo, shit, baby!", Devin exhaled with furrowed eyebrows.

Out the top of my eyes, I saw *near-eruption* written all over his face. I slowed my pace, not because I didn't want that salty taste. I'd gotten past that. I delayed because I remembered my mission. To give him love, like never before.

We switched positions, like tag-team love-wrestlers. Now, it was his turn.

He spread my legs and began french-kissing me down there.

His tongue's probing, excavated the shivers as he tightened his grip on my inner-thighs.

After several minutes of stomach-contracting, thigh-shaking, head-*jerking mouth-love*, Devin reached for his pants. Apparently, so that he could get a condom out of his wallet.

I grabbed him by the arm that was reaching for his pants. He gazed directly in my eyes, as I said sweetly, "You don't need that".

Then, I reached to his *thang* and guided him inside me.

Devin gave me all he had. Went deep. Didn't neglect the sides. Or, the top. Stroked so nicely, my voice had become falsetto.

Both of our bodies poured out more sweat, than a non-freed slave. Our breathing was heavier than John Henry trying to beat the railroad-track-making machine. But we forged ahead anyway.

Our love-making was metaphorically reminding me of home. The slushy sound created by the two additional orgasms I'd had, brought thoughts of cars slushing their way through the rainy/snowy streets in Des Moines. And, Devin's *car* felt right at home in my *garage*.

We'd gone at it, non-stop, for what I'd've guessed was at least 45 minutes or so.

Not so much as even a break, to switch positions. In fact, we never did change positions. Devin stayed on top, with me receiving underneath him.

The only break came, when he backed all the way out for some strange reason.

I figured, Devin was not getting ready to cum, because I'd not heard that engine-revving sound that most guys make.

Strangely, he grabbed a small bottle of lubricant that was hidden underneath a pillow. Began generously *lubing himself*. So thick, it was dripping off of him.

Then he raised my legs, firmly gripping the back of my thighs. Pushed my legs back. Way back. So far back, it was clear, his intent was indeed, my *bottom-shelf*.

Having now put it together in my mind, the reason for extreme lubrication and despite having never talked about such a big moment, I didn't discourage him. Simply*, eye-communicated* for him to be gentle.

As he quickly nudged in 3-inches, before I changed my mind, I sucked in enough air to scuba dive for an hour. My watery eyes, involuntary crossed at the beginning of my first *DNB, dick-n-booty*.

Devin, keeping his *eye-promise*, remained still, allowing me time to get adjusted. Sparingly, I released sighs in a staccato fashion, until I was breathing at a *somewhat* normal pace again.

The pressure from the filling of my *bottom-shelf*, created incredible stimulation for my *top-shelf door-bell*. It had bubbled to capacity.

Devin, patiently waiting for my heavy-breathing to subside, so that he could began his movement, must've noticed my *door-bell's* unusual size.

As he delicately brushed an already lubricated thumb across my, now extremely sensitive *door-bell*, I felt ecstasy like never before!

"Ooo-ooo….Shit….Iighh-yiyi...Ohhmaa…..Uhh-oooph-eee",   I uncontrollably moaned, sounding like a kid that took the *short-bu*s to school.

My hands were wrapped around his wrist, but they didn't have any strength left in them. Well, not enough to remove his hand. They were sapped by what felt like an infinite-orgasm.

The sensation seemed to constantly be escalating with no end in sight. My body's violent tremors began a viscously intense revolving cycle.

Unintentionally, my body earthquaked the *DNB* to more depth, as Devin continued ringing the *door-bell* that was answered by more orgasms, which led back to the deepening of the DNB.

Felt as though I was on a roller-coaster that I couldn't get off of. Though the roller-coaster was doing exactly what was desired when boarding, sometimes the ride had too many twists and turns.

Once Devin began *working* my *bottom-shelf*, I began drifting in and out of consciousness. It was weird. Like I was driving on a highway and had temporarily fallen asleep at the wheel. And I couldn't tell, how long I'd been asleep. Occasionally, I'd *come-to*, to the extreme sensations that were divided only by my hazy lucid states.

As my *bottom-shelf* became more versed, I experienced less frequent black-outs. However, the heavenly stimulation never waned.

Neither did Devin, who appeared to have turned into the *Duracell-battery, Energizer-bunny*. He kept going and going and going. Frantically, *working* my *door-bell*, left to right and up and down. Periodically, filling my *top-shelf* with a finger or two.

Even added lubrication without removing his *thang*. Just poured some down his shaft on the backstroke. Apparently afraid, that if he pulled out completely, I might not let him back in, which wasn't true. Never mind the fact that I was tired and almost *orgasmed-out*.

My feet were tingling with numbness from having my legs in the air for so long. Stomach was cramping from repetitive ecstasy. My *door-bell* was feeling the effects too, having never gotten this much exposure before. Even my face and eyelids were exhausted from all the fuck-expressions they were creating.

In my wildest dreams, I never would've thought the best sex I'd have would come from a *one-position* night. Him always on top.

At this point, even a new position wouldn't have excited me. I was simply ready to be done.

On the contrary, Devin looked renewed. Just warming up.

When Devin finally *did* climax, after what seemed to be an eternity, I arched my torso up to use my body to catch his *jackpot*. As his milky-ness streamed down the front of me, I used my hands to rub it all over my body as though it were baby-oil. Wanting to send the clear message to Devin that I truly treasured his *love-juice*.

Though, I'd been anxiously awaiting his climax for quite sometime, a part of me wished it wasn't over, as I watched Devin's sexy body still jerking.

Couldn't resist grabbing his *thang* in my hand, stroking a couple of left-over blasts out of him, as Devin's face strained and his body convulsed ultimate-satisfaction!

At that moment, I knew Devin was the one.

For me to allow a guy to DNB-me, I knew what I felt, *had* to be real!

And so, after we'd finished showering together, I didn't beat around the bush. Didn't relegate myself to hint-throwing. Or reduce myself to hoping.

Instead, I just did it. I asked.

"Devin, will you marry me?"

Though, I'd gotten it out without hesitancy, immediately I was nervous about getting a declining response.

"Well, that depends?", he said.

Not the answer, I wanted.

"Depends on what?", I hesitantly asked.

Devin, reaching under the other pillow, pulled out a velvet box, as he spoke.

"Well, it depends on whether or not you'll marry me?", Devin charmingly said, opening the box to reveal a ring.

Having successfully wrestled the proposal from me, back to him, in a manner so charming, I would've endured an hour more of the love-making we'd just finished, if he so desired.

I said, "Yes, yes, yes!", hugging and kissing him all over his face.

Though we'd have to keep our engagement a secret and not see each other for several months, until the whole *Rico-Clive-Sgt. Fillmore* situation had diminished, it was a small price to pay for true love.

Homecoming CHAPTER THIRTEEN

June 14th of the next year, I sat in the diner in Iowa, *well-after* closing time, on the eve of my wedding. With me were the only two bridesmaids, Nia and Tyanna, who were also the maids-of-honor.

The new name on the outside of the diner, read Sue's Diner. I'd purchased it with some of the money I'd gotten by selling the *Carmel Club* and *Slick-N-Thick*.

Named it after my mother, 'cause we had a running joke that she worked there so much it oughtta have her name above it.

At least now when customers would tell one of their racially-charged jokes, I'd have the last laugh, 'cause they were paying me!

At just 1-month shy of my 21st birthday, I'd had enough of the fast-life and was looking forward to a more peaceful existence, with my husband-to-be.

Over the past two years, my bridesmaids and I had gone through a lifetime's worth of trials. But, we'd all fought through it. And now, finally, we were all doing well at the same time.

My wedding was the talk of the town. Especially because there was a platinum-selling, Grammy Award-winning artist scheduled to sing –

-- Nia.

Just two weeks earlier, Nia had gotten engaged to her music producer, Miles Vincent.

Most shocking was Tyanna, with her wild self, was also engaged to Herman Williams a.k.a. King Kong. Together, they'd bought both clubs from me and continued producing their own porn-movies. A perfect match, if there ever was one!

The night before my wedding, there was no wild night scheduled for the three of us. We'd already exhausted those days. Well, Nia and I had!

Satisfied, we were, to drink coffee and reflect on how our lives had changed for the better. I knew mine, certainly had. And I owed it all to Devin Lorenz.

I was in the best place mentally, spiritually and emotionally, that I'd ever been. And it wouldn't have happened without him.

I knew in my heart, that he'd've done anything for me.

Two days after our engagement, the two bouncer's bodies surfaced in the Chattahoochee River.

Often wondered if Devin had done that for me? And if *he'd gotten-rid-of* Rico for me as well?

In my life, I'd had many guys *claim* that they'd be willing to die for me. But none willing to kill for me. That's why, occasionally, during our *three-musketeer* coffee conversation, I'd have to be comforted by Tyanna and Nia, just thinking about the depth of Devin's love.

On such a special day, that'd take place tomorrow, it was a shame that Devin would not be there, standing next to me.

Six days after our engagement night, Devin was killed, while off-duty, when he stumbled upon a convenience-store robbery. Though, he was able to shoot-and-kill the armed suspect at the counter, a second assailant shot Devin in the back.

That assailant's bullet, pierced not only Devin's heart, but also mine.

During my grieving, Darren Sharper, the newly crowned heavyweight champion, comforted me. With patience and love becoming of Devin, Darren got me back on *my emotional feet*.

Now, I don't love Darren, more than I did Devin. It's not even like that. It ain't a contest.

I love them both. Just differently. It's hard to explain.

Darren, I feel grateful to, for his understanding and his warmth.

And, I'll be forever grateful to Devin, for showing me how to love and appreciate a good man, like Darren.

THE END

Winston Chapman

Welcomes Your Comments!

Winston@WinstonChapmanBooks.Com

Request For Appearances By Winston Chapman Are To Be Sent To:

Black Pearl Books
c/o Publicist for Winston Chapman
P.O. Box 361985
Decatur, Georgia 30036-1985

OR, E-MAIL TO:

Publicist@BlackPearlBooks.Com

Fun Facts!

ABOUT THIS BOOK

- **Written in 63 days**
- **4-Rewrites**
- **62,615 Words**

Original Title: SHAKE IT FAST!

The title change came at the suggestion of Winston's wife, after their daughter pranced around their home singing Shake It Fast! – At least there ain't no song called *Caught Up!* – yet!

The Cover

MODEL: Cristal is a talented model from Detroit, Michigan now residing in Atlanta, GA.

PHOTOGRAPHER: Ohm, is an Award-Winning International photographer & filmmaker from Thailand. A Law School graduate at the age of 20, his photographic art has been featured in numerous prestigious exhibits and publications across the world.

Tidbits About The Author

Winston Chapman was first published at age 11, when he sent an article to a local newspaper entitled, "Why Dr. Martin Luther King Jr.'s Birthday Should Be A National Holiday". At age 16, he won the title of Mr. Black Teenage World of Minnesota & 1st Runner-Up at the National Competition, as a part of Hal Jackson's Talented Teens program. Known to friends as a "clown", Chapman entered and won his first-ever Stand-Up Comedy contest at age 18, held at the very same club (*First Avenue* – Minneapolis, MN) that spawned such music stars as Prince & The Time. In his adult years, Chapman has enjoyed a diverse array of interesting careers including owning a drycleaners, working in mutual funds investments and producing a sports television talk show.

Learn more about Winston at **www.WinstonChapmanBooks.com**